Death

at Fort York

Title: Death at Fort York / Danee Wilson
Names: Wilson, Danee, author.
ISBN 9781069763808 (softcover)
ISBN 9781069763815 (HTML)

Destiny Press

For Kevin and Nutmeg, who make every day better.

Chapter 1

A sudden, sharp knock at the door startled me. I clumsily splashed tea over the edge of my cup into the saucer as Muffin, my wire fox terrier, bolted from my lap, barking at the abrupt interruption.

"Oh, my. Who could that be, Muffin?" I asked, setting the cup aside. "Go on and see."

She raced from the back sunroom, where I'd been relaxing in peace, to the front door. Full of spritely terrier energy, Muffin ran tight circles, her toenails scratching at the threadbare doormat as she impatiently waited for me to make my way down the hall.

As I opened the door, I was surprised to see my husband, Bill, standing on the front step, his cheeks rosy and droplets of sweat glistening at his temples. Muffin jumped up and down fruitlessly, as he crossed the threshold. He mindlessly patted her head without looking at her. I frowned, wondering what was on his mind.

Before I could speak, he launched into a breathless dialogue: "Beatrix... I'm so glad you're here... I have to show you. We've found something exciting on the skeletons from San Miguel!"

We had returned from the excavation of the medieval cemetery at San Miguel in Spain at the end of August, shipping crates full of skeletal remains to the Department of Anthropology at the University of Toronto from the secluded mountain sanctuary near Pamplona in Navarre. After a student was tragically murdered during the excavations, I begged Bill to take some time off when we returned to Canada. We were supposed to be retired, after all. However, after nearly two months of his bumbling around the house, misplacing things, talking to himself, and bumping into me during meal preparations, I'd sent him back to the university, for both our sakes.

I plainly ignored his excitement; the skeletons were his passion.

"Bill, dear, why didn't you use your key to get into the house?"

He looked at me as though I'd asked for the square root of 117. Then he adjusted his glasses with his index finger.

No response.

"Bill," I repeated. "Where are your keys?"

He blinked a few times and said: "Oh, yes. Sorry, Beatrix. Now that you ask, I'm quite certain I forgot them. They must be back at the lab. I left in such a hurry, I didn't remember to pick up my things. I wasn't really thinking at all. We'll go get them now. You'll come over to see the skeletons, won't you?"

I hadn't felt much interest in the remains we recovered from the cemetery since we came home. One did not simply get over the brutal murder of a young person overnight. I shivered and tried not to think of it. Yet, Bill's childlike enthusiasm piqued my curiosity. What had he discovered on the bones that had him racing home in the middle of the day to find me? A strange disease perhaps? Evidence of syphilis in Europe prior to 1492? Everyone was always trying to find that. Venereal disease was a hot topic at conferences, and finding the characteristic caries sicca, pit-like lesions affecting the bones of the cranium, in a medieval European population would be just the thing to kindle his interest.

"Of course," I said, looking down at the dog. "Are we breaking the rules today and taking Muffy? She could use an outing. My back is a bit achy, and I've not taken her for a walk yet. She's been cooped up in the house and yard all day, the poor thing."

Bill finally took notice of Muffin, bending down to let her sniff at the bristly white hairs of his beard. Prior to San Miguel, we'd had a rule: no dogs in the lab. San Miguel had changed many things, and I didn't like to be far from her, even though we were back in the safety of our home in Toronto where nothing much ever happened.

"I don't see why not," he replied, scratching the fur around her neck. "It's late enough in the day that the labs aren't busy. What do you think, Muffin?"

Bill stood and held a treat out for the scruffy terrier, who rose on her back feet and pumped her front paws in the air. She would perform any number of tricks for a tidbit.

I quickly grabbed a coat, silk scarf, felt hat, and leather gloves. These days I needed to bundle up appropriately for the late-fall chill gusts of wind that often swept through the streets from Lake Ontario, blowing leaves about on the streets and wrapping its cool fingers around exposed skin. As I picked up my handbag and car keys from the mahogany entryway table, I watched Bill through the open doorway. He approached his bicycle, which he'd dropped on the lawn when he arrived. Muffin was, as usual, tight on his heels. Though he'd fashioned a basket to the front for taking her along on rides, and I did have a bicycle of my own that I rode occasionally when my joints cooperated, I had no intention of cycling to the university, even if it wasn't that far away.

"Don't be silly, Bill," I said, closing the door behind me. "We'll be taking the car this time."

Chapter 2

I stepped out of our seafoam green Mercury Meteor and brushed the creases from my plaid wool skirt. I'd very much liked the colour of the car when we decided to replace our old Chev, and Bill had been pleased it was manufactured just down the lake from us, in Oakville. Muffin raced around the car, waiting for me and Bill to gather ourselves before making the brief trek to the Sidney Smith Building, where the Department of Anthropology had relocated from the Royal Ontario Museum in 1961, the year before Bill retired.

"Aren't you going to tell me what you've found?" I asked Bill as we walked, arm-in-arm across campus. The late fall grass was dry, yet the adornment of yellow and orange leaves that crunched softly under our feet lifted my spirits.

"That would spoil the surprise," Bill smiled, a hint of mischief in his eyes.

Though he'd turned 70 that year, there was still something youthful about him, despite the white hair and beard, and the wrinkles that ran across his forehead in lines so straight they might have been traced by a ruler. It certainly wasn't every man his age who could ride a bicycle to the job he'd retired from half a decade before and not regret the experience. Two years his junior, I couldn't say I felt the same way about myself. My age showed beyond the hair my youngest grandchild liked to compare to the snow in the winter. I had slowed down, my joints creaky and tired. Bill, on the other hand, thrived in his eighth decade and I marvelled at his joie de vivre.

As we passed the Sir Daniel Wilson Residence, a far statelier building than the more modern, but brutal, Sidney Smith Hall, a group of rowdy young men tumbled from its front doors, several of whom wore corduroy pants and tight buttoned shirts with bold patterns. Things had changed since the days of drab men's fashions in the 40s.

"Hello, Professor Forster!" A young man called out, waving his salutations, but not stopping to talk.

Bill absentmindedly waved back with his free hand, then letting go of my arm, he stooped to pick Muffin up.

"I'd better keep her under the radar until we get to the lab," he said, winking.

Once inside the room where Bill had been analyzing the remains from San Miguel, he set her down and closed the door. Muffin busied herself sniffing at the corners, probably looking for a mouse or insect to terrorize.

"All right, out with it, Bill," I said, nudging my husband with my elbow and motioning with my chin to the skeletons, laid out in anatomical position on the tables.

"Well," Bill began, approaching the closest table. "It wasn't clear when we excavated the remains, but once they were cleaned and we had a chance to reassemble some of the bone fragments, we realized that these three individuals, who were buried together in a common grave, were the victims of a violent attack. Look at this femur," Bill continued, holding up various fragments from the shaft of the thigh bone. "When I put all the fragments together, what do you see?"

I peered at the diamond shaped hole formed once all the pieces of the puzzle were held in place. It didn't take an archaeologist to know that something sharp had pierced the bone with great force. Given the time period and size, I guessed it to be an arrow.

"Goodness," I said, running my finger over the injury. "It's completely traversed the bone and caused a comminuted fracture. That can't have been a good day at San Miguel. Any chance of an association to a known historical event?"

"Not that we know of," Bill shook his head and replaced the fragmented femoral bones back on the table. "The historical records from the time the cemetery was in use are limited. There may have been a violent attack when the original church was destroyed, but these individuals may well have died at another time altogether."

"What about that radiocarbon dating everyone is always on about?" I asked. "Can you use that to narrow down the time period during which these individuals were killed?"

I was always pleased to apply the knowledge I'd acquired over the years during my work as an archaeological illustrator. Though I saw myself more as an artist, I'd learned a thing or two about archaeology and physical anthropology, having worked on so many digs alongside Bill. He was always keen to share his findings with me and I tried to keep abreast of all the latest advancements in the field. These days, though, it felt that technology was moving at the speed of light, not just in archaeology, and one had to scramble uphill, always a step or two behind the researchers who tossed words like isotopes, radioactivity, integrated circuits at us. The list was endless, and nobody could really pretend to keep up with the times.

"Unfortunately," Bill tempered my optimism in the power of scientific advancement, "bone is not the best material for dating. Libby himself noted that it was likely to be contaminated and thus affect the accuracy of the tests. Perhaps in the future it will become more reliable, but for now, I don't know that it would be the best place to spend the little funding we have."

Willard Libby was the father of radiocarbon dating, proposing a method in the late 1940s to use carbon-14 to date organic materials. According to Bill, however, the method hadn't advanced quite enough to date the skeletons from San Miguel. I was just about to ask Bill another question when the door suddenly swung open. Muffin ran immediately to examine the trespassers, a low grumble coming from deep in her throat.

"Muffin, sit," I said sharply, pointing at the ground.

She plunked her bottom onto the floor, as she was obliged to do, but she whined quietly, waiting for my next command, her front legs shaking as though she were sitting in a freezer.

"Bill, am I ever happy to have caught you," Professor Stephen Blake, head of the Department of Anthropology, said, slamming the door shut behind him. "Beatrix, good to see you."

Despite his words, he nodded curtly in my direction. He was accompanied by Donna, the department secretary, who stood slightly behind Stephen, her brow furrowed. She'd joined the department after Bill retired, but I'd seen her often over the past few years when Bill went to university gatherings and events. I guessed her to be in her mid to late forties. Her grey hair was cut short, and creases fanned away from her eyes even when she wasn't smiling. She could be quite lively outside the walls of the department, but she often clammed up in Stephen's presence.

"What can I do for you, Stephen, Donna?" Bill asked, stepping away from the skeletons.

Stephen hesitated, rubbed his smooth chin, then said: "I'm sure it's nothing and there's some logical explanation for this. But I've just heard from the students over at Fort York. They said that Evelyn was at the excavation this morning, but they haven't been able to find him for hours. He's simply vanished into thin air."

Chapter 3

"What do you mean, vanished?" I clutched the lapel of my coat, aghast.

How could someone simply disappear in the middle of Toronto? I hoped Stephen was right. There must be some explanation as to why Evelyn Volk, a young and ambitious professor of historical archaeology, would have disappeared in the middle of the day, abandoning his students at the excavation he was directing.

Stephen glanced at me briefly and then looked back at Bill.

"Donna was there this morning. Tell them," Stephen ordered.

He turned and looked impatiently at the secretary, reaching around behind her back and pushing her firmly forward as though she were a nervous child at the Christmas concert who didn't want to perform her solo.

"Well," she hesitated and bit her lip, but Stephen clamped a hand onto her shoulder. "Evelyn asked me to do him a favour and drop some journals from his office to the fort this morning. He'd meant to pick them up before he went to the excavation, but he forgot. Normally I wouldn't, but he's such a kind man and..."

"Kind or handsome?" Stephen said bitterly, cutting her off mid-sentence.

Donna blushed deeply and I felt for her. Stephen's remark had been rude and unfeeling.

"Go on, Donna. You were about to say...," Bill urged.

"I was going to say I didn't have a lot on my plate, and I thought a little trip down to the fort could be fun. I hadn't been down to see what they were up to." Stephen squeezed her shoulder, and she flinched. "I gave him the journals and we talked for a few minutes. Then I left him and came back to the university."

"And the students didn't see him after that?" Bill asked.

"That's just it." Stephen took a handkerchief and dabbed the sweat that had accumulated on his forehead. As though realizing what he was doing, he quickly stuffed it back into his pocket. "According to the students, Evelyn gave them a lecture this morning, as he normally does. Apparently, he demonstrated how to load a musket. God only knows why. I've always said the man is a liability, but that's beside the point. Then he gave them work instructions before saying he was going to put the musket away in his office, and that he'd be back a little later to check on them."

"Then what?" Bill asked, tapping the hairs on his upper lip.

"Then nothing." Stephen shrugged his shoulders emphatically. "He didn't come back. After a while, they got

11

worried. They looked around the site for him but could find neither hide nor hair of the man. Finally, Nadya, his graduate student... you've met her before... came back to campus to inform me of what had happened. I told her to send everyone else home for the day, but they'll be back at Fort York tomorrow morning, expecting to be taught something and to dig. What if Evelyn doesn't show up tomorrow? What if that firebrand upstart just plain ran off? Or what if it's something more sinister? Should we call the police? I'm at a loss here, Bill. In all my years, I've never had to deal with something like this. Nobody has ever just disappeared from an excavation."

Stephen's face grew hot and blotchy as he spoke. Though there was plainly no love lost between the department head and the junior professor, who I had heard insisted on pushing the boundaries of the status quo at the university, it was clear Stephen was wavering somewhere between anger and concern. I wasn't sure what to make of it either. I quite liked Evelyn myself, and I knew Bill did, too. He was clever and charming, the centre of attention at any social gathering, though not in a pretentious or obnoxious way. People simply liked to hear what he had to say, and he seemed genuinely to enjoy the pleasure of others' company. I had the impression that Stephen, something of a stick-in-the-mud traditionalist and approaching retirement himself, had started to feel like a dinosaur in the increasingly youthful and forward-thinking department.

"Did you call Evelyn's wife?" I asked.

If Bill were to go missing, I knew any one of his friends or colleagues would contact me first.

12

"I tried," Stephen replied, stuffing his hand into his pocket and fidgeting with the handkerchief. "But she wasn't home. I wasn't sure what else to do, beyond going to the police. I thought that might be somewhat of an overreaction, so I came to see you, Bill. At this point, I just want to make sure the students aren't at the dig alone, until we can sort this out. Would you mind going down to the fort tomorrow to supervise them?"

Stephen then lowered his voice, pleading and desperate. "I'm sure Evelyn will be back by then. He probably stormed off on one of his tantrums and will have cooled down, but just in case he's decided to abandon his position for good, as he sometimes threatens to do, I would feel a lot better if you were there. There's nobody else with time to take this on. Winter is approaching quickly, the funding is running out for this blasted dig, and Nadya may be a brilliant student, but I don't know that she's got the gumption to tell all those young men what do to. They need someone with some authority. She'll make a good lab tech someday, but she'll never advance in field archaeology if she can't hand out orders."

I looked at Bill, then back at Stephen. Had the entire department forgotten Bill was retired and no longer worked for the university? The fact seemed to have eluded Bill himself for some time now. Would we ever get the quiet retirement I'd hoped for?

"Of course," Bill nodded. "Happy to help out where I'm needed. From what I've seen, Nadya is very competent, if a bit shy. I was planning to go down to Fort York, anyway. I bumped into Evelyn just last week and he told me they'd found some bones. He thinks they are probably human and asked if I'd consult before they excavate further. Tomorrow's as good a day as any, and with luck, I can chat with Evelyn himself about what's to be done next."

Stephen ran his hand over his nearly bald scalp. "I hope you're right and that he comes back to resume his duties with his tail between his legs. I'll strangle the man myself if he doesn't show up on time in the morning. Let's go, Donna."

Stephen placed his hand on Donna's lower back and ushered her out of the room.

Chapter 4

"Bill, how did Evelyn seem when you spoke to him last week?" I asked, looking up from my half-eaten dinner of roast chicken with boiled carrots and potatoes.

No answer.

"Bill?" I repeated, placing my hand on his and squeezing it gently.

He looked at me, surprised, then smiled. "Sorry, Beatrix, I was just thinking about what Stephen said."

"I imagined as much," I patted his hand. "I asked how Evelyn seemed when you spoke to him?"

I looked down at Muffin, sitting patiently beside my husband, her eyes fixated on Bill's left hand, waiting for any treat he might sneak to her during dinner.

"He seemed fine, as always," Bill replied, picking up his fork and moving the chicken around his plate. "I spoke to him briefly when he stopped by the lab. He said we could speak more on site and that he was excited to have found some possible remains at the fort itself, rather than at one of the military burial grounds."

Bill explained that over 130 men had died, counting the British, Americans, Indian warriors, and Canadian militia, when the Americans attacked and captured Fort York in 1813. Outnumbered by the Americans, the British retreated, blowing up their stores of gunpowder to prevent the Americans from using them in the war. When the Grand Magazine at Fort York exploded, the casualties were significant.

When it came to burying the dead, Evelyn had told Bill the Americans felt rushed and did a poor job of digging the graves. Many of the bodies were moved to cemeteries after the British came back to the fort, but it seemed some could have been left behind.

"I had no idea there might still be some graves underfoot there," I said, setting my fork down and adjusting my glasses. "Fort York still has some secrets to be revealed."

Fort York was an unusual sight in Toronto. The early 19th century medley of soldiers' barracks, blockhouses, and magazines built of brick, stone, and wood a stark contrast to the modern city growing up all around. Bill and I went there from time to time, taking advantage of the open spaces of Garrison Common Park to let Muffin run. Fort York had originally been constructed east of its current location as a defensive fort to garrison troops in the last years of the 18th century. John Graves Simcoe, lieutenant-governor of Upper Canada, ordered the fort built to protect Upper Canada from an American invasion as British-U.S. relations deteriorated after the War of Independence. During the War of 1812, the fort was moved to the west side of Garrison Creek after the

Americans captured the original fort from the British in April 1813, and returned in July to burn the buildings, destroying what was left of the defenses of the capital of Upper Canada.

Though old maps showed the fort once stood directly on the shores of Lake Ontario, the city had expanded south by filling in the harbour. Originally called York, Toronto had spread its wings of iron, glass, and concrete far and wide, forcing nature to retreat. She was no match for the thieving backhoe and hungry chainsaw. Miraculously, in the early 20th century, the fort was saved from developers and turned into a historical site and museum, a tangible reminder of the city's past even if it felt like something of an anachronism next to the giant pillars of the now complete Gardiner Expressway. Cars zipped along at high speeds, while tranquil Fort York slumbered below, oblivious to the passage of time and growth of the metropolis.

"Indeed," Bill scratched at his beard. "Let's just hope Evelyn walks through the gates at Fort York tomorrow morning with a good explanation for his absence. If not, I think it will be time to call the police."

As I cleared the dishes away from the table, I knew I wouldn't be getting much sleep that night, wondering where Evelyn had disappeared to and why.

Chapter 5

Bill was up early the next morning, the muffled sounds of his rustling in the kitchen reaching our bedroom upstairs. I patted the bedside table until I'd located my glasses. Putting them on, I looked around to see if Muffin was having a lie-in, but failing to discover a furry body lazily stretched out on the quilt, I decided she must be downstairs with Bill.

"Good morning, Beatrix," he greeted me when I entered the kitchen.

"Good morning, dear," I said, noticing the trail of oatmeal that spread across the counter and onto the stove, but pretending I didn't. I wondered how he had even managed such a feat.

"Oatmeal for breakfast?" he asked, pulling the wooden spoon from the pot and turning toward me. Little droplets of beige gruel dribbled over the countertop.

At least it wasn't on the wall, I thought. Yet.

"Sounds delightful," I said, standing on my tiptoes to give him a light peck on the cheek. There were worse things than spilled oatmeal. "Any word from Stephen this morning?" I asked, wondering if the department head might have contacted him with news about Evelyn.

"Nothing," Bill frowned. "Would you mind giving Margaret a call?"

Margaret was Evelyn's wife. She was a fashionable young woman with dark eyes and hair, and though quiet in comparison to her husband, I had always felt they complimented one another. Evelyn loved to throw parties for friends and colleagues, and we'd visited their house on occasion, their two adopted children tucked away in bed while the adults drank wine and socialized downstairs. Margaret was the perfect hostess, impeccably dressed and not a hair out of place, waving her hand grandly around the room while serving staff offered drinks and canapés to guests who balanced a wine glass in one hand and a cigarette in the other. The room blanketed in a haze of smoke was Evelyn's stage as he regaled us with tales of his youthful adventures abroad and university in the United Kingdom before he returned to Canada and the stability of family life. Bill and I were not nearly stylish or young enough for the Volks' parties, sneaking out early before the music got too loud and the guests too tipsy, but we enjoyed the early hours of the events when everyone tried hard to impress the others with their travels and scholarly knowledge. We always went home and discussed the latest revelations before falling into the deep, undisturbed sleep of those who knew they weren't missing a thing.

"Of course," I said, glancing at the clock on the wall. It was 7:15 in the morning, but I guessed she'd be up.

Though Margaret and Evelyn had hired a live-in maid from the Caribbean, Abigail, to help with household chores and care for the children, I surmised Margaret would still need to rise early to see them off to school. I picked up the receiver of the phone we kept on the buffet in the kitchen and opened our small leather address book with my free hand. Placing a glass paperweight on the book to keep it open, I punched the numbered buttons with my index finger.

The phone rang twice before I heard a voice on the other end: "Good morning, you've reached the Volk residence. How may I help you?"

I recognized Abigail's lilting accent and soft voice.

"Good morning, Abigail," I said, hoping I sounded bright and cheerful despite the circumstances. We didn't know yet if there was need to worry. "It's Mrs. Forster. How are you?"

"Ah, hello, Mrs. Forster. I'm well, thank you." She sounded relieved to hear my voice. "Are you calling for Mrs. Volk?"

"I am, indeed. Is she up?"

"Yes, she's just waking the children now. Give me a moment, and I'll get her."

"Thank you, Abigail."

There was a clunking noise as she set the receiver down and then silence. After a minute, I heard Margaret's voice.

"Beatrix, how are you?" she asked. Her voice sounded as it always did over the phone, a little breathless. It had always seemed practised, as though she modelled it after the late Marilyn Monroe's manner of speaking.

"I'm well, thank you, dear. How are you?"

"Oh, just the usual morning struggle. We're getting the kids up, and you know how much they enjoy leaving their warm beds in the morning. Maybe Abigail told you already."

"She did," I said, wondering how to approach the subject of Evelyn. I looked up at Bill who was watching me, listening to one half of the conversation. "I'm calling about Evelyn. Have you seen him since yesterday morning?"

"That's an odd question," Margaret hesitated a moment, then lowered her voice. "I saw him yesterday morning before he went to Fort York. I'm sure you know he's directing the excavations there. Is that what this is about? The dig?"

"Yes, that's what I'm calling about. Stephen said yesterday that after his morning lecture, Evelyn didn't go back to supervise the students. Did he come home yesterday at all?"

Margaret paused, then said slowly: "I can't say I've seen him since he left in the morning."

"Aren't you concerned he didn't come home after work?" I asked, trying to keep my voice from sounding accusatory.

If Bill had not returned home after going to the university, I'd have been beside myself.

"Oh no, Beatrix. That's nothing to worry about," Margaret responded, her words tumbling out. "Evelyn does this sometimes, staying out all night. If he has too much to drink with friends in the evening, he'll often stay over, and I might not see him for a day or two. You shouldn't be concerned at all."

"What about the excavation?" I pushed, hoping to get to the bottom of the story. It was one thing for a man to stay over with friends after a few drinks, though that bothered me given Evelyn had two young children at home. It was quite another to disappear in the middle of a workday and not tell anybody. "Nadya said he went to his office for something in the morning and didn't come back. Donna dropped some things off for him, but nobody seems to have seen him since."

"I'm not sure," Margaret said. She took a deep, audible breath. "You know Evelyn. The slightest chance of fun or adventure will have him running off in all directions. I know it sounds bad... unprofessional, I mean. You don't think Stephen will cause any trouble, do you? He doesn't like Evelyn much."

"I don't think it's that," I told her, wrapping the phone's cord around my finger. "He seemed genuinely worried. Bill and I will go down to Fort York this morning, and I hope we'll see Evelyn there."

"I'm sure he'll be there, Beatrix. If he comes home before then, I'll give you a call, so you don't have to go for nothing. I'm sorry you've had to worry, but I'm sure Evelyn's fine. It's just the way he is."

"Thank you, Margaret," I replied. "I'm sure you're right and Stephen is worrying for nothing. If we hear anything, we'll let you know, as well."

"That would be appreciated. Talk soon."

Margaret sounded almost defeated. As I hung up the phone, I felt sorry for her. I'd imagined her life was perfect domestic bliss. The charming husband, beautiful home, hired help, two adorable young children, the latest fashions. What more could she ask for? She had the life many women her age dreamed of. And yet, it seemed their marriage wasn't as idyllic as they'd let on at their parties. No husband and father should be staying out all night, leaving his family alone and not knowing where he might be.

Chapter 6

With Muffin trotting between us, Bill and I walked up the path to the gates on the west side of Fort York. At quarter to nine in the morning, it was quiet, the manicured lawns of the historic site healthy and glistening in the morning sun despite how late it was in the season. As Stephen had said, winter would be here before we knew it, freezing the ground and blanketing the buildings in snow. The fort, bordered by the railway to the north and the new expressway to the south, was a silent witness to the city's history and how close it once came to becoming the territory of our neighbours to the south.

In the spring of 1813, the American army captured Fort York, setting fire to the parliamentary buildings, Government House, and other public property before abandoning the site to attack Fort George in Niagara, across the lake. By late summer of 1814, the British hadn't forgotten the afront at York and set fire to much of Washington D.C., including the White House. The War of 1812 finally came to an end in early 1815, both sides paying the price of a lengthy war in blood, thousands of lives and limbs lost, but with little to show for it.

I tucked my silk scarf deeper into my coat as we passed between the brick buildings that had been, in 1815, newly constructed soldiers' barracks for the British army. I had decided to accompany Bill to the fort, but had no intention of digging. I dressed as I would for any other outing in the city. Bill, however, had donned his archaeology garb of khaki pants, leather boots, and the heavy red and black plaid Mackinaw jacket he wore to excavate when the weather was cooler. That morning, I tied a red kerchief around Muffin's neck so she would be easier to spot if she wandered off, which she almost certainly would the moment Bill and I got distracted. I felt anxious as we walked toward the excavation area, my stomach unsettled. I wondered if we would see Evelyn.

Instead, I spotted Nadya, one of Evelyn's graduate students, wave as we approached. Both Bill and I had met her before. She had a reputation for being an excellent academic, but her shyness was viewed as a flaw in the male-dominated field of archaeology. Passion and talent weren't enough to ensure success, and I didn't doubt she was aware of the fact. Nadya wore her dirty blonde hair tied back into a knot at the nape of her neck and no makeup on her face.

"Good morning, Nadya," Bill said, reaching out to shake her hand.

She accepted his hand but didn't maintain eye contact.

"It's good to see you again, dear," I said squeezing her arm. "Professor Blake asked Bill, I mean, Professor Forster, to come by until we can track down Professor Volk."

"There's still no word from him?" She looked down at me intently, chewing on her lower lip.

Nadya was a tall girl, not quite Bill's height, but close enough that she hovered over me like a pelican over a seagull.

"I'm sorry, Nadya, we don't have any news. However, I did speak with Mrs. Volk this morning and she wasn't concerned, so I don't think you should be either."

"Oh, that's good," Nadya said, glancing away from me and down at Muffin, who sat primly by my feet.

Nadya crouched down to pat the little terrier who was a sponge for attention. She ran her hand over the handkerchief around Muffin's neck.

"I like her scarf, Mrs. Forster," Nadya said, looking up.

I laughed. "Yes, I thought red would be easy to spot in the distance. No doubt as soon as we look the other way, she'll run off to explore the grounds. Like a naughty child, this one."

Nadya smiled and stood.

"What time will the students arrive?" Bill asked.

"I wasn't sure what might happen today." Nadya shoved her hands into the pockets of her jeans. "I told them to come a little late, around 10:00, just in case. I hope that's alright. We normally get started at 9:30."

"Sounds reasonable," Bill replied. "It'll give us a chance to look around. Do you mind giving the grand tour, Nadya?"

"No problem, Professor Forster," she nodded.

Nadya walked around the demarcated area of the excavation, on the south boundary of the fort. She explained that they were excavating the foundations of two buildings that had been lost over the years. The excavation area lay along the fortification wall and earthworks. She pointed to the eastern part of the excavation trench and noted that the building that once stood there was the cookhouse. Next to it, on the west side, had been soldiers' barracks, probably similar to those we'd walked past when we entered the fort. Nadya lit up as she explained the findings, showing us a few trays with an assortment of artifacts pulled from the excavation. There were broken ceramics, fractured animal bones, both metal and bone buttons, unidentifiable objects of various materials, the tip of a bayonet, half a riding stirrup, a key, and the ubiquitous white clay pipes found at historical archaeology sites across North America.

"Nadya," Bill interrupted suddenly as she was holding up a broken glass artifact from one of the trays. Knowing Bill, his mind had wandered to other subjects. "I saw Professor Volk last week and he asked me to come down to offer my opinion on some bones you'd found. He thought they might be human. Where are they?"

"Oh yes, the bones," Nadya shook her head. "Of course, you'd want to see those straight away. Sorry, Professor Forster. I should have thought of that first."

"Not to worry, Nadya," Bill said, taking his glasses off and polishing them with a cloth he kept in his jacket pocket. "I'm simply curious. That's all."

I, on the other hand, was more curious about the whereabouts of the excavation's leader.

Chapter 7

As Nadya led us back through the Fort York gates where Bill and I had entered that morning, I decided to ask her about the events of the day before.

"Nadya, do you mind telling us what happened yesterday? With Professor Volk, I mean. Was he acting strangely at all?"

Nadya stopped and looked at me. "No, there was nothing unusual that I noticed. He seemed himself and was excited to show the students how to load a musket. It wasn't necessary. It's not like they needed to know how to load one for the dig, but one of the students, I think it was Anthony, asked about how the flint worked after he found one in the excavation area. Professor Volk thought it would be fun to do a demonstration of how a flintlock musket functioned. Of course, it's too dangerous to fire a weapon here. He didn't do that. Just loaded it, and explained what would happen if he pulled the trigger."

I didn't think I knew any of the students participating at the dig. The name Anthony didn't ring any bells, but perhaps my memory wasn't what it used to be.

"What happened after he showed everyone how to use the musket?" I asked.

"Well...." Nadya looked at me and then down at the ground. She kicked at the grass with her boot. "Then he said he'd take the gun back to his office and come back to supervise the excavation work. After some time went by and he didn't come back, I walked over to check his office, but he wasn't there. I told the students we should have a look around the grounds, just in case. We didn't find him. That's when I went to campus to tell Professor Blake. I figured he would know what to do. I hope it was the right thing."

"Of course, it was," I reassured her. She looked worried, as though she would get into trouble because Evelyn had gone missing and she'd reported it. "We want to find out where he is. That's all. Make sure he's alright."

"Where are you taking us, Nadya?" Bill interjected, looking around. We'd passed through the gates and stood back on the path where we'd entered.

"Didn't Professor Volk tell you he opened some test pits outside the walls of the fort?" Nadya asked. "That's where we found the bones. They're in one of the test pits out here."

"No, I hadn't realized." Bill scratched at his beard. "I suppose that makes sense. From what I've read, the battlefield and the range of the explosion of the Grand Magazine would have extended well beyond the area delimited by today's fort."

"Exactly." Nadya smiled, transported back to the world of archaeology.

As the three of us, with Muffin bouncing ahead, walked toward the test pit, I noticed a young man in a yellow rain jacket approach the grounds of the fort. It seemed odd since it wasn't raining, but I thought perhaps he was one of the students, and a rain jacket was a good way to protect clothing from the muck of an excavation.

Chapter 8

The test pit was nothing more than a one metre by one metre square dug into the grass beyond the western boundary of the fort. To the east, past a dry moat, the fraise of sharpened stakes pointed menacingly toward us from an earthworks rampart constructed to defend the fort. The approaching enemy might have felt intimidated by the wooden spikes jutting into their path, something pulled from a medieval war saga, but in the contemporary era of peace and tranquility they were harmless, a mere decorative feature of the old fort.

Nadya crouched down, kneeling on the grass, and pulled back an olive-green tarpaulin that had been folded several times and placed carefully over the bones that had been revealed prior to Evelyn's disappearance. Bill got down beside her and pulled a metal dental pick and delicate paintbrush from his pocket. There was little to see beyond a small area of dense dirt-stained matter, which I presumed to be bone given what Evelyn told Bill. Bill immediately flicked dirt from the edges of the bone with the dental tool and brushed away the loose soil. He repeated the action several times until more and more bone was revealed.

"What do you think?" Nadya asked, leaning into the pit to get a better look. "Is it human?"

"Looks like it," Bill replied, brushing more dirt away. Muffin moved in to see what the fuss was about, but I called her back. She was an avid digger when given the opportunity, creating great craters in the backyard if she sniffed out a vole or mouse, but her skills were undesirable at an excavation. "It's a tibia, but I want to see if it's in anatomical connection to the fibula, femur, and talus. There were a lot of medical waste pits in those days. Soldiers suffered traumatic amputations on the battlefield. You wouldn't believe the damage a speeding cannon ball can create when it hits flesh and bone. And of course, there were also surgical amputations, when limbs were so damaged they couldn't be repaired. This could be a pile of discarded limbs, or it could be a complete burial. We'll have a better idea once more has been uncovered."

I shuddered at the thought of pits full of amputated limbs. The conditions for soldiers in those days were ghastly and the field of medicine wasn't particularly advanced in the early 19th century. Surgeons were known to hack off limbs quickly and efficiently, a skilled practitioner executing an amputation in a matter of minutes, start to finish. Without anaesthetic in those days, their patients bit down on a piece of wood to prevent them from breaking their teeth during the agonizing procedure. If they were lucky, they might get a swig of liquor before the battlefield surgeon began his grisly work, but many were not so fortunate. Surviving the amputation in less-than-optimal conditions was another story.

"Well?" Nadya prompted Bill. "Anything?"

Bill laughed. "Patience! I thought archaeology would have taught you that important life lesson by now."

Nadya pulled her head out of the pit and sat back. "Oops! I got excited."

"Come on, Bill," I intervened. "Put us both out of our misery. What are your thoughts?"

"I can't say with one hundred percent certainty." Bill looked up at me, his hands on either side of the pit to support him. "But the tibia is connected to the femur as it should be. The patella has shifted a little to the side, but that's not unusual. Of course, this could be an entire amputated leg, but given it seems to be completely straight and facing up it is highly likely this is a complete individual, not just an amputated limb."

Nadya grinned and quietly clapped her hands together at Bill's proclamation. He wasn't the only one excited at the prospect of a dead body. I looked around us and realized Muffin had taken advantage of our distraction and run off somewhere. Now I'd have to track her down. Frankly, one disappearance was plenty.

Chapter 9

Once Bill was satisfied and decided the direction the test pit should be extended to excavate the skeletal remains, we returned inside the walls of the fort with Nadya. She would have to meet the students soon and as far as I could see, looking out around the vast expanse of Garrison Common for the tri-coloured body and red scarf, Muffin must have gone back through the gates. How far could she have wandered in such a short time?

"How many students are there?" I asked Nadya as we trudged over the grass.

"It's a small group, Mrs. Forster," Nadya said, looking over at me. Her initial shyness seemed to have diminished as we got down to the business of archaeology, which was evidently a source of great pleasure for her. "There are just four students: Anthony, Brian, Marco, and Christopher. They're all master's students because the undergrads are in classes during the fall. Do you know any of them?"

I shook my head. "I'm afraid I don't. Other than the students at San Miguel, who were primarily undergraduates and mostly with a focus on physical anthropology, I haven't been much involved with the student body in the past few years. Bill might be familiar with the names."

Bill said nothing and seemed not to be listening to the conversation. He strode along ahead of us, his long legs propelling him quickly toward the excavation area. A man on a mission. Though Nadya was clearly capable of keeping pace with Bill, she politely hung back with me, my stout legs working hard to keep up.

"All the students are men, I take it?" I asked.

"It's the way things are, isn't it?" She sighed, tucking a loose strand of hair behind her ear. "At least, in archaeology."

"Take heart, Nadya," I said. "Things are changing. Progress is slow and it comes in waves that are sometimes unpredictable. There will be setbacks because people fear change, but with time, I'm confident that women like you will lead the way. We've already taken great strides forward from when I was a young woman. I was told, over and over, until it rang true in my ears, that women were put on this earth to be wives and mothers. Luckily, I met Bill, and he wasn't so narrow-minded about women's roles in society as my parents had been. I worked as much in archaeology as any man can hope to, even if it wasn't my intention."

Nadya's eyes welled with tears, so I said no more. I knew firsthand the struggles women faced in the field. I didn't want her to feel vulnerable when we were about to meet the students. Women were so frequently criticized for their emotions; it had become cliché. A woman could never be a strong leader because she was too emotional. Of course, those who said such things viewed tears as emotions, but never anger and violence.

Back at the excavation site, there were four young men idling around, their bags tossed casually to the ground nearby. They looked as though they could have been on the album cover for a popular music group, each one dressed in near identical clothing, matching the young man next to him. Straight-legged blue jeans, leather boots, and thick tartan jacket buttoned up against the cool, early-November weather. The only originality in their ensembles could be found in the various colours of plaid. I couldn't help but smile at how comical they looked.

"Hi, Nadya." One of the boys stepped forward as we approached and nodded at her. Unlike the others, he had dark skin and tightly curled hair. "Any word from Professor Volk?"

"Hi everyone," Nadya replied, shifting her gaze from the students to the grass to the excavation area. "Sorry, Anthony, we haven't heard anything yet. I think you probably all know Professor Forster, and this is his wife, Mrs. Forster. They've come down to help out until Professor Volk comes back."

Anthony stepped forward to shake my hand. He was tall and lean, and made me think of a younger Sydney Poitier. After returning from Spain, Bill and I had gone to the theatre to watch *In the Heat of the Night*, the latest Norman Jewison film starring Poitier and depicting the devastating impact of racial bigotry in the southern United States. Though perhaps not to the same degree as what was depicted in the film, I imagined that Anthony's life in Toronto might not be so easy given that the majority of Toronto's population was of European descent. Canadians were no more immune to prejudice than anywhere else in the world, though we liked to believe in our superiority when it came to tolerance.

"Pleasure to meet you, Mrs. Forster," Anthony said, smiling. His grip was gentle, but firm.

"The pleasure is mine," I said cheerfully.

The young men each shook Bill's hand and then introduced themselves to me. Brian was a tall, yet plump, red-haired fellow with a jovial presence. He still looked very young, with exaggerated dimples creating cavernous pockets in his cheeks, and his green eyes sparkled when he smiled. Marco was more serious, with tanned skin and dark hair. He mumbled a little when he spoke and was much shorter than both Anthony and Brian. Finally, Christopher, who had very pale skin, blue eyes and chestnut hair introduced himself, but he noticeably didn't extend his hand to shake mine. In fact, he struggled to look me in the eye. I wasn't sure if it was shyness, like Nadya, or dislike.

As Bill chatted with the students and Nadya about details of the excavation, I remembered Muffin. She'd been off exploring on her own long enough, and though she was mostly well behaved, she was still a terrier at heart, and I liked to keep her in sight. I'd brought her leash along in my purse, in case she got it into her head to be too adventurous. I pulled the long, red leather strap from my bag and waved it at Bill so he'd know I'd gone to look for her.

Chapter 10

I walked across the clipped lawn, the soles of my flat brown oxfords sinking into the soft ground with each step. Every now and again I'd whistle, hoping Muffin would hear me and come racing over. The one-storey building directly north of the excavation area, constructed of stone, was my first stop. I read the sign, posted for visitors to the site, indicating that it was a magazine, constructed in 1815 below grade to protect it from enemy fire. It would have stored casks of gunpowder, artillery cartridges, muskets, and other weapons used for battle in those days. I walked down the steps to the door on the south side of the building. It had a green tinge to it, being made of copper. They couldn't use iron on the exterior surface of the magazines because the slightest spark could have resulted in the explosion of the entire store of ammunition. Of course, the British had intentionally blown up the Grand Magazine as the Americans approached Fort York in 1813, but the accidental explosion of a magazine would have caused great injury to those within the walls of the fort. Copper, being a soft metal, would dent if struck but not create sparks. Since the door was fully closed and latched, I knew Muffin wouldn't be inside. She was clever, but thankfully not crafty or tall enough to open doors.

I carried on, around the stone magazine into the extensive span of the fort's grounds. During the early morning it had been quite calm despite our proximity to the lake, but the wind had picked up and a sudden strong gust nearly tore my hat off. I clamped a gloved hand over my head to prevent it from taking flight and wished that hat pins hadn't gone out of fashion decades ago. I pushed on, the wind whipping the hem of my skirt against my legs, thinking that what was practical should never be out of style. Ahead, a long, one-storey brick building caught my eye. The western-most entrance on the south side of the building was closed, but the next access to the east was open, the wooden door banging against the brick wall when the wind picked up. I recalled from previous visits to Fort York that this building had been the officers' quarters in the days when the British army was stationed here. Compared to the soldiers' quarters, the rooms for the officers were almost luxurious, though not compared to our 20th century standards of living. I knew that the open door would be temptation enough for a curious wire fox terrier.

As I approached the brick building, I saw the man in the yellow rain jacket leaving the east side of the building. He noticed me staring at him, smiled, and waved in a nonchalant manner. I waved back, still clutching the red leash in my hand. I wondered who he might be – did he work at the fort or was he a visitor? It was clear now he wasn't one of the students. There weren't many visitors, but the historical site wasn't closed to the public during the excavations either. Though Fort York occupied a large swath of land in the centre of the city, it felt as though people had forgotten it existed or had simply ceased caring about the history it represented. What relevance did an old fort have for urbanites who drove to work in automobiles, went shopping at Eaton's department store, and spent the weekend at the cottage in the Muskokas? The past had been enveloped in dust and cobwebs as developers still pushed and shoved to convince the city to tear the fort down to build shopping malls or new skyscrapers that blocked out the sun. I turned back to look at the landscape behind me, the expressway blocking much of the view that once existed, but you could still just see the recognizable red Tip Top Tailors sign in the distance, another relic of days past.

I stepped through the entryway and into the building, pulling the door shut behind me. I imagined it wasn't meant to be left open and at the mercy of the mercurial Toronto breeze. To my left there was a small room with a small black fireplace decorated to look the way it had when an officer of the British Army lived there. There was a wooden table, laid out with a blue and white china tea service, and a desk in the corner, with various writing materials displayed, as though the officer had just stepped out for a moment and would be back to enjoy his tea. The next room down the hall had a single bed, pushed up against the wall, with rough-looking bedding. A mannequin wearing the recognizable red coat with gold buttons of the army stood motionless in the corner, a pair of worn black boots adorning its feet. What appeared to be a taxidermied cat lay curled in a ball as though sleeping near the fireplace. Some chicken wire stretched across the doorway prevented me from inspecting the animal more closely to confirm my suspicions that the cat had once been a living and breathing being. Though it was a museum and historic site, it gave me the sensation that I was intruding on the life of the imaginary officer who occupied these rooms.

When I arrived at the last room at the end of the hallway, the door slightly ajar, I knew I'd found Evelyn's field office for the Fort York excavations. There was a 'No Entry' sign beside the door, but I paid it no mind. A modern desk had been placed in the middle of the room with a wooden chair tucked under it. There were piles of papers and magazines on the desk, a stained coffee cup on a bright ceramic coaster, a handful of pencils in another cup, and some sketches easily distinguishable as scale maps of the excavation area. In a corner of the room, there were a few stray hand tools, still dirty and piled on top of one another, but no pickaxes or shovels. He must have had access to another area at the fort to store the larger tools essential to any dig. Next to the excavation tools, propped against the wall, I saw the musket Nadya had mentioned. I was no munitions expert, but the glossy wood and untarnished metal made me think it was a replica and not an artifact of the War of 1812. Knowing how volatile and dangerous muskets could be if not handled properly, and sometimes even if they were, I didn't touch the weapon. However, I did wonder if it was still loaded or if Evelyn had disabled it before he disappeared the day before.

I was about to leave the office when something in the large, brick-lined fireplace built into the wall grabbed my attention. Among the blackened ashes was the scrap of a white page that had escaped the destruction of the flames. I crouched down, my knees protesting the movement with a sharp twinge. I could read a handful of words along the top of the page that had not been burned away.

lyn Volk   Analysis of clay tobacco pipes at historical si

The rest of the title of the article had been consumed by the fire. It appeared the page belonged to an academic journal, and I wondered why Evelyn would burn his own published work. I was also surprised that the city had given him permission to have a fire at a historic site. Though it was cool outside, surely it would be considered too dangerous to use the fireplace in these old buildings. A stray ember could destroy the quarters before the fire brigade could even be called. I thought back to what Stephen Blake had said about Evelyn the day before, that he was a liability. Is this what he'd meant? That Evelyn didn't follow the rules or placed his own convenience above safety? Perhaps. Stephen and I knew Evelyn in very different ways. To me, Evelyn was Bill's charming colleague, young and adventurous, but he'd seemed harmless. To Stephen, he was something else altogether. I'd imagined a professional rivalry, but after speaking with Margaret it seemed there was more to Evelyn than I would have guessed.

I stood up and winced at the pain in my lower back. I took a moment to straighten my knees slowly and curl my spine forward to counteract the discomfort that issued from my lumbar vertebrae. The cooler weather tended to bring on additional bouts of rheumatism. I was about to leave Evelyn's office when I heard the distinct sound of growling, followed by several high-pitched yips coming from a nearby room. As

I turned to leave Evelyn's office, I wondered what could be provoking Muffin?

Chapter 11

I followed the sound of Muffin's excited yapping as best I could, but I wasn't certain of the exact layout of the building. I walked briskly down the hallway, retreating the way I'd entered, my heavy footsteps echoing in the void. I glanced in at each room, but there was no dog. The sound of her agitated barking was farther away. At the end of the hallway, I turned left into what might have been a sitting room. Still, no small dog. The next room was a large dining room, set for the officers to take a meal. The farther I went into the maze of rooms, the closer her barking seemed.

I stepped into another hallway or foyer of some sort and there she was, the mischievous little terrier with her kerchief tied around her neck.

"Goodness, Muffin," I said, beginning to unwind her leash. "What are you barking at? There's nothing here."

I looked around the small space that had a doorway I could see led into the kitchen. There was shelving on the far wall with various odds and ends, plates, jugs, containers displayed. As far as I could see, Muffin was barking at the hatch door that probably provided access to the cellar. I clasped her leash onto her collar, half-hidden by the scarf around her neck, thinking she would settle once she was under my control. She barely even noticed that I'd touched her and kept staring at the door.

"What is it, Muffy?" I asked, following her intent gaze. "Come on, now. I'll show you there's nothing to see."

I bent over, despite the tenderness in my back, and pulled at the handle on the door. It was awkward and heavy. At first, I couldn't get it open. I let go of Muffin's leash and tried pulling with both hands. The hinges squealed, but with significant effort I was able to pull the door up and lean it against the wall, so it remained open. I could see that there were stairs, but they led to an opaque darkness. I looked around, wondering if there was anything I could use to light the passageway. It was too dark to risk going down. I watched as Muffin started toward the stairs, but I quickly stepped on her leash.

"Oh, no you don't," I said, leaning over and grasping the red leather in my hand. "You're not going anywhere, little vixen."

I pulled her toward the kitchen which was a medley of the old and new. Though much of the kitchen had been staged to look as it had in the early 19th century, there was a cabinet near the door which held a variety of modern objects. I brief scan of the items gave me exactly what I needed – a silver Energizer flashlight. I hoped the batteries were still working. I clicked the button and fortunately, the bulb flicked on. I returned to the hallway and shone the light down the stairs. As I glimpsed the bottom of the staircase, I immediately dropped the flashlight at my feet.

"Oh, no," I whispered. "Oh, no. Not again."

Chapter 12

I took a deep breath, then grabbed the flashlight in one hand and picked up Muffin and tucked her under my other arm. She weighed only about 17 pounds, but she squirmed like a worm at the end of a hook as I held her at the top of the hatch door. I shone the light down the stairs again. Evelyn's body lay on its side at the bottom. He could have been sleeping, but I knew he wasn't. I watched for a few seconds, hoping to see the rise and fall of his chest, but he was deathly still. Near his head, there was a small blood stain on the stone floor, but I couldn't see the injury. I set Muffin back down on the ground and she pulled hard to get to the stairs.

"Oh, dear, Muffin," I said, yanking on her leash to get her to follow me away from the scene. "We need to get Bill."

I walked as quickly as my legs would carry me back toward the excavation area. Once we were away from the cellar, Muffin trotted along beside me as though she were a proud show dog, and I were a skilled handler. How easy it was for her to forget what she'd found.

As we got closer to the dig, I saw Bill's jacket.

"Bill!" I shouted, waving my free arm in the air. "Bill, come here!"

Bill saw me, my arm flailing desperately, and ran. I knew he would recognize the agitation in my voice.

"What is it, Beatrix?" he asked. "Are you alright?"

"It's..." I couldn't say it. I fought back tears, choking on the thick feeling in the back of my throat. "It's... him. It's Evelyn, Bill. Muffin found him in the cellar of the officers' quarters."

"What?" Bill arched his eyebrows. "Where is he now? Is he alright?"

I shook my head and leaned my head into his chest. He embraced me and held me tight for a few moments.

Once I had recovered, I pulled away from him, looked up and said: "He's at the bottom of the stairs. Muffin was barking at the trap door, and when I opened it, there he was, lying down there. I don't know exactly what happened, but if he'd fallen down the stairs on his own, would the door have been shut above him?"

"Good Lord!" Bill took off his glasses and rubbed his eyes on the sleeve of his jacket. "It must have been an accident. Who would want to hurt Evelyn?"

I looked over to the excavation area where Nadya and the students were watching us, little gophers peeping out of their burrows. My heart thudded in my chest, and I hoped Bill was right. Perhaps Evelyn had fallen down the stairs and pulled the door shut in a failed effort to break his fall. Of course, there was always the possibility someone pushed him, closing the door above to hide their crime long enough to make an escape.

Chapter 13

Bill took one look at Evelyn's body, splayed at the bottom of the cellar stairs, and turned away from the horrible sight.

He wiped the back of his hand over his brow and sighed: "I think we'll need to call Arthur, just in case this wasn't an accident. Do you mind waiting here with Muffin and I'll go find a pay phone if there isn't one at the office?"

I nodded but said nothing. Arthur was my cousin and happened to be a homicide detective with the Metropolitan Toronto Police. I was already eighteen when Arthur was born, something of a late arrival for my aunt and uncle, and I'd looked after him from time to time before I left home. He was a cheery, rambunctious child in those days and now, all these decades later, I still found it hard to reconcile the little boy he once was with his very serious work as a detective.

We saw each other a few times a year for family gatherings, but I couldn't say that we'd remained particularly close. His work and family kept him busy, and when we were younger, the age gap was significant. However, I felt reassured that should it turn out Evelyn hadn't fallen down the stairs accidentally and died at the hands of someone else, Arthur would work hard to find the killer. He was a dedicated officer, though he had been accused of being overzealous in his work at times. Beyond our familial relationship, Bill also had a professional connection to Arthur. On occasion, Arthur had called Bill to consult when human skeletal remains were found, and I knew each had great respect for the work of the other.

When Bill returned from making the call, I told him I would ask Arthur if it would be alright for me to go with him to inform Margaret. I knew she would be distraught, a young widow with two children to care for. Women often found themselves in vulnerable situations when their husbands passed away suddenly. Many had spent little or no time in the work force prior to marriage and had limited skills to take over as the family's primary breadwinner. I didn't know what the Volks' financial situation was, but I knew they led a lavish lifestyle of parties, live-in help, and had a beautiful home in the affluent neighbourhood of Forest Hill. Perhaps she would be fortunate and not have to go to work to put food on the table.

"I'm sure Arthur will be pleased for Margaret to have some support when he delivers the news," Bill agreed. "We'll have to send the students home, and I can go later today to discuss the situation with Stephen. I suppose they'll cancel the dig. He may not like the idea, but he'll have to put some faith in Nadya to wrap things up and close the site. I don't imagine he'll trust her to take over in Evelyn's absence."

"No," I mused, twisting Muffin's leash around my wrist as we waited for Arthur to arrive. "Stephen certainly didn't give the impression he had much confidence in Nadya. Perhaps she just needs someone to believe in her to take on directing an excavation. Margaret told me a few months ago that Evelyn thought Nadya's doctoral research would be brilliant. I think he was very proud of her and her accomplishments. His nature made him overshadow his students, but by all accounts, Nadya has a bright future in archaeology ahead of her."

"Quite true," Bill said. "Evelyn had a knack for recognizing and nurturing talent, and Nadya is no exception. He has always been very good with the graduate students, perhaps a little too familiar sometimes, in my opinion. But he's young, closer to their age. I mean was... I just can't believe he's gone. Just like that."

Bill glanced nervously at the staircase. It felt strange to me to be talking about Evelyn when he was just a few feet away, obscured by the darkness of the cellar. I couldn't see him, but I could feel his presence nearby.

When Arthur walked around the corner into the small hallway and we locked eyes, I was relieved.

"Thank goodness you're here," I said.

"Trixie, Bill," he said giving me a firm squeeze and shaking Bill's hand. Arthur was one of few people in my family to still call me Trixie. It was a nickname I felt I'd outgrown long ago, but he'd used the moniker since he was a child, and it didn't bother me coming from him. "It's good to see you, even under the circumstances."

"I'm glad to see you, too, Arthur," I said, lifting my glasses and wiping a stray tear away with my handkerchief. I snapped open my purse and placed the handkerchief back inside. "The body's down there, in the cellar."

I pointed to the darkness that enveloped the staircase, where Evelyn's body lay. When Arthur approached the cellar with a younger policewoman in tow, I took a few steps back and stood next to Bill. Arthur used an industrial strength flashlight and climbed down the stairs, his burly frame struggling in the narrow space. I could see into the basement now that it was illuminated. Arthur stared at the body for a few moments, said something in a low voice to the woman I assumed must be his partner, and then waved one of the investigators that had accompanied him to come down into the basement.

"You can start setting up a perimeter," Arthur said, climbing halfway back up the stairs and pulling a notebook from the pocket of his grey wool overcoat. He was not a tall man, but he exuded confidence within his milieu. "I'll need to see the other side of his head once we get the requisite photos. Looks like he might just have taken a tumble down the stairs, but I'd like to confirm that with the coroner."

After handing out instructions to the members of the police team, he returned to me and Bill. Muffin stood on her hind legs to greet him, and he scratched her under the chin.

"Hi there, Muffy girl," he cooed. "Who's a good girl?"

His levity in the situation was odd, but I realized he'd seen enough dead bodies in his career that nothing could faze him anymore.

"It's getting crowded in here," Arthur said. "Let's take this outside."

We followed Arthur past the gaping mouth leading to the basement and through the kitchen. He opened the door, and we stepped outside into a recess that existed between sections of the building.

"She found the body," I stated, looking at Muffin and wondering how she could have known. Had she smelled the early stages of decomposition? I could only imagine that the cellar was cool, and Evelyn had been dead less than twenty-four hours according to Donna's and the students' accounts of when Evelyn had gone missing. I hadn't detected the distinct odour of decay, but perhaps she could, her sense of smell more sensitive than humans could even conceive. "She was in there, barking at the hatch door. Once I opened the door and found a flashlight, I saw him lying there."

"Your fingerprints will be on the cellar door. Is that correct?" Arthur looked at me earnestly.

"I'm afraid so," I said. "I had no idea what I was about to find."

"It's fine. Just something to note when we collect evidence. I need you to tell me everything you know," he said, adding our names and the date in his book. "There's no detail too small."

"Does that mean you think he was murdered?" I gasped, squeezing the strap of Muffin's leash firmly in my fist.

Chapter 14

I was startled when Arthur was suddenly called back to the scene by one of his colleagues, who popped his head through the open door and motioned for Arthur to step inside. While we were speaking to my cousin, relaying all the information regarding Evelyn's disappearance we'd gathered from Donna, Nadya, and Stephen, I could see through the window into the kitchen that a man I assumed must be the coroner and the police team had removed the body from the basement and placed it on a black bag on the long kitchen table. Arthur went in and we instinctively followed him. Nobody said anything. Arthur leaned in and examined the right side of Evelyn's head, then he examined the left side. He tapped his pen a few times on his lip.

"Bill," he commanded, beckoning my husband with his hand. "Come here a minute. Not you, Trixie, just Bill. I don't want you to see this."

I was glad he hadn't asked me to inspect the wound I knew must have affected the right side of Evelyn's head. I already had an empty, sickly feeling deep in my stomach that could have been hunger under other circumstances. Though Bill and Arthur had worked together on the skeletonized remains of homicide victims before, Bill wasn't the obvious choice to discuss trauma to the recently deceased. I watched the two men discuss the wound with the coroner, in lowered voices. Just out of earshot, I watched Arthur point at something with his pen and Bill lean in to examine the injury. They both pulled away from Evelyn's corpse and Arthur used his pen to scratch at his beard which had once been a rich, nut brown, but these days was streaked with coarse, gray hairs.

"Pretty gruesome, huh?" A woman's husky voice next to my ear made me jump. "Ever seen anything like it?"

"Pardon me?" I asked, looking at Arthur's partner, surprised by her high spirits.

She appeared to be in her early thirties, dressed in black trousers and a black coat that was belted at the waist. Her dark hair was cut short, her smile expectant.

"Oh sorry, ma'am," she said, still smiling. One of her front teeth was crooked and overlapped the other slightly. "I thought you'd seen. You didn't know the poor fella, did you?"

I realized Arthur must not have told her anything about who we were and our relationship to Evelyn.

"We did," I said gently. "He was my husband's colleague."

The woman's smile disappeared instantly, and she blushed. "Oh, I'm so sorry, ma'am," she stammered. "I didn't know. I thought you were just a visitor and happened upon the scene. I didn't mean to be insensitive. I get carried away sometimes and forget my manners. I'm Detective Constable Silva, by the way. But you can call me Mariana."

"It's fine," I said, shaking her bare hand with my gloved one. "Everyone reacts to these things differently. I'm Beatrix Forster."

I was about to say more when Bill returned to where I stood near the door.

"What was it?" I asked.

"Looks like a large caliber gunshot wound, with no exit wound." He stuffed his hands in his pockets as he spoke. "They'll be able to recover the projectile during the autopsy, or whatever's left of it, but given what we know of Evelyn's activities yesterday and the size and shape of that injury, I don't think it was any modern weapon that killed him."

"Oh, my goodness," I whispered, knowing very well that Bill was referring to the musket Evelyn loaded to show the students. "I saw the musket before, in Evelyn's office. We'd better tell Arthur so he can check for fingerprints."

A gunshot wound to the head certainly ruled out an accidental fall down the stairs, and with the probable weapon safely stored in Evelyn's office, it wasn't suicide either. It was clear now Evelyn had been murdered, but why and by whom?

Chapter 15

Arthur hustled us outside once more, to stand behind the officers' barracks. He pulled a package of cigarettes from his pocket and during a lull in the wind, he lit the end of a white cylinder before placing it between his lips and inhaling deeply. I got the feeling he'd been craving one since his arrival.

"I need to speak to those students before they run off," he said, pointing in the direction of the excavation with the cigarette pinched between his fingers, though neither the students nor the excavation area were visible from behind the building.

"That sounds fair," Bill said. "We can make the introductions."

"You can listen in," Arthur said, putting his lighter back in his pocket. "And tell me if you think they're lying, but don't get involved. You're the only ones who know them. Just keep in mind this is police business. They're all adults and you don't need to protect them. Got it?"

I didn't remind Arthur that I'd only just met most of them that day, except Nadya. I felt it could be insightful to hear what they had to say, and I'd already formed basic first impressions from their introductions that morning.

After Arthur marched us across the grounds of the fort, back to the excavation area, I was out of breath, my chest heaving as I gulped air into my lungs as quickly as I could. Once we arrived, I noticed that Mariana had stayed behind at the scene. Arthur would be interviewing the students by himself.

"We'll start with the girl," he said, looking at Nadya while he puffed on his cigarette.

"Nadya, please come here," Bill called over to her, where she stood awkwardly with the students.

"Am I in trouble?" she asked, glancing from Arthur, to me, to Bill.

I guessed that at this point the students were well aware we'd found Evelyn's body, but they probably knew little else.

"How did you know Professor Volk?" Arthur began, dropping the cigarette to the ground and stubbing it out with his shoe.

"He's my doctoral supervisor," Nadya said.

"What's a pretty girl like you doing a PhD for?" Arthur asked without smiling, while every bone in my body cringed with shame.

Nadya shrugged but said nothing. What could she say? With one question, Arthur had expressed exactly what he thought of female academics.

"Tell me what happened yesterday, after you last saw the professor?" Arthur pulled his notebook and pen from his pocket and flipped to a fresh page.

"I told the Forsters," she began, shakily.

"The Forsters are not the police," he interrupted.

"S-sorry," Nadya stammered. "Professor Volk gave us his morning lecture, which finished around 10:30. He demonstrated how to load a flintlock musket."

"Did he shoot the musket?" Arthur asked.

"No," Nadya shook her head. "It wasn't possible; it's a public space. Donna, the department secretary, arrived just a few minutes before the lecture ended. Professor Volk said he was going to put the musket away in his office, organize some things, do a little paperwork, and come back to see how the work was going. He told me to supervise while he was gone. Donna went with him because she was dropping some things off. After I put the students to work, I went to dig at one of the test pits outside the wall. After a long time passed and he hadn't come over, I went to check with the students to see if he was with them, and then I walked over to see if he was still in his office. After a lecture, he usually goes back to his office, but never for this long. I'm sure it was more than an hour."

"The professor was shot at close range with the musket," Arthur said. "You didn't hear the gun go off?"

Nadya looked on the verge of tears. She bit her lip.

"No," she mumbled. "I'm sorry. I wish I'd heard something, but I was far away."

"What time did you go look for him?" Arthur asked.

"I'm not sure exactly," She hesitated, kicking the toe of her boot into the dirt. "Maybe around 11:45 or noon? I may have lost track, but I felt certain more than an hour had gone by since the lecture. I don't wear a watch to excavate because dirt gets in all the cracks."

Arthur nodded and made a note in his pad.

"The professor's quite a good looking fellow from what I saw," Arthur began. "And young, for a professor."

I wasn't sure where Arthur was going with his statement, but I already didn't like it.

"You're young and attractive, as well," he continued, pointing at Nadya with his pen. "Was there anything beyond a professional relationship between you?"

Nadya's head shot up and her mouth fell open. I desperately wanted to intervene on Nadya's behalf, the poor girl, but the truth was, I didn't know the answer to Arthur's question. Could Nadya have had an inappropriate relationship with her supervisor? From what I'd heard, her work was unimpeachable, but these kinds of relationships between professors and students did happen from time to time. Over the years, Bill had recounted several cases that were quickly swept under the rug by the department, the girl being pushed out of the university and the professor receiving a slap on the wrist and then, when nobody was looking, a slap on the back. Nadya would know the risk to her reputation and career if she were involved with Evelyn. Would she have put all she'd worked for in jeopardy for a married man?

"No, absolutely not," Nadya said firmly once she'd recovered from her initial shock. "Professor Volk was my supervisor, nothing more."

Chapter 16

Next, Arthur wanted to speak to the "red-haired one". Brian approached, smiling nervously. He extended his hand to Arthur, but my cousin ignored it. Brian retracted his outstretched appendage as if he'd just seen a snake, and the smile disappeared from his face.

"I'm Brian," he said. "Brian Wilson. Not of the Beach Boys..."

His voice trailed off. Had the circumstances been different, his reference to a more famous Brian probably would have made Arthur chuckle, but in the role of homicide detective, my cousin was cold and untouchable.

"I know who you are," Arthur said. "You do understand that your professor was murdered, correct?"

Brian hung his head in shame, his cheeks aflame.

"I do, sir," he said. "I'm sorry."

"Now," Arthur tapped the pen on his notebook. "After the professor left to go back to his office yesterday, what did you do?"

Brian looked up.

"Who? Me?" Brian sputtered, his voice high and pitchy. "I... um... well, I..."

Brian glanced over at the other students, then down at his boots.

"Out with it, boy," Arthur snapped. "I have a murder to investigate. I don't have time for nonsense. What did you do?"

Brian twisted a short strand of ginger hair between his fingers.

"I needed to take care of some business. Know what I mean?"

I wasn't exactly sure I did know what he meant. What kind of business would Brian have during school hours? Did he mean drugs? I looked over at Bill, but he was shading his eyes against the sun, and appeared to be watching a large bird circling overhead. I didn't know if he'd even heard what Brian said. The look on Arthur's face made me relax slightly, though I was still confused. The corners of Arthur's mouth twitched into a smile, his moustache covering more of his top lip as he tried not to laugh.

"What do you mean?" I couldn't help asking, completely bemused.

Arthur finally laughed, his guffaw a loud, honking noise like a goose.

"Sorry, Mrs. Forster," Brian said. "I didn't want to seem ungentlemanly in front of you. I needed to use the bathroom, but the bathrooms here aren't that great, you see. There's a gas station on Bathurst I go to sometimes. They don't mind if I buy a few snacks and things. Takes a little while to walk there, but I can use the east entrance to the fort, so I don't have to go all the way around."

The joke was apparently on me. Brian had needed to relieve himself. Arthur understood perfectly. My neck flushed, and I smiled.

"Did you see anyone on your way out?" Arthur asked, regaining his composure. "Anybody you didn't recognize?"

"There were a few visitors hanging around here and there" Brian said. "But it's pretty quiet here most of the time. Not a lot of people come to the fort beyond tourists and school children. I did see lots of people once I got to Bathurst, but not before that."

"Did you recognize any of the visitors you saw?" Arthur demanded.

"No. They were all strangers, sir."

"How long were you gone?" Arthur persisted.

"I'd say about forty-five minutes, maybe a little longer." Brian blushed again. "I was back at the excavation area when Nadya came to ask us if we'd seen Professor Volk. Around 11:45 it would have been."

I knew Arthur wouldn't be able to do much with that until he'd confirmed Evelyn's approximate time of death with the coroner. He jotted the time down in his notebook.

"You understand, Brian," Arthur said, "I'll be checking your alibi with the clerk at the gas station."

Brian nodded.

"I won't be learning from them that you lied, will I?" Arthur asked.

Brian's eyes grew wide.

"No, sir."

After Brian, Arthur asked to speak with Marco, who trudged over to us, hair hanging in his eyes, hands shoved deep into the pockets of his jacket.

"Hello," Arthur said, giving Marco the once over, eyes starting at the leather boots and finishing at the mop of dark hair on Marco's head. "I'm sure by now your peers have told you what happened to your professor."

Marco nodded.

"How do you feel about that?" Arthur asked, staring intently at the sullen student.

"Bad?" Marco's intonation made it sound more like a question than a statement.

"I should think so," Arthur stated. "Marco, what kind of name is that? Italian?"

Marco pushed some hair out of his eyes and assented with a nod.

"And where were you when the professor was murdered?" Arthur asked, though I wondered how he expected the students to know when Evelyn had been killed exactly.

Based on what the students had reported, we knew he'd probably died sometime between 10:30 and noon. Donna could probably narrow that down more since she'd gone to Evelyn's office with him after the lecture. In fact, she was likely the last person to see him alive, before the killer, of course, unless she'd shot him and pushed him down the stairs herself.

"After Professor Volk left," Marco began quietly, "I stayed in the pit to excavate, like he told us to do. I was there working the whole time, until Nadya came and asked us if we'd seen him. Then she went to check his office. When she came back again, she asked everyone to look for him."

"How long was she gone?" Arthur asked.

Marco raised his eyebrows. "Maybe thirty minutes? It takes a few minutes to walk over there," he murmured. "I'd say we all started looking for him sometime between 12:15 and 12:30 maybe. I didn't actually look at the time, but my stomach was rumbling by then."

"Can anybody corroborate this story?" Arthur asked, scribbling in his book. "About you working from 10:30 until Nadya came over?"

Marco shook his head, stringy hair grazing his eyebrows.

"Not really," he replied. "Everyone went off after Professor Volk left. I was the only one working at first. Anthony was the first to come back and start working with me. A bit after 11, I'd say. I'm not sure. Nobody wears a watch, only the professor. We've gotten good at estimating the time, but nobody's perfect."

"What about the others?" Arthur said, pointing with his pen at the group of students who stood watching us. "What were they doing?"

"As far as I know," Marco replied, looking straight at Arthur, "Nadya went to excavate the test pit; Brian went for his usual bathroom break at the gas station... he has performance anxiety; Anthony went to make one of the instant coffees they have for us at the blockhouse over there, and I honestly don't know where Christopher went. Off to smoke somewhere, maybe? He does what he wants, and nobody asks questions. Only Professor Volk stood up to him. Even Nadya's afraid to tell him what to do, and she's in

65

charge when Professor Volk isn't around. He tells her to supervise us while he's gone, but she usually disappears to a test pit and leaves us alone. As you can imagine, not a lot of work gets done when neither of the supervisors is around."

I realized that, up to that point, none of the students could be completely certain where the others had been, until Anthony joined Marco in the excavation area after a coffee break. They might have seen each other wandering off in various directions, but after Evelyn left, they each had gone their separate ways for a time. Of course, it was likely a coincidence, and they were probably telling the truth. They hadn't known yesterday when Evelyn walked away that they'd be needing an alibi the next day. I couldn't help but think it was convenient, though, and thought of an old Agatha Christie novel I'd read years ago. What was it called? Murder on the Orient Express?

Chapter 17

At the end of the leash, Muffin lay on her back, exposing her belly in hopes that someone might scratch her. She wriggled on the lawn for a few moments and finally gave up, getting to her feet with bits of grass clinging to the fur on her back.

"Bill," I said to my husband, who seemed to fade in and out of the conversation Arthur was having with the students, "why don't you hold her for a bit? She's getting antsy, but I don't want to let her off the leash. Not with everything going on."

Bill stooped to pick her up and I handed him the leather strap that I'd kept around my wrist until then.

"Who's next?" Bill asked Arthur.

"The coloured boy," he said, motioning to Anthony.

Anthony stood next to Arthur and the difference in stature was striking. Anthony was about Bill's height, and he hovered over my cousin, forcing Arthur to look up to maintain eye contact.

"What was your relationship with the professor?" Arthur asked.

"He was my supervisor," Anthony said. He still held his work gloves in his right hand. "I'm doing my master's degree. He agreed to supervise me in my last year of undergraduate studies. It's my second year of my master's now."

"That's quite an achievement for a coloured student," Arthur mused, looking at Anthony.

Once again, I winced on the inside. Arthur wasn't wrong, but I didn't think he'd said it because he understood the barriers faced by some of the students at the university. Ontario had closed the last racially segregated school only two years before, and universities continued to openly discriminate against Black students. Getting a foot in the door wasn't easy and studying for a master's was certainly a testament to Anthony's fortitude.

"I've worked hard to be here," Anthony replied, squeezing his gloves slightly. "It's always been my hope to work at War of 1812 sites and help preserve and share the story of my ancestors."

"Your ancestors?" Arthur scoffed.

"Yes, sir." Anthony's face remained inexpressive. "My ancestor fought in the War of 1812 for the British as part of the Coloured Corps. My family's been in Toronto, York in those days, a very long time. They knew back then that, if the Americans won the war, it wouldn't be good for them."

"How did you feel about Professor Volk?" Arthur swiftly changed the subject, likely ashamed that the young man had taught him a thing about Canada's history.

"I liked him alright," Anthony said, glancing at me then back to Arthur. "He was good with his students, respectful, you know."

"Was he closer to any of the students?" Arthur asked.

Anthony frowned. He seemed confused.

"Not sure what you mean, sir," he said.

"Did you notice him paying more attention to his female students?" Arthur said plainly.

"No way," Anthony said. "Nadya was his only female student, but he wasn't like that from what I saw. He was respectful, like I said. To all of us."

"What did you do after the professor left to go to his office?" Arthur continued, flicking the skeleton of a dead leaf from the sleeve of his jacket.

"Usually, after the morning lecture, I get coffee from the blockhouse," Anthony said. "We keep tools there, but the staff here set up a little area with instant coffee and sugar, things like that. I work evenings at a grocery store to pay for school, so I feel sluggish sometimes in the morning. The coffee gives me a good jolt and I'm ready to go back to work."

"Did you see anybody at the blockhouse or on your way there?" Arthur glanced at Anthony before jotting something down in his notebook.

"Brian walked with me as far as the blockhouse. He's regular like a clock but doesn't like to use the facilities here. Everyone knows about the visits to the gas station. It's hard to keep a secret here when there's so few of us. He normally goes out the east entrance to get to the gas station and he walks with me to the blockhouse. Everyone's got their rituals when the professor is gone. Other than Brian, I couldn't really say. There were some visitors to the fort, I suppose,

69

wandering around, but nobody that caught my notice for any reason."

"How long does the professor usually take to go to his office after the morning lecture?" Arthur asked.

Anthony paused a moment, then said: "I'd say we're free for at least thirty minutes, but sometimes a little longer. It depended on what he needed to do in his office. As long as you're back at work within an hour you're usually safe. It's easy enough to say you just stepped away for a minute to do something. Nadya's nice. She wouldn't rat on anybody, and there isn't much discipline here anyway, even when Professor Volk is around."

"What do you think of your fellow students?" Arthur changed his line of questioning abruptly.

"They're cool enough," Anthony said, shoving his gloves into the pocket of his jacket.

"Cool enough?" Arthur repeated, his eyebrows knitted together. "Care to expand on that?"

Anthony shifted his weight from one foot to the other.

"Christopher," he said, then hesitated. "You didn't hear it from me, but Christopher's one we all watch out for, even Professor Volk."

I looked over to where Christopher stood, slightly apart from his peers, with a deep crease drawing his eyebrows together. What could Anthony mean when he said they all watched out for Christopher?

Chapter 18

Christopher's eyes narrowed down to slivers, the pale blue of his irises glimmering through the slits left by his eyelids. He looked angry, a few lines forming around his eyes.

"How did you feel about Professor Volk?" Arthur asked him.

"Didn't like him much," Christopher replied. "Can I smoke?"

Arthur was beginning to nod his assent, but Bill interjected: "Not near the excavation. You know that, Christopher."

Christopher huffed audibly but didn't produce a pack of cigarettes. I wondered if, at the mention of smoking, the weight of the cigarettes in Arthur's own pocket had become more noticeable.

"A lot of people liked the professor," Arthur said. "Why didn't you?"

"Just different points of view," Christopher said, running a hand over his short blonde hair.

"About what?" Arthur pushed.

"Archaeological methodology," Christopher snapped. "You want me to go into the merits and failings of processual archaeology?"

It was a dangerous fib. I didn't believe for a second that Christopher's main complaint about Evelyn was their difference of opinion on processual archaeology. He was counting on Arthur not knowing what that meant, but he knew very well that Bill and I did. Still, I had a strong feeling that Christopher had no intention of being cooperative with the police. He behaved like a spoiled child with a sliver in his thumb. Grumpy, whiny, and feeling as though he'd been irreparably harmed. Why he was this way, I couldn't guess, but I'd seen students like him before.

Falling for the bait, Arthur changed the subject.

"When Professor Volk went to his office, what did you do?"

Christopher rolled his eyes skyward as though struggling to remember what he'd done just yesterday.

"I suppose I went for a walk."

"You suppose?" Arthur's nostrils flared, and I recognized the tell-tale sign of his losing patience.

"Yes, I suppose," Christopher repeated, unfazed by my cousin's irritability.

Had Christopher been interviewed by the police before? He didn't seem as nervous as the others.

"What about inappropriate relationships with students?" Arthur asked. "Aware of any of those?"

Christopher snorted. "Do you mean Nadya? I doubt it. She's a 'not that kind of girl' girl, if you know what I mean. You know what they're like. She'd have more fun if she'd just relax a little, worry less about school and have a drink or two at parties. Instead, she's all work and no play. You know what that makes her."

It didn't take a psychiatrist to realize that Christopher was a cruel boy who seemed to enjoy the suffering of others. I also had the feeling he was hiding something. However, I realized Arthur wasn't going to make progress with this interview unless he had something to hang over Christopher's head, of which, at this point in the case, there was nothing and we were all at the mercy of Christopher's childish whims.

Chapter 19

Once Arthur realized he would get nowhere with Christopher, he wrapped up the student interviews and asked me and Bill to accompany him to the university to speak with Donna. Bill dismissed Nadya and the students, telling them to cover the test pits and any delicate features in the excavation area, then go home until further notice.

Bill, Muffin, and I rode in our car and Arthur took his to the university. We found the department secretary in her office, seated behind a large desk with a pencil tucked behind her ear. The office was lined with bookshelves that boasted the burgundy, leather-bound copies of theses and dissertations of students who had long ago finished their studies at the University of Toronto. She smiled when she looked up from her work, but when she saw us, it fell instantly from her face.

"Have you found him?" she asked before anyone could speak, standing up from her desk.

"I'm very sorry, Donna," I said. "Professor Volk has been murdered. This is Detective Sargeant Campbell; he's the homicide detective leading the case."

Donna's lip trembled and tears formed in her eyes. For a moment she covered her mouth with her hands.

"What? How?" she mumbled, grabbing the purse on her desk and rummaging through it hurriedly.

She pulled out a white handkerchief and dabbed at her eyes, then walked around to stand in front of her desk.

"He was shot with a musket," Arthur said quietly. "We'd like to ask you a few questions, Mrs.?"

"Ewen," Donna said.

She backed up against the desk, bumping a framed photograph which fell and clattered against the wood. She winced at the sound, but did nothing to right the frame that had toppled over behind her.

"It's my understanding," Arthur began, stepping closer to her, "that you accompanied Professor Volk from the excavation site to his office at Fort York after his morning lecture. Is that correct?"

Donna nodded. "Yes, he wanted me to bring down some journals that had arrived at his office on campus and drop them off. I wouldn't normally do something like that, but he's such a friendly man and it was just a small favour. Hardly any trouble."

Bill and I stood slightly behind Arthur. Muffin was tucked under Bill's arm, but she didn't struggle to escape. She quietly surveyed the unfolding drama while I nervously stroked her ear. I still hadn't recovered from the shock of finding Evelyn's body and wished I could retreat to my home instead of helping interview witnesses. Bill had been very quiet, and I wondered how he was processing the death of his friend and colleague.

"Did he have the musket with him when you went to his office?" Arthur asked.

"Yes." Donna looked up at Arthur. "He was carrying it with him. When we got inside, he put it against the wall in the corner."

"Did he at any point unload it?" Arthur continued, noting Donna's responses in his notebook.

"I don't think so." Donna hesitated, pulling the pencil from behind her ear.

"You don't think so?" Arthur queried, his eyebrows arched.

"I mean no," Donna said quickly. "He didn't unload it while I was there. Just leaned it against the wall. He was in a hurry to get the journals from me. I don't think he was paying much attention to anything else."

Arthur nodded, then asked: "Then what happened?"

"We spoke for a few minutes. I gave him the journals he requested, and I left to come back to the university."

"Was there anybody else in the officers' barracks?" Arthur asked.

"No, of that I'm certain." Donna tapped the pencil's eraser on the wooden desk. "There was a sign outside saying the building was closed during the excavations. I supposed it was so they could store the artifacts safely, and so Professor Volk could work in peace."

I hadn't noticed the sign that morning, but perhaps it was obscured by the open door. I wondered if Nadya left the door open accidentally the day before when she went looking for Evelyn, or if someone else hadn't closed it properly behind them. I was reminded of the man in the yellow rain jacket leaving the building that morning. He might have left the door ajar, the wind catching it and blowing it wide open. Yet, if he had seen the sign noting the building was closed to visitors, why had he gone in?

"What did you talk about with the professor?" Arthur asked.

"Not much, I suppose," Donna glanced at Arthur and then dabbed at her nose with her handkerchief. "The usual pleasantries. He thanked me for bringing the journals and I asked him about Margaret, his wife, and the children. I couldn't have been there more than five minutes. I needed to get back to the university. I didn't want Professor Blake to check in on me and wonder where I might be. I just can't believe Professor Volk is dead. Those poor children... I can't imagine. What a horrible thing to have happen. Who would do such a thing?"

Donna looked at me and then Bill when she said this. I knew she liked Evelyn, but then again, most people did.

Arthur ignored her question. "Did you speak to anyone before you left? The students, I mean."

"No, I didn't go past the excavation again." Donna blinked and tucked her straight hair behind her ear. "I left through the exit on the west side, closest to where I parked the car. I can't say I saw the students when I was leaving. Sometimes when they are crouched down you can't see them at all. However, I can't say I was looking for them either. I was in a hurry to get back."

Chapter 20

I sat beside Margaret Volk on an orange sofa in her formal living room. Across from us was a stone-framed fireplace with the charcoal remnants of a handful of logs. Arthur sat patiently in an armchair, his notebook balanced on his right leg. When we arrived, Abigail had quickly shuffled the children out to play in the backyard, leaving us alone with Evelyn's widow. Bill had stayed at the university to speak with Stephen and then taken Muffin home, but I wanted to see if I could be of any help to Margaret and anticipated I would stay after Arthur left.

"Mrs. Volk," Arthur said when Margaret's tears had subsided a little, "when was the last time you saw your husband?"

Margaret sniffed, wiped her nose with a handkerchief, and looked at Arthur. Her mascara left black streaks under her eyes.

"I told Beatrix this morning that the last time I saw Evelyn was before he went to work yesterday."

"And you weren't concerned when he didn't come home after work?" Arthur asked, leaning forward as he spoke.

Margaret glanced at me and then back to Arthur.

"No," she squeaked. She'd lost the breathless tone of voice she had on the phone that morning. "It wasn't unusual for him to do that. I mean, sometimes he stayed out late and if he'd had a few drinks, he might stay with a friend instead of coming home."

"Did that bother you?" Arthur raised his eyebrows. "Your husband not coming home to you and the kids?"

"I have Abigail to help me." Margaret squeezed my hand. "She does more than Evelyn would."

"Can you think of anybody who'd want to harm Evelyn?" Arthur asked.

"Of course, not," Margaret responded quickly, glancing once more in my direction. "Everyone loved Evelyn. Isn't that right, Beatrix?"

I nodded my assent. "Yes, that's what I would say about Evelyn."

I didn't want to say I'd been surprised by his treatment of her. She didn't need the judgement right now, just a supportive friend.

"Nobody at the university? One of his students? A former flame?" Arthur persisted, tapping his notebook with the point of his pen.

Margaret's eyes were red, and she looked on the verge of tears again.

"No," she insisted. "Like I said, everyone loved Evelyn. He was a wonderful husband and father, well-respected by his colleagues and students. Nobody would have wanted to hurt him, I swear. It must have been a stranger, someone who didn't know him. A robbery or something."

Arthur scribbled a note onto his pad and closed it. I thought about what some of the students had said earlier, but didn't put much stock in it – professors always had some detractors amongst their flock, Christopher being one of them.

"It wasn't a robbery, Mrs. Volk," Arthur said, looking directly at Margaret. "He had his wallet with him when he died. I want to be honest with you. There's no point beating around the bush. I believe this crime was committed by someone he knew, and I have every intention of getting to the bottom of it. I know this is difficult, and I won't take up more of your time today, but I may have more questions for you."

Margaret thanked him and stood to show him out, still the perfect hostess even in the midst of a tragedy. I put my hand on her arm.

"I'll show him out, dear," I said, getting up from the brightly coloured sofa. "You sit down a moment and then if you'd like, I'll stay and make us some tea."

Margaret nodded and fell back down onto the sofa, her shoulders hunched and chin tucked toward her chest. She looked genuinely bereaved.

Chapter 21

I walked Arthur to the door and stepped outside with him. He quietly closed the door behind us.

"What do you think, Trixie?" he asked, pulling his pack of cigarettes from his pocket and tapping the box against his palm until one came loose.

"What do you mean?"

Arthur put the cigarette in the corner of his mouth and flicked a lighter with his thumb. He took a long drag before he responded, blowing the smoke away from me.

"Do you think she's telling the truth? What kind of father stays away all night in the middle of the week?"

"I agree it's odd," I began, looking at the immaculate front lawn, "but I don't believe she'd have reason to hurt him. Do you?"

Arthur exhaled a puff of vaporous smoke and said: "I've seen angry wives do many things to their husbands. If he's having an affair, she'd have the motive. She wouldn't be too pleased if he had an inappropriate relationship with, say, one of his students. I'll have to speak with the maid. Once we have an estimated time of death from the pathologist, I can check Mrs. Volk's alibi. The maid will know if she was home or not."

"I doubt Margaret would know how to fire a musket," I interjected. I couldn't imagine the petite woman killing her husband in cold blood, even if he were having an affair.

"Good point, Trixie." Arthur flicked the cigarette with his thumb to loosen the ash. "But as far as we know, the musket was loaded when the professor brought it back to the office. It doesn't take a genius to point and shoot once it's all ready to go, especially at close range. Had it not been loaded, I'd say you were right. We'd have narrowed down the suspect pool to the students and perhaps the secretary, depending on how much of the lecture she actually saw. Anyway, I have the feeling that your friend in there is hiding something, I just can't quite put my finger on it yet. A professor at the university earns decent money alright, but enough to afford all of this?"

I wasn't sure what exactly he thought Margaret might be hiding, but in this he was correct. Bill and I could never have afforded the Volks' lifestyle. I'd always imagined there was another source of income or inherited wealth, but it wasn't my business where their money came from. I didn't plan to ask directly, but perhaps Margaret would be more open once Arthur was gone. The disadvantage the police faced was that nobody really liked talking to them. They were their own worst enemy.

"Was he killed in the office?" I asked, changing the subject when I remembered I hadn't noticed any blood while I was in there. Then again, I hadn't known to look for it.

"I'll let you know when we have a better idea of the sequence of events," Arthur winked.

At least with Arthur in charge of things I'd be kept more in the loop than if it were a stranger investigating Evelyn's death.

Chapter 22

Back inside Margaret's elegant foyer, complete with a sparkling crystal chandelier, I took a deep breath before walking down the hall to the kitchen at the back of the house. The kitchen had been remodelled to keep up with the changing fashions in home décor. The wallpaper had larger-than-life florals in oranges and yellows and the cabinets were a warm mahogany. Everything was spotless and gleaming, the room giving off a bright and cozy atmosphere that felt at odds with the tragedy of Evelyn's death. I found Abigail at the stove, a kettle of water on one of the burners.

"You've beat me to it, Abigail," I said, resting my hand on the countertop. I hadn't realized how tired I was.

"Tea can't remedy the situation, Mrs. Forster." Abigail smiled at me sadly. "But it's a good place to start. Why don't you have a seat? You look like you could use a rest."

Abigail motioned to the kitchen table with one of her slim hands.

"I won't say no to that," I replied, pulling a wood chair out and seating myself. My skirt was uncomfortably snug at the waist, but at least I was off my feet. "Where's Margaret?"

"She's gone outside to tell the children," Abigail said, looking toward the door. "They'll be a wreck, Mrs. Forster. They adored their father."

"I can imagine. How long have you worked for the Volks, Abigail?"

"I started just after they adopted the children." Abigail stared at the kettle, as though lost in thought. "That would have been about six years ago. I'd only just come to Canada, and I was placed with the Volks right away. Some of the girls who come get moved from house to house until it's a good fit, but we all got on from the start. I was so happy to have a good position and a little money to send home each month."

I nodded. Many people came to Canada for the economic opportunities it presented. However, not everyone found what they were looking for.

"Of course," I said, watching Abigail remove the kettle from the stove and pour the hot water into a teapot, which was a matte pale blue with a classical scene in white relief on the side. Her movements were graceful and delicate, and I wondered if in another life she might have been a dancer. "Do you go back to visit often? You're from Antigua, if I remember correctly."

"That's right, Mrs. Forster." Abigail looked over at me, nodding slightly, but then returned her attention to the tea. "I'm from Antigua and all my family is still there, including my daughter, but I haven't been back since I left."

I was surprised. I didn't know Abigail had a daughter or that she hadn't been back to her home in all these years. I realized how little I had spoken to Abigail in the time I'd known her and felt sorry I hadn't made more of an effort to get to know her. Suddenly, Abigail whirled around to face me, her eyes wide.

"I shouldn't have said that," she whispered. "The Volks know I have a daughter, but the government does not. The program to come to Canada was only for young, unmarried, and childless women. I lied on my application. If it got out, it might affect my status here."

"Mum's the word," I said, pressing a finger to my lips. "I don't know anyone at immigration to tell, anyway."

Abigails shoulders dropped, and she looked relieved.

"It must be very difficult being away from your family," I said. "I know it's not my place to pry, but is it money that prevents you from returning?"

I hoped Abigail would not be offended by my asking, but I hated the thought of her being separated from her own child for all these years.

"Oh no, Mrs. Forster," Abigail said emphatically, crossing the kitchen to stand by the table. She gripped the back of a chair, her knuckles turning pale. She lowered her voice: "It's not money. The Volks pay me well enough. I can pay for my daughter's education, everything she needs. It's that Mrs. Volk, she doesn't like me to be away for too long, what with Professor Volk being gone so often. She needs me."

The muscles in Abigail's face tightened and she glanced nervously at the open doorway to the kitchen.

"I'm sorry, Abigail," I said, standing up from the chair. "It wasn't my business to ask. However, under the circumstances, do you mind if I ask about Professor Volk?

Do you know where he goes when he doesn't spend the night at home?"

She shook her head and went back to the kitchen counter, carefully arranging the matching teapot, cups, cream and sugar on a silver tray.

"I couldn't say," she said, without looking at me. "But I know it's something nobody is supposed to know. They always say it's because he's been drinking and needs to stay with friends, but even at parties, he doesn't drink much. He may be many things, Mrs. Forster, but he's not an alcoholic."

Evelyn had a secret, and whatever it was, the family preferred people think he had a problem with alcohol than whatever the truth was. If Abigail didn't know where he went on the nights he didn't stay at home, did Margaret? Was Margaret hiding something or was she truly in the dark when it came to her husband's nocturnal activities?

Chapter 23

Back at home that evening, after Bill picked me up at Margaret's house, we sat on the sable leather chesterfield in the living room. It was dark outside, and I'd drawn the curtains to prevent the neighbours from seeing in. Not that there was anything to hide. Muffin lay between us on her side, and I scratched her exposed, pink-skinned belly covered in soft tufts of white curls.

"What did Stephen say when you spoke with him?" I asked Bill.

He was fidgeting with his watch, holding it up to the light.

"Hmm?" he mumbled.

"What did Stephen say?" I repeated.

"Oh, Stephen." Bill set his watch down and looked at me. "He was sorry to hear about Evelyn, but he insisted that the excavation must carry on. He wasn't sure they'd be able to procure funding for next year and with winter on its way, he worried the project would never be complete if things didn't move forward now. With or without Evelyn. He's not wrong, I suppose, but the way he expresses himself is unfeeling sometimes. I'm glad Margaret didn't have to hear the conversation."

"What's his plan, then?" I asked, astonished by Stephen's callous reaction to the death of a colleague. "I mean for the dig? Will Nadya take over?"

"I thought he might suggest that," he replied. "She's the one who knows the site best and the findings will be critical for her dissertation, but you know, Stephen. Not one to feel comfortable with a perfectly competent student taking the reins. He's asked me to oversee the whole thing."

I sighed. "Why am I not surprised?"

"I reminded him that I'm not an expert in historical or even military archaeology," Bill said, taking my hand. "He said he didn't care; he just needed someone he could trust in charge. I did get permission to expand the test pit with the human remains, though. At least I'll be of some use to Nadya in that sense."

"It's because she's a woman," I said. "He doesn't need to say it; it's obvious. He doesn't trust her to supervise a team of young men because she is a young woman. How could she possibly exercise authority over them?"

"True," Bill replied, smiling at me. "He hasn't spent enough time with you to know the kind of authority women can wield."

I laughed. "What are you trying to say, Bill?"

"Absolutely nothing." Bill leaned over and kissed me on the cheek, his prickly beard tickling my face.

"I supposed you've accepted his proposition?" I asked, already knowing the answer.

"I didn't see how I could say no," he shrugged.

"Never one to say no to an excavation," I teased him.

Chapter 24

The next morning, as I prepared Muffin's breakfast in the kitchen, I wondered if I should tell Arthur what Abigail had said about the Volks. It seemed to confirm his suspicion that Margaret was either knowingly or unwittingly hiding some secret about Evelyn. How much she knew about Evelyn's outings was yet to be determined, but there was something to conceal. After I'd mulled it over while watching Muffin scarf down her food in a few hasty gulps, I decided to let sleeping dogs lie, as they say, and keep the information to myself for the time being. I didn't want to cause problems for Margaret, if whatever Evelyn had been doing had nothing to do with his murder.

"Bill," I said, turning to the kitchen table where my husband was drinking coffee and reading the morning's newspaper.

No response.

"Bill," I repeated, going over to him and tapping him on the shoulder.

"What is it, Beatrix?" he asked, startled.

"I'll come with you to the site today," I said, pulling out a chair and sitting down.

I ran a hand over the curlers I hadn't yet taken out that morning. It made me miss the days at San Miguel, on the remote mountain top, when I didn't need to worry about societal expectations regarding women's appearances and I let my hair do as it pleased. At my age, what did it matter what I looked like? And yet, here I was, like every other woman my age in the city, tightly winding my hair around dozens of curlers each night and then hoping to get a decent sleep with lumps and bumps all over my head.

"Is that to work or to ask questions?" Bill set the newspaper down on the table.

"Perhaps a little of both," I responded. "It will give me a chance to ask Nadya and the students some more questions."

"Nadya, yes," Bill said. "But not the students. They won't be back on site again until tomorrow. I thought it best for me to have some time to discuss the next steps with Nadya before they come back."

I nodded. "Probably a good idea. I'll come anyway. Maybe Arthur will be around, and I can find out if Evelyn was killed in his office or somewhere else."

"It's not our job to investigate his murder, Beatrix," Bill warned me. "We had no choice at San Miguel, but Arthur can handle this case. He won't be pleased if you stick your nose where it doesn't belong."

"I thought you'd be a little more interested in what happened to Evelyn," I said, tapping my fingernail on the side of my teacup. "He was your colleague, and your friend."

Bill spread his hand out over the newspaper, his fingers leaving gaps where I could just make out a few words here and there.

"Of course, he was," Bill sighed. "I'm just not sure we can offer much in the way of help. Arthur has been doing this work for decades. Getting involved could be dangerous, Beatrix. You don't know who might have wanted to harm Evelyn. Some killers will go to great lengths to prevent the police from uncovering their identity."

"Perhaps you're right," I agreed. "However, I don't think asking Nadya a few questions about Evelyn and the excavation will put me next on the killer's list."

Chapter 25

Back at Fort York, Bill and I walked together to the gates of the historic site. This time, I decided to keep Muffin on her leash as there was now an active crime scene where she would not be welcomed. The wind blew ferociously from the south, tearing at my freshly styled hair. I'd left my hat at home, knowing it was no match for a blustery Toronto day, but now I wished I'd at least thought to bring a woolen toque. The sky was overcast, and I felt the chill of the wind deep in my bones. There was a police officer stationed just outside the gates. He looked barely out of his teens.

"Good morning," he greeted us, but held up his hand to signal we should stop. "This is a crime scene. I'm afraid you can't go inside today."

"Good morning, officer," Bill said. "I was under the impression that the archaeological excavation would be able to continue since the crime scene was on the opposite side of the fort. Perhaps we could speak with Detective Sergeant Campbell. We were with him yesterday."

"Oh, yes. Sorry, sir," the officer muttered, his cheeks burning. "I didn't know who you were. Your colleague is already there. Detective Sergeant Campbell said you could move forward at the excavation area, but you won't be able to access anything from the officers' barracks and mess until the full crime scene has been processed."

"Of course," Bill nodded. "We completely understand and thank you for allowing the work to proceed. It's a considerable favour to the department and the university appreciates it."

The young man, dressed in his freshly pressed uniform, waved us through the gates.

"I suppose we won't be disturbed today," Bill said.

"Bill," I stopped in my tracks and grabbed his arm. "Did you see a man in a yellow rain jacket here yesterday?"

Bill paused, looking up toward the sky. He scratched at the edge of his ear lobe.

"I don't think so," he hesitated. "Why do you ask?"

"I saw someone yesterday," I said, feeling silly I hadn't remembered the incident sooner. It had completely slipped my mind. "He was coming in while we were looking at the test pit and then later when I went to find Muffin, I saw him leaving the officers' quarters. Not from the door near Evelyn's office, but by another door on the east side of the building. It was odd. He didn't seem concerned I saw him, but I wonder if it had something to do with Evelyn's death."

"I suppose it could be someone who works at the fort," Bill mused. "Or a curious member of the public. The site is open to the public despite the excavations."

"True," I mused. "It could be unrelated. I think I should tell Arthur, though, in case it's relevant."

While Bill went to speak with Nadya, I returned with Muffin to the brick building that had once housed the officers who lived at Fort York. It had been cordoned off with police tape that snapped and fluttered in the wind. I shivered from the cold and the stark reminder of my grisly discovery the day before. I saw Mariana step out of the barracks and waved.

"Hello, Mariana," I called out. "Is Arthur here?"

"Hiya, Beatrix," she said, ducking under the police tape and striding toward me. "He's not at the moment. Something I can help with?"

"Well, yes," I paused, wondering if I should wait to speak with Arthur. Mariana was here now, though, so I decided it was best to share what I knew. "I saw something yesterday that I forgot to mention to Arthur with all the commotion. I don't know if it's important, but it could be. Arthur mentioned no detail being too insignificant."

"Excellent," Mariana said, motioning with her hand for me to follow her. "Let's go inside. This wind feels like it might make a Mary Poppins out of me."

She wasn't wrong. The gusts had nearly blown me over a few times as I walked to the barracks. I hesitated, looking at Muffin.

"It's fine. Nobody needs to know," Mariana whispered.

I stooped to pick Muffin up and Mariana lifted the police tape for me to walk under. Just inside the door, she leaned over to pick up a yellow and orange Thermos. I was beginning to wonder if everything these days was manufactured in bright, sunny colours.

"Coffee?" she asked, loosening the lid.

I shook my head. "Thank you, no. I had tea at home this morning."

"It's my vice," she smirked. "Can't go without it or I'd be sleeping on the job."

She poured a small amount into the lid and drank it in one long swallow. I thought she must have a gut made of steel to handle the acidity of regular black coffee consumption. It wasn't for everyone.

"You know," she said, holding the empty cup and pointing at me with her index finger, "he wasn't killed in the office."

Did she know I'd asked Arthur where Evelyn had been murdered?

"He wasn't?" I shifted Muffin's posterior onto my hip. She always started to feel heavy after I'd held her a few minutes.

"No!" Mariana smiled. "I would've thought he might've been since the musket was in the office and all. But get this - we found blood in the officers' mess behind the table. And there were also scuff marks on the floor leading to the cellar that nobody noticed at first. Just a few black streaks on the floorboards from the soles of the professor's shoes. Pretty cool, huh?"

It wasn't cool, as she said. We were discussing the murder of a young husband and father, but I realized Mariana was so eager to share the information that I could possibly extract details of the case without seeming to pry.

"Indeed," I smiled. "You must enjoy your job."

"I love it. I couldn't imagine a better job."

"Do you mind if I put her down?" I motioned to Muffin with my chin. "She gets heavy after a while."

Mariana looked around and then grinned. "Go on. Nobody here to see anything."

I set Muffin on the floor made of slats of rough wood. She immediately began sniffing at the boards.

"Mariana," I said, turning to face her. "Do you have any suspects? I was so shocked by Evelyn's death. I couldn't imagine anybody wanting to harm him. Have you perhaps spoken to Arthur on the subject?"

Mariana tucked a few short hairs behind her ear. "It's probably the wife. That's usually the first suspect in a case like this."

"And if Mrs. Volk has an alibi?" I asked.

Mariana frowned and said: "Then we're at square one again. Someone from the university, probably. Maybe one of his students? The secretary, perhaps. At this point, she was the last one to see him alive, should the simplest explanation be the correct solution. If only Occam's Razor could be applied to police work. Unfortunately, cases like this can become quite tangled as they unfold. It's early stages yet, Beatrix, but we'll find who did this. We have a high success rate. You know that, I'm sure."

I smiled. I did know. Arthur had a habit of reminding everyone at family gatherings.

Chapter 26

After I'd given all the details I could about the man in the yellow rain jacket to Mariana, providing another potential suspect to mull over, I returned to the excavation site with Muffin to see what Bill and Nadya were doing. The trek back across the fort was as miserable as when I'd walked to the officers' barracks, the frigid wind biting my nose and lips. Everyone kept reminding us that winter was approaching, but some days it seemed it was already here. All that was missing was a dusting of snow to confirm that Old Man Winter had arrived. Before I knew it, I'd have to pull out my furs to contend with the freezing weather that sucked the life out of the city each year. Bill didn't mind the cold so much, but each year, I felt more and more I was ready to insist on escaping to some place warmer for the season.

I found Nadya alone at the main excavation area that ran along the southern boundary of the fort.

"Where's Professor Forster?" I asked.

Nadya looked up and pulled herself out of the trench. She brushed the dirt from her gloves.

"He's gone over to look at the bones," she said, motioning west with her head.

"Of course, he has," I laughed. "How do you feel about the excavation going forward?"

She looked down. "I guess it's good the project will move forward, but I feel bad because of what happened to Evelyn. It feels like things should just stop for something like this, but life goes on. I can't stop thinking about Mrs. Volk and the children. Yet, if Professor Blake hadn't insisted we carry on, I'd be in trouble for my PhD. I'm glad Professor Forster is here. He'll be able to manage the students."

"I believe you can manage the students as well, Nadya," I said. "It's a matter of gaining confidence in your own abilities and authority. Professor Volk wouldn't have chosen you to help him run the dig if he hadn't thought you were capable. They are your students now. Professor Forster is simply here to help out when you need him. I know he has faith that you can run things on your own. Plus, he'll be busy working on the bones and forget all about you. You'll see."

Nadya smiled and pulled at the fingers of her gloves.

"How did you and Professor Volk get along?" I asked, trying not to let my question sound like an interrogation.

She removed the gloves and squeezed them with her fingers.

"We got along pretty well," she responded quietly, "but it wasn't perfect. I respected him, but we didn't always see eye to eye on everything to do with the dig and my research. It had been difficult these past few months, but I wouldn't have changed supervisors over it. I still wanted to work with him. He just has a strong personality; that's all."

Nadya's shyness and reluctance to lead made me think Evelyn could easily have walked over her in their relationship as student and supervisor, even if he hadn't meant to. He was the kind who wanted to be the star of the show and Nadya would happily fade into the background. I'd seen this kind of thing before at the university. It wasn't necessarily those who were academically brilliant who found the limelight, but rather those who sought the validation of their peers and craved attention.

"Yes, he wasn't one to sit quietly in the corner." I shoved my hands deeper into the pockets of my coat to keep them warm. With Muffin's leash still around my wrist it was tricky to get my entire left hand inside the protective burrow of the lined pocket. "Did he have any rivals or people who didn't like him at the university?"

I had long been on the periphery of the drama that inevitably unfolded in the department. Bill occasionally brought tidbits of gossip home, but mostly he didn't notice the interpersonal theatre of the university community. He existed in his own world, and sometimes I was glad of it. Bill didn't always recognize or even understand the ills of society, wrapped in the protective blanket of his research and skeletons.

"He was very popular." Nadya pulled the elastic that held her hair back and released a jumble of tangled hair onto her shoulder. She was pretty but didn't take much care about her looks the way I'd seen other young women primp and preen at the university. Eyeliner, lipstick, perfectly coiffed hair. Nadya was a natural beauty. "I mean, most people liked him. Not everyone, though. Professor Blake didn't care for him, but I think that was jealousy. Professor Volk was younger and on his way up the academic ladder. Professor Blake is near retirement. Also, Professor Volk had an argument with one of the students last week. I'd forgotten about it, but he and Christopher got quite heated about something. I couldn't hear the conversation. They seemed fine after that, though Christopher is difficult to get along with on a regular day."

"Why is that?"

"He's an entitled brat," Nadya spat out, then covered her mouth. "Sorry, Mrs. Forster. I didn't mean to say that about one of the students. I know how unprofessional I must sound."

"Don't worry, dear," I said, reaching over and patting her arm. "I won't tell Christopher what you said. Could it relate to Professor Volk's death?"

Nadya shook her head. "I don't think so. Christopher is the son of a donor to the university. He is constantly inappropriate to me, but there's little I can do except try to stay away from him. Last year there was an incident with a girl at a party. It would have been a scandal, but it was hushed up before it got beyond the department. What would be the point of my complaining to the university if they didn't do anything for the other girl?"

"What other girl?" I asked, glancing down at Muffin who still sat patiently beside me, tethered at the end of her leash.

"We aren't really supposed to talk about it." Nadya's words tumbled out of her mouth and she glanced around, though we were the only ones in the vicinity. "I don't know much, just what a friend told me. Christopher was at a party at one of the residences on campus. I was there, too. It was mostly people from the department. Honestly, I didn't actually see anything, Mrs. Forster, but my friend told me that Christopher and one of his friends took a girl who was extremely inebriated to one of the bedrooms. Nobody knows exactly what happened because Christopher and his friend denied everything, but the girl made a complaint about them the next day. I heard the police came, but since it was her word against theirs, she was basically told to keep her mouth shut or she'd get kicked out of the university. It didn't matter. She left after a few months anyway. Christopher and his friends never left her alone after that."

"Oh, my," I breathed. "That's shocking."

I rolled my fists into little balls in my pockets. This was not the first time or the last time a woman would be assaulted on campus and be forced to pretend it didn't happen or told it was her own fault for dressing a certain way or drinking too much. The situation had evidently scared Nadya, and she didn't feel she could defend herself against Christopher's unwanted advances. It wasn't fair, but she was right to worry about the consequences of any complaint she might make.

"That's a terrible story, Nadya," I said. "I'm so sorry to hear that these things are still happening at the university. Every woman knows what it is to feel helpless in these situations. Did you tell Evelyn you were having issues with Christopher?"

Nadya crossed her arms and kicked at the dirt.

"I did, but I begged him not to say anything. He was angry, but he promised he wouldn't speak with Christopher about it."

Had Evelyn broken his promise to Nadya and confronted Christopher? Had Christopher seized the opportunity of the loaded musket to prevent Evelyn from making a complaint at the university? Christopher may have survived one scandal, but would a second tarnish his reputation and make the university reconsider?

Chapter 27

Outside the gates of the fort, I saw Bill kneeling over the test pit. His back was to me, but I could tell from the repetitive movements of his arms that he was working to uncover more of the remains.

"Bill," I called out as Muffin and I got closer.

No response.

Perhaps the wind was carrying my voice away from him. I let go of Muffin's leash and she ran to him, sidling up under his arm and sniffing at his jacket collar.

"Oh, hello, Muffy," Bill said, smoothing the fur on her forehead. He turned around to look at me. "Hello, Beatrix! What have you been up to?"

"I couldn't find Arthur," I panted, trying to catch my breath after the exertion of battling the gusts of wind, "but I spoke with Mariana about the man in the yellow jacket. She told me that Evelyn wasn't killed in his office but in the officers' mess and dragged to the cellar. I don't know that this detail makes much of a difference, but now we know."

"Hmm," Bill mumbled, pulling Muffin tight against his jacket. "I wonder if Arthur has a prime suspect in mind already."

"Mariana said he thinks it's likely to be Margaret, but I can't imagine her doing something like that. Their relationship may not have been ideal, what with all his nights away from home, but to kill someone is extreme. Divorce isn't as taboo these days, especially under certain circumstances."

I considered sitting on the grass with Bill and Muffin, but the thought of bending my joints to get down and then having to get back up again deterred me.

"Any progress here?" I asked.

"Yes," Bill immediately let go of Muffin and swivelled to look into the area he'd been digging. "Have a look, Beatrix. I've uncovered a bit more within the test pit. I'll have one of the students extend it tomorrow, but we've got a right tibia and fibula here in supine position," Bill lightly tapped the bones with the handle of his paintbrush as he mentioned them. "And then just south of that we've got a left tibia and fibula here, also in supine position."

He didn't have to explain what he meant. I understood. In anatomical position, the bones of the lower leg, the fibula was lateral to the tibia. If the person buried was in supine position, meaning they were buried on their back facing up, their left tibia and fibula would have been north of the right leg in an east-facing burial. Thus, what Bill was telling me, was that there was more than one individual in the grave Evelyn and his team had inadvertently discovered.

"Wonderful," I said, leaning over to examine the bones. "Are they from the War of 1812?"

106

"Too soon to say," Bill replied. "It does appear to be a historic European burial, though, since the Indian peoples would typically have buried their dead in a flexed, not supine position. We'll know more if these people were buried in uniforms – buttons are a good way to identify soldiers."

I thought back to what I'd learned about the War of 1812 over the years. Though they used to teach about it in school when I was a girl, it had been overshadowed by the Great War and World War II when it came to Canadian military history. These days, it was a conflict many had forgotten. Were it not for the concrete presence of Fort York, I wondered if Torontonians would have relegated the War of 1812 to a neglected past of conflicts of lesser importance to those that our century had witnessed and our friends and family had fought, bringing home the scars of modern warfare, some visible on the surface, some hidden deep within. I seemed to recall that in the early years of the 19th century, more soldiers died of disease than of trauma resulting from battle. It was a sad statistic, but when war was a death sentence for many and the injuries from canon balls and musket fire were so horrific, there was no good way to die.

Chapter 28

I left Bill at Fort York and returned home. I wanted to prepare a meal for Margaret and drop it off later that day. Even with Abigail's help, I knew she would be struggling to come to terms with Evelyn's death. There was little anyone could do in these situations, but removing the everyday burdens at a time of loss and grief was a small gesture. I pulled raw ground beef from the refrigerator while Muffin danced around my feet, nearly tripping me.

"Muffin, sit," I told her, pointing at the ground.

She planted her rear on the floor and watched me intently, her short tail vibrating, as I pulled other ingredients from the kitchen counter and cabinets. Garlic, onions, soda crackers, dried spices, eggs. A large meatloaf would last them a few meals. I was chopping the onion when the doorbell rang. Muffin barked and ran to the front door. I brushed my hands on my apron and silently cursed Bill and his forgetfulness. He must have left his key at the excavation and walked home, since I took the car. I had planned to pick him up later in the day, but he must have decided to return home early, walking the hour or so it would take for him to get to our house on the west side of Toronto.

When I opened the door, I was surprised to see my daughter, not my absentminded husband.

"Goodness. I wasn't expecting you," I said, hugging her tightly. "What a pleasant surprise."

"I wanted to check on you and Dad," she said, brushing some windblown hair away from her face and bending over to scoop Muffin into her arms. "I heard about Evelyn. How is Dad taking it?"

In all the commotion I'd failed to remember that our daughter, Shirley, worked in the same department as Evelyn. As a cultural anthropologist, she wouldn't have known him as well as Bill did, but she knew who he was and, by now, everyone in the department would have heard the shocking news. Shirley had taken after her father, doing her PhD in anthropology and securing a professorship at the University of Toronto after she graduated. There weren't many women in her position, and I was proud of her significant accomplishments. Swimming against the stream wasn't easy, but she'd fought the current and come out with the career she'd dreamed of since she was a little girl.

"He's working," I said, leading her into the kitchen. "What else would he be doing?"

She smiled stiffly and boosted Muffin higher in her arms. The little terrier sniffed at her ear.

"Sit down." I pointed at a chair at the kitchen table. "I'll make us some tea."

"I won't stay long, Mum. Don't go to any trouble."

"It's no trouble," I insisted. "Sit down. I'm sure you've been busy. It feels as if we haven't seen you for weeks."

"Don't start with the guilt trip," Shirley said in a low voice.

"I'm not, dear." I stood on my tiptoes to reach the tin of tea, my plump abdomen pressing into the counter, nearly winding me. I exhaled sharply as I set the tin on the counter. "I'm just glad to see you. I know how busy you are with work and the children."

I filled the kettle and set it on the stove, twisting the temperature control knob all the way to high. While the water began to heat, I pulled out a chair and sat across from my daughter. She held Muffin on her lap.

"What's being said about Evelyn?" I asked.

"From what I can tell, most people are genuinely shocked," she said. "He was well liked by a lot of people. There's speculation, of course. Some are saying it had to do with money, some that he was having an affair, and his wife had had enough, but it's just the rumour mill working at full force. I don't put much stock in the gossip. They probably don't know any more than what they read in the news rags."

I nodded. "Hmm. I imagine you're right. Nobody suspicious of any of Evelyn's students then?"

"What do you mean?" Shirley asked, fiddling with the red handkerchief around Muffin's neck. I'd forgotten to take it off when we got home.

"They aren't suggesting one of the students had an axe to grind?"

"Are you talking about someone in particular?" Shirley raised her eyebrows.

She was always quick to pick up on what had been left unsaid. A critical thinker, Bill always said of his daughter.

"I suppose I am," I sighed, standing up when the kettle began to whistle. The high-pitched wail startled Muffin, and she jumped off Shirley's lap to run around and peer expectantly at the stove. "It's just the kettle, Muffin. I heard some awful things about a student named Christopher. I don't know his last name, I'm afraid, but his parents are donors to the university."

"Ah, Chris Pearson." She leaned her elbows on the table. "Yes, I'm sure everyone in the department knows about Chris. No relation to the Prime Minister, by the way. He's a horrible boy. I'm quite sure if it weren't for his father, he'd be in prison, not at the university."

"What do you know about the situation with the girl from last year?" I inquired, hoping Shirley might have more information than Nadya.

I poured hot water into the teapot and replaced the lid, the china clinking delicately as the top slid into place.

"Pumping me for information, are we?" Shirley arched her eyebrows again.

"That's exactly what I'm doing," I confessed, leaning my posterior against the lower kitchen cabinets.

"Well, it was quite hush-hush," Shirley sighed, "and frankly, I think there was money involved to pay off the police. I don't know exactly what happened to that poor girl in that room, but I can tell you the powers that be were worried about a scandal of that size. The girl... I don't know her name... made the mistake of believing in the justice system when justice is reserved for a select few, and she wasn't one of them. It's disgusting and everyone ends up complicit, because if we want to keep our jobs, we have to toe the line."

"I'm sorry, Shirley," I said, shaking my head. "I wish I had the solution, but I don't. We just keep fighting and hoping that one day things will get better."

"I know," she nodded, looking defeated. "I just get so frustrated at times. I want to scream. Anyway, if you're asking me if I think Chris Pearson would murder someone with the right motivation, then my answer is yes. I absolutely think he would."

Chapter 29

After Shirley left, I made a quick call to the police station saying that I had information for Arthur, who, I was told, was out on an investigation. I had no doubt he was working on Evelyn's case. I finished the meatloaf for the Volk family, steam rising from the block of compacted beef as I put the hot dish on the counter. Once it had a chance to cool a little and I'd dressed to go out, I placed the glass casserole on the back seat of the Meteor, wrapped in a towel to keep it safe for the drive over. Muffin jumped into the front seat, where she curled into a tight ball. I hustled around to the driver's seat, worrying I might not arrive before they had their dinner. I slid into the car, my wool skirt gliding over the smooth vinyl upholstery. When I pulled the seatbelt taught over my torso, I remembered how we'd all had to get used to the awkward restraint less than a decade before, always forgetting to use it and the discomfort of wearing it for long periods. Now it was second nature for me, a feature that made me feel just a little safer. Behind the wheel, I felt small, barely able to reach the pedals and see over the dash at the same time. I could swear I had shrunk over the past few years, like a sweater washed in boiling water. I hastily checked all the mirrors and slowly backed out of the driveway onto our quiet street.

At Margaret's house, I parked in the long driveway and rolled down the windows a little.

"I won't be long, Muffin," I said, as I stepped out of the car. "You stay here."

She didn't even flinch when I spoke to her. Muffin loved car rides and often fell asleep the moment the wheels were in motion. If anything caught her attention, she would look out the window and bark a little, but she was accustomed to staying in the vehicle while I ran errands on cooler days. In the summer, much to her dismay, she had to stay home.

Abigail answered the door and smiled.

"Hello, Mrs. Forster," she said quietly. "How are you?"

"I'm well thanks, Abigail. How is everyone here?"

"Coping," Abigail nodded. "Doing the best they can."

"I understand," I said, pushing the casserole dish toward her. "I don't want to disturb you, but I thought I'd bring by a meal. You can reheat it in the oven. It's CorningWare, so you can pop it straight in. The heat won't hurt it."

"That's very kind of you." Abigail took the meatloaf from my hands. "Why don't you come in. I'm sure Margaret would be glad to see you."

She glanced down the hall, lowered her voice, and said, "She doesn't have many friends, Mrs. Forster. I think she feels very much alone right now."

"Oh, I had no idea." I was surprised. How could she not have friends with all the parties she and Evelyn had thrown? Had everyone there been his friends and not hers? "Of course, I'll come in, if you think she'd like a visitor."

I removed my shoes, thankful I'd worn a pair of slip-on deerskin penny moccasins I ordered from the Sears catalogue for ten dollars at the beginning of fall. I couldn't believe shoes had reached such an exorbitant price, but these were the times we lived in. Abigail led the way to the living room, where Margaret sat staring into a cup of tea. She didn't look up when we walked in.

"This tea must be freezing by now," Abigail said gently, reaching for the cup. "Let me make you something fresh. Here's Mrs. Forster come to visit you."

I sat down next to Margaret on the orange sofa, where we'd been the day before. I was surprised to find her alone in the living room, a space usually reserved for receiving guests, but perhaps she had lost all sense of formality in the wake of her husband's death.

"How are you, dear?" I asked her.

She looked at me, her eyes red and bloodshot.

"Oh, Beatrix," she sobbed, leaning over and placing her head on my shoulder. "Thank you for coming. I haven't got much in the way of family."

"Of course," I replied, wrapping my arm around her and squeezing. "I'm here as long as you need me."

She didn't act like a woman who'd killed her husband two days earlier. Would she be this upset if she'd done it herself? I let her cry, handing her a handkerchief out of my purse. She sniffled, wiped her nose, and sat up.

"How are the children doing?" I asked.

"Oh, they're hanging in there." She dabbed at the corners of her eyes, remnants of kohl staining the lash line below her eyes, but it didn't appear she'd applied fresh makeup that day. "Children are more resilient than their parents, not that Evelyn and I are Bobby and Sandra's biological parents. I'm sure you know that."

I did know. I wasn't certain if Evelyn and Margaret had adopted because they weren't able to have their own children or for some other reason. Bobby and Sandra were the same age but looked nothing alike. Bobby had dark hair and eyes, and olive skin, while Sandra was blonde with blue eyes. Of course, genetics were a mystery at times, but it seemed unlikely that Sandra and Bobby were biological siblings.

"Yes, of course," I said. "Where did you adopt them from, if you don't mind my asking?"

Margaret shrugged. "I don't recall all the details. Evelyn organized most of the paperwork and such things, but I think the mothers were at Bethany Home on the east side."

I shuddered involuntarily. I'd heard of the infamous home for unwed mothers from a friend of mine. Society's views of unmarried, pregnant women were unkind at best, and downright vicious at times. Our interpretations of morality could be unforgiving and primitive. Of course, I hadn't experienced a home like that myself, or adopted from one, but my friend told chilling tales of physical and emotional abuse during the pregnancy and the forced surrender of their babies into the adoption system. These women were not given a choice of keeping their infant children, the newborns wrenched away and never seen by their grieving mothers again. In some cases, the staff went so far as to tell the mothers the baby had died at birth in the hopes that she would never try to find her child beyond a tiny grave at the cemetery.

"I've heard of it," I said, but kept tight-lipped about what I knew. Perhaps Margaret was aware of the environment her children had come from, but I doubted it. Most people were blissfully ignorant of the social ills that happened around the corner from them on a daily basis. Most people thought the birthing homes for unwed mothers were a blessing for these poor girls who got themselves into trouble before wedlock. "Margaret, this is an odd question, but do you think Bobby's and Sandra's mothers would be able to find out your and Evelyn's identities?"

I had walked into the Volks' home thinking that Christopher Pearson was the best suspect in Evelyn's death at this point, despite what Arthur might think about Margaret. However, the fact the children had come from Bethany House provided a new alternative. A woman might hold a grudge long after the birth of her child if she were coerced into giving up her baby. If I'd learned anything from the detective programs Bill and I watched on television, it was that you had to consider all the possibilities.

Margaret's eyes grew wide. "Are you suggesting one of the biological mothers killed Evelyn?"

I shook my head. I didn't want her to be upset or plant the seeds for wild ideas in her mind. I had no evidence. It was simply a thought that had crossed my mind.

"I'm not suggesting anything, Margaret. However, it's a line of inquiry that Arthur could look into."

"The adoption was closed," Margaret said, shaking her head, "but you never know who has connections or enough money to bribe someone. I suppose it could be possible this whole thing is related to the adoption."

I squeezed her hand and faced her on the sofa. "I don't want you to rush to any conclusions, but I think the more you can tell Arthur about pretty much everything in your and Evelyn's lives, the better. He's a clever man. He just needs something to go on."

I didn't want to tell her she was Arthur's prime suspect until he found another lead he found more compelling.

"Well, I'm glad you don't think I did it, Beatrix. I'm sure lots of people think I did, but I swear I wouldn't have hurt him. We didn't have the perfect marriage... I can admit that... but I would never have wished him dead."

"I know," I said. "That's why I'd like Arthur to have various avenues to investigate."

Abigail appeared with the tea. The bone china cups tinkled against the saucers as she walked across the carpet, her tiny feet sinking into the thick cushioning layer that had likely been laid over the original hardwood of the house.

"Abigail, you're a godsend," Margaret breathed. "What would I do without you?"

Abigail smiled and handed each of us a teacup.

"Thank you, Abigail," I said, inhaling the fragrant aroma of the milky blend.

"One more thing, Margaret," I said, as she took her first sip, the steam dissipating as it brushed across her delicate nose. "Did Evelyn mention any conflicts with students recently?"

The teacup clinked as Margaret replaced it on its saucer. She looked serious.

"Well, now that you mention it, there was something." She paused, took a deep breath, and continued. "He didn't say exactly what happened, but last week he came home in a mood. I asked, but he didn't want to tell me. He just said he wished he could focus on research and excavations and didn't have to bother with the students. Some were a nuisance and others were a menace, he told me."

"Is that the word Evelyn used, menace?"

"It is. He said menace."

Menace. That was exactly the word I would have used to describe Christopher Pearson.

Chapter 30

Over a simple dinner of fried fish, scalloped potatoes, and cooked carrots, Bill and I discussed my suspicions.

"I have a few thoughts," I told him, cutting my carrots into bite-sized pieces. "The most likely is Christopher Pearson, of course. Shirley came by today and told me what a horrid creature he is. She thinks he would be capable of murder, and I think she may be right. Nadya said he had an argument with Evelyn last week. She wasn't sure what they had discussed, but it's possible Evelyn threatened to make a complaint about him if he kept harassing Nadya, which, apparently, he has been doing. Whether Chris actually believed himself to be in danger of expulsion from the university is something to consider. If he felt protected by the power his parents obviously wield, he wouldn't have much motivation to hurt Evelyn, but on the other hand, if Evelyn had something that would threaten his position, he might have decided to act first."

"That seems plausible," Bill mused. "Have you spoken to Arthur about this?"

"Not yet. I keep missing him, but maybe this evening I'll find him at home if he's not burning the candle at both ends."

"I know you want to help, Beatrix," Bill said, moving a cheese covered potato around his plate with his fork. "But you should leave this in Arthur's hands. He's competent and, regardless of whether Christopher is the culprit or not, the person who killed Evelyn could be extremely dangerous."

"Who would hurt a little old lady like me?" I teased.

Bill smiled, but he said: "Don't make light of it, Beatrix. You know full well the kind of lowlifes that exist in this city. The bigger Toronto gets, the more crime it attracts. We would have asked the same question of Evelyn - who would have guessed he would wind up dead at Fort York?"

"You're right, Bill." I stopped smiling. He had a point. "I'll be careful. But, I'll ask you this one favour. I'd really like to speak with Christopher and frankly, I don't want to do it alone. Will you go with me to talk to him?"

Bill pushed his glasses up the bridge of his nose with his index finger and smiled.

"It may be against my better judgement, but I'll go with you. He'll be back at Fort York tomorrow morning. Then we let Arthur handle things. The good thing about my position is that I can't be intimidated by a malicious student. The university can't exactly fire me, can it?"

Chapter 31

The next morning at Fort York, Bill and I pulled Christopher aside to ask him some questions while Nadya began work with the other three students. Once again, I'd decided to keep Muffin on her leash. She sat quietly by my feet, surveying the grounds of the fort. Without even really knowing him, I despised the young man with the icy eyes that matched his heart, but I tried to keep my voice even and polite. I always remembered the adage: you'll catch more flies with honey than vinegar. In my experience, it wasn't wrong.

"Hello, Christopher," I said, looking up at him to keep eye contact. With Bill at my side, I would feel less intimidated by his sour face and the lack of manners I'd seen the other day. "Do you prefer we call you Chris or Christopher?"

"I don't give a fig, lady," he said, his eyes squinty as though he could spread hostility through his gaze. "Call me whatever you like."

I squeezed Bill's hand behind my back, hoping he wouldn't react. I always got a queer feeling in my gut whenever someone called me lady. One could be certain it wasn't used in a pleasant, courteous manner, but Bill and I both needed to keep our cool for this conversation. Bill usually had an even temper, but he wouldn't be pleased by Christopher's lack of respect.

"Alright, Christopher," I said. "I'll get to the point since you're not one for pleasantries. What were you arguing with Evelyn about last week? Evelyn's wife told us he'd had a run-in with a student."

Christopher laughed. The sound was like a train screeching into the station. It made the hairs on my neck stand up.

"That fag?" he spat. "I was just giving him a warning. Those perverts think nobody sees them cruising at night in Allan Gardens. We see them alright, give them a good beating or call the fuzz to take care of them. A criminal record is worse for some of them than a beating anyway."

The vehemence with which he spoke frightened me, but I kept my face as expressionless as I could muster. I knew the young people referred to the police as the fuzz. I'd learned the term reading the popular novel, *The Outsiders,* released earlier in the year. I wasn't sure exactly what he meant by cruising, but from the context and words he used, I could make an educated guess. Is this what Evelyn had been doing the nights he didn't go home to Margaret? Cruising in Allan Gardens?

"So, you saw him with another man at the park?" I asked.

He shifted his weight and stuck his hand in his pocket.

"I saw him there at night," he said, though he now seemed hesitant. "Why else would he be there?"

"Why were you there? What takes you to Allan Gardens at night?" I asked, pointing an accusatory finger at him.

"I told you, lady," he looked away from me. "We go there to pound queers. The fuzz does it, too, before taking them down to the cooler where they belong."

I was thoroughly disgusted, and had I believed the police would do anything about it, I would have called them immediately. I knew too well, though, that they had no interest in preventing offences against homosexual men and as Christopher noted, often committed said crimes themselves. I couldn't even turn to Arthur. He'd made his views on the subject clear in the past. Relations between men were illegal and though assaulting someone was also against the law, it was easy for the perpetrator of the crime to use the moral panic defense and enjoy impunity despite their offense. The victim easily became the accused in these situations. Newspapers, even the more legitimate ones, loved to report on tawdry cases, printing the names of men arrested for morality crimes for all to see, knowing the consequences it would have for their careers and reputation. It was clear just which way justice in Canada, if it could be called that, swayed.

I bit my lip briefly to calm my nerves, then said: "What you are telling me is that you saw your professor walking at night in the park. I don't believe that is a crime. In fact, sometimes Bill and I walk in Allan Gardens at night. Would you attack us? Pound us as you say?"

I lied. Bill and I never went to Allan Gardens at night. Perhaps during the day to visit the botanical gardens housed in a handsome glass conservatory, but never past dark. The neighbourhood was known to have its share of social issues, though it was news to me that it was a place for men to congregate and seek one another's company.

"I wouldn't do that," Christopher mumbled, all his righteous indignation blown out of him. "We're only after the perverts; we don't hurt normal people."

I decided not to bring up the situation at the party the year before. It wasn't clear to me if Christopher was telling the truth, but it could explain why the story surrounding Evelyn's absences from home seemed so odd. Being an alcoholic would be better tolerated by society than being a homosexual. Or perhaps Christopher had seen Evelyn in Allan Gardens, made an assumption about his reasons for being there and decided to use that as leverage against him in some way. Had Evelyn decided to fight back and things got out of hand? Is that why Evelyn was dead now instead of going home to his family? Because of a misunderstanding?

"Do you have any more questions, Beatrix?" Bill spoke for the first time since we'd pulled Christopher aside.

I shook my head, glad that Bill let me handle the situation my way.

"In that case, I'll say what needs to be said." Bill let go of my hand and took a step toward Christopher. He may have been a 70-year-old man, but he still presented an imposing figure. "This whole conversation has been excessively disrespectful, young man. To my wife, to me, to your professor, who is only recently deceased. This kind of behaviour will not be tolerated while I'm in charge. If I hear that kind of language again, or see any kind of disrespectful behaviour, you will not continue at this site. You can run to daddy if you like. However, I'll remind you that I cannot be fired from the university because I don't work there, and your threats won't work on me. Do I make myself clear?"

Bill's tirade was all the more dramatic because he didn't raise his voice once. Christopher stood in silence before him and nodded his head. My husband hadn't stated the obvious and perhaps Christopher hadn't thought of it, but the university could remove Bill from the project at any time. As he'd said, he didn't work for them; he was technically little more than a volunteer at Fort York. However, if Christopher weren't clever enough to connect the dots, then who was I to point him in the right direction?

As Chritopher slunk back to the excavation area, I leaned into Bill's arms and let him hold me for a few moments. Muffin stood on her hind legs and rested her front paws on my skirt, begging for attention. We'd hardly given her the consideration she was used to since Evelyn died, and I felt sorry for her. Yet, there were urgent matters at hand. Bill and I had discussed homosexuality in the past and I knew his thoughts about the topic that was regularly debated in the court of public opinion. An anthropologist at heart, he'd explained to me that homosexuality had not only existed for thousands of years but that attitudes toward it had varied across cultures and time periods - from acceptance or even reverence to denial or abhorrence. He didn't believe it was anyone's business what adults did together in a free and democratic society. It was evident, however, that our society was not yet liberated in that sense.

Regardless of Bill's or my feelings toward the subject, Christopher's story didn't necessarily mean that Evelyn was homosexual. It was possible he'd been at the park to cruise, as Christopher suggested, but there could be other reasons, about which I could only guess. Perhaps Evelyn was simply passing by on his way to some other place and Christopher had misconstrued the situation. Still, it was an avenue worth investigating, if I could get someone to be forthcoming with information.

Chapter 32

"What do you think, Bill?" I asked. We were still out of earshot of the excavation, out of sight of the crime scene, on the east side of the stone magazine where the British had stored their kegs of gunpowder.

"About what Evelyn was doing at Allan Gardens?" he asked.

"Yes," I nodded. "Do you think he was cruising, as Christopher said?"

"I don't actually know what cruising means..." Bill's voice trailed off.

"I don't either," I smiled. "But based on the context, I imagine it means men looking for other men with whom to engage in certain kinds of activities."

"Yes, I see. I suppose that's one way of putting it, Beatrix." Bill smoothed the hairs of his moustache with his finger. "It would potentially explain why he might be out all night, not going home to Margaret and the children. The question is: did she know about it, or did he lie to her about his whereabouts?"

"If she knew he was attracted to men and engaged in relations with them, why would she stay with him?" I wrinkled my nose, pondering the situation. "She's young and attractive. She could find someone who would come home every night. Divorce isn't so frowned upon these days, is it?"

Bill shrugged. "Well, depends on the religion, I suppose. It's certainly less stigmatized than homosexuality, but perhaps not fully accepted in some circles. Toronto hasn't forgotten its puritanical past."

"Toronto the Good we shall remain," I quipped, pulling at Muffin's leash to keep her from eating the grass. "Whether we like it or not."

"What are you going to tell Arthur, now?" Bill asked.

"I don't know, yet," I said. "There's no real evidence that Evelyn was homosexual, and you know Arthur's opinions on the topic. Telling him could affect how he views the case and impact his investigation in a negative way. Of course, I believe he would try to remain objective, but would he succeed?"

I hadn't fully thought it all through. Should I hide what I knew from my cousin, despite his being the best chance there was of finding the killer? Or would his personal beliefs cloud his judgement and result in a witch hunt. I didn't believe him to be a malicious person, like Christopher, but I knew he would feel it was his duty to uphold the law. If Evelyn were homosexual, would anybody involved even feel safe speaking with Arthur, telling him the truth? It seemed unlikely. Self-preservation was deeply ingrained in marginalized groups. Finding Evelyn's killer might not be their top priority if their own safety were at stake, and I couldn't blame them for that.

Chapter 33

I pulled into Margaret's driveway after dropping Muffin at home. I wondered how I could politely intrude on her personal life and ask her about what Evelyn had been doing the evenings he stayed out all night. She wouldn't like the meddling, but it was better coming from me than the police. Arthur wouldn't be far behind me, asking the same questions once he'd spoken to Christopher or someone else who might know something. Toronto was a large city, but in some ways, we lacked the anonymity afforded to other urban areas. Gossip was a form of currency like any other and Toronto was a magnet for information.

As usual, Abigail greeted me at the door. Though she was probably only in her early thirties, she looked tired, as though she had aged since the day before. I wasn't surprised given the strain she must be under. Her skin, normally glowing and bright had a dull pallor and I questioned if she was getting any sleep.

Instead of taking me to the formal sitting room, as she usually did, Abigail led me to the back sunroom. With the sunshine bright and unencumbered by the clouds that day, the space was warm and inviting, despite the cool air outside. The sunroom looked out onto the backyard, which had been carefully landscaped. The lawn was still lush and green, the fallen leaves carefully raked away out of sight. I thought of our own yard, where the leaves would sit through the winter untouched, covered by a layer of snow, until spring, when Bill would eventually push them into the planters to compost. The Volk children were nowhere in sight, and I'd started to feel they were invisible phantoms in their own home.

"Oh, hello, Beatrix," Margaret sighed as I entered. "Have a seat."

She motioned for me to sit on a rattan two-person sofa with a floral seat cushion. Margaret lounged in a matching chair.

"I don't wish to disturb you, Margaret," I began, hoping I wouldn't upset her. She wasn't as pleased to see me as she had been the last time I was there. "But I've heard some information about Evelyn, and I wanted to ask you about it."

She looked up from pulling at the threads of a white throw she had draped over her legs.

"What did you hear?" she asked, leaning forward.

"This won't be easy to hear," I said slowly. "One of his students said he saw Evelyn in Allan Gardens at night to meet other men."

After a moment of silence, Margaret giggled, covering her mouth like a little girl. Then she pulled the throw closer around her body.

"Don't be silly, Beatrix," she said, regaining a serious countenance. "Of course, Evelyn wouldn't be going to Allan Gardens to meet men. What a ridiculous idea. Perhaps he was in Allan Gardens, as his student said, but he wasn't there for anything illicit, I can assure you. You know, Evelyn. Do you really think he would be so vulgar?"

I didn't know what to think anymore. I felt sure that Evelyn had been up to something, but it wasn't entirely clear what that was. Did it have to do with men? Was it about money? The anonymous man in the yellow rain jacket? Something relating to his students? Or even the mothers of his children? There were so many possibilities, it was hard to narrow things down. I desperately wanted to speak with Arthur, but I worried how things might turn out if Evelyn had indeed engaged in relations with other men. As Margaret continued to deny Christopher's accusation, I thought of someone I could speak with who just might be able to shed some light on the situation. It was a long shot, and could potentially be viewed as impertinent, but finding a killer had to take precedence over common courtesy, especially if a few uncomfortable questions could reveal the information I needed to understand better who Evelyn was.

Chapter 34

I hadn't seen Eduardo Reyes Iglesias since we left San Miguel at the end of the summer. He was a kind and intelligent young man who had developed an interest in archaeological illustration when we worked together in Spain. Though his father, one of Bill's colleagues, hoped for him to follow in his footsteps and become an expert in Mesoamerican archaeology, Eduardo had discovered he didn't love field archaeology quite as much as his father wished. Since I didn't know where Eduardo lived or his phone number, I had called Donna, the department secretary, to find out if he had any classes that afternoon. She was obviously surprised by my question and asked if it had anything to do with Professor Volk's death. I lied and said I just wanted to see how a former student was doing. Luck was on my side, and it turned out Eduardo had a course in archaeology methodologies at 4:45pm in Sidney Smith Hall.

After I left Margaret's house, confused by her reaction to my questions about Evelyn, I drove to the university. Without Bill, the walk across campus to the home of the department was gloomy. The trees had few, if any leaves, remaining, and the sun had already begun to dip in the sky as sunset approached. I'd decided to try to catch Eduardo before his course, but if I didn't hurry, I'd miss him and have to wait. I wanted to get home to let Muffin out, so I pushed my legs to go as quickly as they could. By the time I reached the steps up to the unimaginative, box-like concrete construction, I could feel beads of sweat drip down my lower back. Once indoors, I unbuttoned my coat and pulled off my leather gloves as I walked down the hallways. There were handfuls of students here and there, their voices echoing in the vast, nearly empty hallways, but this late in the afternoon the crowds of young people had dispersed to nearby bars and cheap diners, or walked to Yorkville, a seedy neighbourhood of coffee shops and music venues. It was popular amongst the Toronto youth, and they flocked to the area like ducks to a young child with a bag of breadcrumbs in the park. Their treat? Popular artists like Joni Mitchell and Gordon Lightfoot had all performed in the past few years in the neighbourhood. Of course, that was music for the younger generations, and Bill and I rarely set foot in Yorkville.

I stood outside a classroom on the main floor of the building. It was 4:25 and I anticipated the students would begin to arrive soon. I'd popped my head in to see if Eduardo had already taken a seat in the small classroom, but only a few students were settled into their places. There wouldn't be much of a crowd for the course, I guessed.

Down the hall I could see a bespectacled student with dark hair approaching. Eduardo looked much the same as he had when we left San Miguel, but his hair was a bit longer, tucked behind his ears. I wondered if he planned to grow it long the way some of the men did these days. He grinned as soon as he saw me.

"Hi, Mrs. Forster. What're you doing here?"

"Truth be told, Eduardo," I said, reaching over to shake his hand, "I'm here to see you."

"You are?" Eduardo clutched his books to his chest with one arm.

"Indeed, do you have a spare moment before class?"

"Definitely. I can spare two for you."

We laughed. It felt easy speaking to him. I'd enjoyed his company at San Miguel, and we'd developed a bond. I was sorry I hadn't reached out once we were back in Toronto, but life was like a herd of wild horses, running off into the distance and leaving all our plans and best intentions in a cloud of dust. I motioned for Eduardo to follow me away from the door as privacy was needed for the conversation we were about to have.

"I'm about to ask you something very personal," I began, looking into his eyes, but wishing I could walk away without saying anything. "And for that I apologize. I wouldn't wish to intrude on your life, and I wouldn't ask if it weren't important." I watched Eduardo's face grow serious. "I'm sure you heard about what happened to Professor Volk."

Eduardo nodded, looking down at his suede oxfords.

"I did," he mumbled. "It's terrible what happened. There's a lot of rumours floating around about it."

I nodded. "I imagined there might be. I hope that what I say will be held in confidence. I know you young people love a good tidbit of information, and I don't blame you."

"Of course, Mrs. Forster," Eduardo said, running a hand over his smooth hair. "I won't say anything to anyone."

"Please forgive my assumptions," I said, my throat feeling hot and blotchy, "but I didn't know to whom I could speak on this particular subject. Christopher Pearson said he saw Professor Volk cruising in Allan Gardens, and I wondered if you might know something on the subject or know someone who might."

Eduardo's face relaxed. While at San Miguel, he had told me that he wasn't attracted to women. He'd been afraid to tell me at the time, rightly so, given the dangers homosexual men faced under the law and in society. In England, only a few months before, the Sexual Offenses Act was passed, legalizing homosexual acts in private. However, in Spain as in Canada, not only were such relationships illegal but so demonized by society that men who were outed in public could face various forms of persecution. Men like Eduardo lived precariously on the margins, waiting for progress to catch up to the realities of life.

"You don't need to feel embarrassed, Mrs. Forster," Eduardo said, adjusting his glasses. "I'm glad you came to see me. Honestly, I didn't really know Professor Volk well, but I've seen him around and we have a mutual friend, you could say."

My heart beat faster. Had I finally found someone who might know what Evelyn was doing the evenings he didn't go home?

"I don't know about Allan Gardens," Eduardo continued. "It's possible he was cruising, but I find that unlikely. Allan Gardens has become popular for cruising again, but it's a risk. The police and bashers are familiar with it. It was a bit passé for a while, but some of the other spots are no longer safe, so people have been returning, little by little. Maybe Professor Volk was there for some other reason or to help someone in trouble. I couldn't say, but he didn't seem the type to go cruising and I know he had been with one person for a while. That would be my friend, Walter. We took an art class together a couple of years ago and we've been friends since. I knew he was involved with Professor Volk, but because of the professor's family situation they kept things quite private. Only a handful of their close friends know about the relationship. It's pretty hush-hush. Walter definitely won't want to talk to the police, but if we go together, he'll talk to you. He's very open about things with people he trusts, and I know he'll want Professor Volk's killer caught. Beyond a tight circle, he can't speak about this with many people. Walter was devastated by what happened, but he probably won't even go to the funeral."

I hadn't anticipated this turn of events. Evelyn had been engaged in a secret relationship with a man named Walter. Had it been Walter who killed Evelyn in a lover's tiff? Had Margaret found out about Walter and decided to kill Evelyn? Did Christopher Pearson invent the story about Allan Gardens and happened to stumble upon Evelyn's sexuality by accident or was the story true? Had Evelyn been cruising and what would Walter have thought of that? The web of deceit had grown complex, and I wondered if we'd ever be able to unravel it.

Chapter 35

When I walked through the front door, Muffin greeted me immediately, sniffing at my skirt and standing on her hind legs until I scratched her head and ears. I set my keys and purse on the entryway table and began removing all my outerwear.

"Is that you, Beatrix?" Bill called from the kitchen.

"Yes, it's me," I shouted back. "I'll be there in a minute."

I trod over the carpet in the hallway in my stockinged feet, wondering where I'd left my slippers this time.

"Did you walk home?" I asked Bill, as I stepped into the kitchen. "I'm sorry I was too late to pick you up. I was over at the university."

"I didn't," Bill said, turning to look at me. The wooden spoon he held dripped tomato sauce onto the linoleum floor. "Nadya has a car and offered to drive me home."

"Careful, Bill," I said, reaching for a roll of paper towels on the counter. "You're spilling sauce on the floor."

"Darn it," Bill said, turning back to the stove and shoving the spoon back into the pot.

"I'll get it," I said, slowly kneeling down to wipe up the small spill. Before I could, a pink tongue happily licked the sauce off the floor. "Goodness, Muffin, you speedy devil. Bill, wet this paper towel for me, would you?"

Once I was down, I didn't want to repeat the action. Though I'd started to think that if I ever stopped kneeling down, I'd lose the ability to do so. My joints would grow so stiff they'd simply stop bending at all. Bill handed me the damp paper towel, and I wiped up where Muffin had licked the floor. I used the chair at the kitchen table to support me as I stood back up.

"What are you making, Bill?" I asked, glancing into the pot that bubbled on the stove.

"I opened the spaghetti and meatballs you had in the pantry."

I rolled my eyes and put my hands on my hips. "Oh, no, Bill. You didn't."

"Was I not supposed to?" He looked at me, his eyes innocently wide behind his glasses.

"That was for the children, not for us." I shook my head. "We don't need to eat tinned spaghetti, we can eat proper food."

I'd purchased some tins of Chef Boyardee for our grandchildren when they came over, though they were starting to get a bit old for it. I'd have to put it on the grocery list for next time. I sighed. At least Bill had prepared something for dinner.

"Sorry, Beatrix," Bill smiled. "I thought it would be easy, and I wanted to make sure there was something to eat when you got home."

I put my hand on the small of his back and leaned my head against his arm. I couldn't fault the man for trying. If Evelyn's death had taught me one thing, it was that life was unpredictable and could be cut short when we least expected it. There was something to be said for appreciating the small things while we still could.

Chapter 36

After a hearty meal of mushy spaghetti and soupy meatballs, Bill and I settled into our armchairs in front of the television. We enjoyed watching *Wojeck*, a program on the CBC about a city coroner investigating crimes while also shedding light on the societal issues of our time. Black and white images flickered on the screen. As I watched, I realized how much the show provided insight into what could be happening behind the scenes with Evelyn's case. I wondered if the coroner was anything like Marty Wojeck.

Just as things were starting to get interesting, the telephone rang. I looked over and saw that Bill was fast asleep, his mouth hanging open, a gentle rumble coming from his throat. I sighed and struggled to push myself out of my chair. I reached the phone in the kitchen on the fourth ring.

"Hello?" I said, pressing the receiver to my ear.

"Trixie. Glad I caught you," Arthur said, sounding pleased. "I heard you were trying to reach me. Sorry I didn't get through sooner. Was it something important?"

I hesitated, perhaps for too long. What should I tell him? Would he unnecessarily make life difficult for Evelyn's friends and family if he knew what Eduardo had revealed? Would Evelyn's reputation be tarnished in the tabloids and Margaret would have to deal with the fallout? I knew how much she valued her position in society. Eduardo had also told me very clearly that Walter would not want to speak to the police. I could understand that under the circumstances.

"Heavens," I said, trying to sound carefree. "I didn't even remember I'd called you. Did Mariana tell you about the man in the yellow rain jacket I saw the morning after Evelyn was killed?"

"She did," Arthur confirmed. "Was that the only thing you wanted to tell me? He may or may not be related to the case, but Mariana is trying to track him down. The officers have talked to the staff at the fort, but they aren't much help. They don't keep records of who went in and out of the fort and what time. Completely useless. He's not an employee, but other than that, we're empty-handed."

I ran my finger over the lace doily I kept under the telephone.

"Let me think," I mumbled, trying to buy time. "The gray matter isn't what it used to be."

Arthur laughed. "You're telling me, Trixie. I swear I'd lose my own head if it weren't attached to my body."

"Have you learned anything new about the case?" I asked, thinking I could avoid Arthur's question with some of my own.

"That we have," he said. "Evelyn had family money and lots of it. There was no shortage of wealth there, and with his parents deceased and no siblings to make any kind of a claim, the inheritance will go entirely to Margaret and the children. Did you know they were adopted? Evelyn's kids, I mean."

I nodded even though Arthur couldn't see me.

"I didn't know about the money, but I did know about Sandra and Bobby. I suppose the money explains how they afforded such luxury on a professor's salary. The children, though, they're what I wanted to talk to you about. Not specifically them, as such, but their mothers. I don't believe they are biological siblings, so there must be two mothers. Margaret told me she thought the children had come from young women staying at Bethany House. I don't know what you know about the place, but I've heard awful things. They force those poor girls to give up their babies, even if they have the means and would like to keep them. All because they are unmarried. I could see a woman holding on to that anger for years. What if one of the mothers tracked down Evelyn and Margaret and confronted Evelyn at Fort York? Perhaps it's a far-fetched idea, but I just can't think that a woman would forget having a child ripped from her arms, never to see it again."

"That's not such a bad idea," Arthur admitted. "I'll have Mariana look into the identity of the birth mothers for the Volk children. They probably wouldn't be able to track down the adoptive parents. Those things are pretty sealed up for exactly the reason you mention, but if the birthing house had a breach of personal information, we could try to find out. Don't get your hopes up, though. It's a long shot."

"I see," I said softly, wondering if I were making a mistake keeping important information from Arthur. "Do you have any other suspects?"

"I know you won't like to hear this, but it's looking more and more like Margaret might have been involved."

"Is that so? I wouldn't peg Margaret for a killer, Arthur."

"Nor would I," he coughed on the other end of the line. I guessed he might have increased his smoking due to the stress of the case. "But she doesn't actually have an alibi for the time of the murder. Evelyn was killed after 10:40, when the secretary last saw him, and before noon, when the grad student went to look for him. The pathologist's findings confirm this timeline. The maid at the Volks' said that Margaret took the kids to school, dropping them off that day and she didn't come back home again until after one in the afternoon. I asked Margaret, and she said she'd been out shopping to clear her mind, but she didn't have any receipts to show for it. What rich lady goes shopping and doesn't buy anything?"

"Goodness, it's not looking good for her, is it?" I said.

I didn't want to believe it of Margaret, but Arthur was building a case against her.

"It's not," he agreed. "Of course, this is between us. I can count on you, Trixie, can't I?"

"Of course. I wouldn't interfere with a police investigation. However, I may as well tell you that I'll be going to see her tomorrow."

"Be careful if you do," he warned me. "And you let me know if she says anything incriminating."

"I don't think she will," I said, but I'd begun to doubt Margaret's innocence myself. If she had found out about Walter, she might have done something drastic. "I can't imagine her shooting a musket, though."

"Easy as point and shoot, like I told you," my cousin scoffed. "At close range, you'd have to be blind to miss that target. Though I guess the killer didn't know to aim at the chest, not the head. Anyway, I never thought we were dealing with a professional. She probably did it for the inheritance. It's a lot of money, Trixie, the kind most people don't even dream of."

According to Arthur, Margaret had the motive, means, and opportunity to kill Evelyn. Yet, surely someone must have seen Margaret at Fort York that day, if she had killed him. And what about Evelyn's secret life? How did that play into things? Arthur was unaware at the moment, but I didn't doubt he'd figure things out soon enough once he started asking the right questions of the right people. Would Margaret have killed Evelyn for money or for his affair, or possibly both?

Chapter 37

The next morning, while I prepared a lunch for Bill to take to Fort York, I thought about how much I would have liked to see Arthur question and arrest Christopher Pearson. Even if he didn't stay in jail because he wasn't guilty of Evelyn's murder, seeing him behind bars, if even for a moment, would have warmed my heart. However, I wasn't ready for Arthur to know what Christopher had told us, whether it was the truth or not. Arthur would be a bloodhound after a scent, if he knew about Allan Gardens or Walter. Perhaps his focus would shift away from Margaret, but he wouldn't handle male suspects as delicately as he'd handled her.

As I mixed leftover shredded roast chicken, mayonnaise, and chopped celery in a bowl, Bill popped his head into the kitchen.

"Can you take Muffin to the site today?" I asked.

I was supposed to meet Eduardo that morning to visit his friend and I didn't know how Walter would react to dogs.

"Yes, I can," Bill said. "Do you think you'll have time to drop by the site today? I'll have a couple of the students open up the grave some more, so there should be something more to see by the end of the day."

"I'll do my best, Bill," I said, smearing the chicken salad on a slice of homemade bread. "I'll be meeting Eduardo's friend this morning and then I'd like to speak with Margaret again. Give her a chance to share anything she may have been hiding, but it's possible she really didn't know what Evelyn was doing. Maybe she really believes he would go out drinking and stay with friends. Wives are often the last to know what their husbands are up to. That could be the case."

"She'll be shocked if she didn't know," Bill shook his head. "I don't know what's worse. Arthur thinking she killed her husband for money or her finding out what her husband was doing when he was away from home."

"I don't want to rush to conclusions, but I'll try to get her to open up. And yes, I'll try to get down to the excavation today after my errands. I'll drive you home, so you don't have to bother Nadya."

"Sounds like a plan," Bill said and kissed me on the cheek.

Chapter 38

I dropped Bill and Muffin at Fort York and drove to Cabbagetown on the east side of the city. The neighbourhood had a bad reputation and was known to have many rooming houses and run-down properties. The northern part of the area, where I parked, was nicer, but people generally knew to stay away from south Cabbagetown. I parked on a quiet street of Victorian row-houses and towering trees that had been growing for many decades. The sidewalk was peppered with dead leaves and there was a dampness to the air where the branches cast shade over the street. I thought the houses could be beautiful with a little paint and sprucing up, but I knew that the 19th century-stained glass and brick façades hid all kinds of horrors on the inside of the homes. Bill and I had needed to do many renovations on our own Victorian home near High Park, and we were well aware of what lay beneath hardwood floors and behind printed wallpaper. The entire neighbourhood of Cabbagetown looked haunted, and I thought that it would be the perfect place for a good fright on Halloween.

I saw Eduardo waiting for me ahead, on the sidewalk beyond a small wrought-iron fence that separated the front yard from the pavement. He was dressed casually in blue jeans and white canvas tennis shoes, a white t-shirt and black leather jacket.

"Good morning, Mrs. Forster," he said. "How are you?"

"Very well, thank you, Eduardo. How are you?"

"Good, thanks." He made a sweeping gesture. "This is Walter's house."

We stood in front of a semi-detached red brick Victorian home. Unlike some of the neighbouring properties, the front yard was carefully kept and though the flowers of summer were long gone, nothing was overgrown. A few purple cabbages even grew near the front step. I wondered if they were for consumption or an ornamental nod to the name of the neighbourhood.

"I appreciate your meeting me here," I said. "I hope Walter won't mind us dropping by. Were you able to reach him last night to let him know we were coming?"

"I did," Eduardo replied. "He's pleased you're visiting, and he wants to help however he can. He just wants to avoid the police if possible. Everyone in his circle knows he's gay. It's no secret, but nobody likes police attention, you know."

"What do you mean by gay, dear?" I asked. "That he's carefree?"

Eduardo laughed at my old-woman naïveté.

"It means homosexual, Mrs. Forster. That's how we refer to ourselves. It's better than other terms that get thrown around."

"Oh, I see," I said, making the connection. "I like it, too. Sounds more cheerful."

"Precisely," Eduardo adjusted the arm of his black, plastic-framed glasses. "Walter is a bit more in the public eye than your average Joe. He's an up-and-coming athlete and has a real chance at winning national championships and even going to the Olympics."

"Goodness," I said. "That's exciting. What sport is he involved in. I must say, I don't follow many sports."

"Neither do I," Eduardo grinned. "You might like this one, though. He's a gymnast."

"Oh, that's delightful," I smiled. "We used to do some gymnastics when I was at school, but I was never any good at it. I do occasionally watch it on the television. I wonder if I've seen Walter before."

"You may well have," Eduardo opened the little gate that led to a flagstone path. "I guess you'll find out."

I followed him up the front steps to the door. It had been recently painted a turquoise blue and the stained glass at the top was pristine, not a single cobweb or speck of dust clung to the corners. A herculean feat at any time of year, I knew from experience. The elements, and spiders in particular, were relentless when it came to making a clean home filthy. Eduardo knocked on the door and within moments it was flung open to reveal a young man in an old-fashioned black smoking jacket, black pants, and velvet slippers.

Eduardo was right about my recognizing the man, but not for the right reason. I hadn't seen Walter on television, but I had seen him just the other day at Fort York. He motioned for us to step inside. Hanging behind him on a coat hook was the yellow rain jacket.

Chapter 39

As soon as I saw Walter's jacket, questions tangled my thoughts. Why had Walter been at Fort York the day after Evelyn was murdered? It was clear now he didn't work there, and it was unlikely he was visiting the fort to learn about its history. He must have been there for Evelyn. Had he shot Evelyn the day before and returned to remove some piece of evidence he left behind? Or had Walter tried to visit Evelyn, completely unaware that Evelyn was already dead? Did he find the body and choose not to call the police, or had he seen nothing and found out about his lover's death in the newspaper?

"Pleasure to meet you, Mrs. Forster," Walter said, extending his hand. "Eduardo told me all about you and how you solved a murder at San Miguel."

"Nice to meet you, as well, Walter," I said. "Eduardo is too kind."

"Come in and sit down." Walter motioned for us to sit in the front living room, which was furnished with antique pieces and a burgundy velvet sofa.

Despite his youth, it looked like the sitting room of an old, noble family in Eastern Europe. Unlike how I imagined other houses in Cabbagetown, Walter's had been renovated, the walls painted, and the old hardwood gleamed with a fresh coat of stain.

"Could I get you any coffee or tea?" Walter asked, as Eduardo and I sat down on the sofa.

"Coffee, please." Eduardo held his hands together in a gesture of prayer.

"I'd love a tea, thank you," I said, not wanting to be difficult, but I knew I couldn't stomach coffee this early in the day. "Can we help you at all?"

I didn't want to trouble the young man in a time of grief, but he waved away the offer and glided into the kitchen.

"How beautiful," I said to Eduardo when we were alone.

I pointed to a painting, if it could be called that, across from us. It was on black paper with the image of a man skating on a pond in antique skates that were traced in gold. In the background there were other skaters. It was a picturesque winter scene that romanticized the season most Torontonians loathed.

I nudged Eduardo. "It almost makes me think I should like winter."

Eduardo chuckled. "There's nothing that would make me like winter, Mrs. Forster. Walter drew that himself."

"A young man of many talents," I said, impressed.

Walter returned with a loaded tray. A teapot and one teacup, a French press that was still brewing, two coffee mugs in a matching striped pattern, cream and sugar. He carefully placed the tray on the coffee table and sat in a high-backed chair next to us, tucking both his legs up under him.

"I suppose Eduardo told you about my relationship with Evelyn," Walter began, his expression serious but not unfriendly. His frankness was refreshing. "I know you must wonder about our age difference. We are twelve years apart, but I'm mature for my age and Evelyn had a youthful spirit. We genuinely cared for one another. It wasn't as lurid as some would have you believe."

"I'm very sorry for your loss," I spoke softly.

I felt sorry for him. He would not be allowed to grieve for Evelyn in the same way Margaret would.

"Thank you, Mrs. Forster." Walter got out of his chair and kneeled on the floor, pressing the plunger down on the French press. "It's been difficult. I heard about Evelyn from a friend, but of course I saw it in the newspaper, too. Eduardo said you had some questions as you're looking into his death yourself?"

"That's correct," I said, glancing at Eduardo and then back to Walter. "I believe I saw you at Fort York the day after Evelyn was killed."

Walter's face lit up with recognition. "That's right. I do remember seeing you there. I couldn't place you at first, but I knew I'd seen you somewhere."

"I imagine you were there to visit Evelyn."

Walter passed me the teacup. His hands shook a little and the contents of the cup splashed over the edge.

"I'm so sorry," he said, his eyes welling with tears.

"Not to worry," I said, reaching with my free hand to squeeze his shoulder. "It's only been a few days. Of course, you're shaky. Anyone would feel the same in your situation."

"I do want to help." Walter stood and returned to his chair. "I was there to visit Evelyn the day you saw me. I was supposed to see him the day he died, but didn't make it. He called me on Sunday night, telling me he had exciting news about an article he'd just published in one of the archaeology journals. He wanted to show me and asked if I'd come down to Fort York around 10:30 in the morning. I was late leaving, and I missed the streetcar. It took ages for the next to arrive, and by the time it came, I knew I'd be too late to see him. I tried calling him that night to explain why I hadn't come by, but he wasn't at home. I decided to try again the next day much earlier, but of course, I didn't find him. I waited as long as I could, but had to run for an appointment. I thought I just had bad timing, but I was very wrong. That's when I saw you, Mrs. Forster. I was just leaving Evelyn's office, and I imagine you were about to go in."

"Yes," I said, smoothing a wrinkle in my skirt. "I went over to have a look around and that's when I found him."

"Was it horrible?" Walter asked, wiping a tear off his cheek with a long index finger.

"I didn't see much, Walter," I told him. "My husband and I called the police after I found him. You didn't see Evelyn's body or signs of a struggle in the building?"

Walter shook his head. "I didn't even know to look. I thought it was bad luck, and I'd missed him again the second day. I had no idea what had happened."

I wanted to believe Walter. He seemed genuinely affected by Evelyn's death and I felt he was telling the truth. However, it was always possible he was a very good actor.

Chapter 40

I realized as I took Eduardo to the university that I hadn't driven this much in years. Now that we were retired, Bill and I did many of our errands together and there was little need for me to drive all over the city these days. I felt a renewed sense of independence - no children to chauffeur, no husband to drive me, and a lightness knowing that despite my age I could go anywhere I liked whenever I pleased. Well, of course there were limits to that, but it was freeing. Nobody could suggest I wasn't capable or that I was too old to be a competent member of society.

When I left Eduardo on St. George Street near Sidney Smith Hall, I drove immediately to Forest Hill. I didn't know how Margaret would react to my telling her I'd met with her husband's lover, but it was important to find out just how much she knew about Evelyn.

To my surprise, Margaret was in the yard with Sandra and Bobby when Abigail showed me in. Dressed in matching light blue wool coats and hats they politely said hello after being prompted by their mother. Then Abigail whisked them away inside.

"Let's sit outside, shall we?" Margaret asked, walking toward a patio set of white-painted wrought iron. "We won't get many more days like this."

She was right. In her backyard, we were protected from the wind and the sun shone pleasantly on the back patio. The sole source of warmth would eventually make its way behind the trees, but it would be nice to have some fresh air while the sun's rays could still reach us. I was worried Margaret would not want to see me after my last visit, but she was welcoming as she always had been.

"I believe your cousin thinks I killed Evelyn," Margaret said, folding her skirt over her leg as we sat down.

"He did mention that wives are often the prime suspect in a man's death." I didn't want to confirm or deny her suspicion after I'd told Arthur our conversation would be confidential.

"Do you think I did it, Beatrix?" Margaret asked, she narrowed her eyes at me.

"I don't believe so, but I do think you are either hiding something from me, and I'd guess the police, too, or you are very much in the dark about your husband's activities."

Margaret's eyes widened and she had the appearance of a child about to be scolded.

"I ... I ..." Margaret stammered. "I suppose with those detective skills you've figured things out. In my gut I knew you would, but of course, I had hoped I would be spared somehow. Better you than anybody else, though."

She looked down at her fingernails, neat and tidy with a shiny coat of red polish.

"I know that Evelyn was having a relationship with a young man," I said.

"Oh, you know about Walter, too, then," she sounded defeated. "Who else knows?"

"Their mutual friends, I suppose, and Bill, but beyond that I don't know."

"Do the police know?" Margaret looked at me.

"Not yet, I don't think," I said, "but it may simply be a matter of time. Once Arthur starts to dig a little, he'll get wind of it."

"Oh God, Beatrix," Margaret whimpered. "This is what I was afraid of."

"What were you afraid of?" I leaned toward the grieving widow. "Why don't you start from the beginning, dear? When did you find out about Evelyn?"

Margaret ran her fingers over her eyebrow and closed her eyes a moment.

"I'm sorry I lied to you," she began. "I only did it to protect Evelyn's reputation and for the children. Please don't judge me. I did what I felt I needed to do. You know how cruel society can be with those trash tabloids everyone reads. When I first met Evelyn, I had nothing. No family, no money, no prospects for a career, absolutely nothing. He was charming, good looking, and had everything I didn't. His family was wealthy. He was nearly finished his PhD and was sure to get a position at the university, and for whatever reason he seemed to like me. I was working as a waitress and barely getting by. You can imagine how I felt when this glimmering white knight showed up to rescue me from a life of poverty. There was of course a catch. He was honest with me nearly from the start, but it hurt to know he would never really love me in that way all women hope their husbands will love them. Evelyn told me one night over a beautiful candlelit dinner that even though he liked me very much, he wasn't attracted to women. Not just me, no women at all. At first, I was scandalized. I knew what he meant by that, and I'd read countless stories in the newspapers – sex perverts they called them. In the eyes of the law, they were criminals, and I hadn't been taught any better along the way. I was about to leave him alone at the table, run home and cry, but he asked me to sit down and discuss a proposition he had for me."

Margaret looked at me but then glanced away into the distance. I knew sharing this story was hard for her.

"You probably don't know what it's like to go to bed hungry, Beatrix," she began, "but in those days I did. Evelyn offered me everything except a husband who would be madly in love with me, and I decided that night that I couldn't survive without food and shelter, but I could survive a marriage without attraction and true love. Evelyn suggested that we would live as husband and wife, but he would ask that I look the other way when he stayed out all night sometimes with a man. At first it was difficult, staying at home alone while he was away, but I got used to it. When we adopted the children and hired Abigail, things got much better. I can't bear to be without her, and I love having Sandra and Bobby. Then when Evelyn left, sometimes for days at a time, I didn't care so much. I have a better life than I did before and for that I'm glad. Evelyn may not have been the perfect husband, but he was a good man, and he made sure we wanted for nothing. I want to be sure that the children have good memories of their father; they shouldn't feel shame for something they had no control over."

Margaret ran her hand over the purple silk scarf she wore around her neck. She looked delicate and frail. I understood now why she didn't like Abigail to be away, but it wasn't fair to Abigail's own child to be gone for years without seeing her. Margaret stared at me with pleading eyes, and I realized how imperfect families were. Under the façade of a happy marriage was often something quite different. The members of the family putting on a cheerful face for company all whilst withering away on the inside. I wondered if Evelyn had been happy with the arrangement or if he'd longed for a day when he could have lived freely with Walter and hosted parties at the house in Cabbagetown instead of Forest Hill. It turned out Bill and I had never truly known Evelyn. He was never permitted by society to exist as himself in public. He had to hide away with only certain friends privy to his genuine self. Had we, as a society, been more forgiving and accepting as we'd been taught by religion, would things have been different? Had someone killed him for his relationship with Walter? Certainly, Margaret knew the whole story and chose this life, even if it weren't ideal. Why would she change her mind now and kill him for it? It didn't make sense. Perhaps it was for the money as Arthur suspected. Or was she entirely innocent of Evelyn's death?

Chapter 41

Muffin came racing over to see me as soon as I breached the perimeter of Fort York. I was so glad to see her, the happy little terrier, bouncing around. It had been a long, hard day and I could feel myself begin to wane. I just wanted to sit at home with Bill and not worry about who killed Evelyn, yet I couldn't let it go. I didn't want everyone's life, Margaret, Walter, the children, to be fodder for the gossip rags. Once the police knew, it was only a matter of time before personal details would hit the papers. Even the more reputable newspapers published scandalous stories of arrests by the police morality squad. Anything to sell a paper. That's the way it had always been. I dug inside my purse and found a small piece of dried beef for Muffin. She lay down in the grass when I gave the command, and I tossed the piece of meat for her to catch. In one gulp it was as though it had never existed. Chewing her food was not Muffin's area of expertise.

I realized as I approached the excavation area that not a soul was around. Where were Bill and the students? Had they gone off to look at some of the other buildings on the grounds of the fort? I glanced back at the officers' barracks and mess and saw that police tape still blocked access to the building. It seemed unlikely they were there, unless the police had additional questions for all of them at once.

"Muffin, where's Bill?" I asked, looking around.

I looked at my watch, noticing that it was 4:45. Had Bill and the students gone home? I walked a little closer to the excavation area and saw that a few bags were still near the dig. They must be somewhere around here, I thought. I glanced to my left and saw that the door to the stone magazine was still closed as it had been on previous days. I decided to check one of the two-story white clapboard blockhouses first. In the days the fort was used for active military service, the purpose of the blockhouse was to defend the fort, allowing its occupants to fire at the enemy in various directions and giving them some form of protection as their adversary advanced.

"Let's go, Muffy," I said, striding toward the blockhouse.

Once more, I was thankful I hadn't worn a heeled shoe. Vanity was a sure path to injury at my age. Muffin leaped and ran ahead of me without a care in the world. If only humans could be so gay as our canine counterparts. I laughed on the inside at my unintended double entendre. I'd have to remember now that the word had multiple meanings. Good thing Eduardo had taught me a thing or two, or I'd be as every other elderly woman, completely in the dark when it came to contemporary linguistics. I didn't like to be too out of touch with youth culture when I had grandchildren. With one already attending university, it was often difficult to feel relevant. No amount of Chef Boyardee could remedy that.

Fortunately for my joints, which had already begun to express their irritation at my increased activity, the door to the blockhouse was open and I guessed I'd find Bill and the others inside.

Muffin ran over the threshold first and I heard a voice from within say: "There you are, Muffy. Where have you been?"

I stepped into the old building, the air not much warmer than it was outside, and saw Bill, Nadya, Brian, and Marco inside.

"Good heavens, Nadya," I breathed, aghast when I saw her. "What's happened to your face?"

Bill was sitting in front of Nadya with a first aid kit open on his lap. There was a ragged injury to the left side of her face and though it was clear Bill had already cleaned up some of the wound, a small amount of blood still seeped out. Scattered around Bill were various bits of gauze and cotton balls stained red.

"Thank God, you're here, Beatrix," Bill said. "Someone attacked Nadya. Anthony found her lying unconscious in here. He's gone to get the police, if they're still around, and to call for an ambulance."

"Oh my, that's awful!" I exclaimed, sitting down in an empty chair next to Nadya. "Are you alright, dear?"

"I think I'm ok, Mrs. Forster," Nadya said slowly. "I just feel a bit shaky, that's all. It's probably the shock more than anything."

"Did you see who attacked you?" I asked, brushing some hair away from the wound.

"I wish I had," she said, looking down at her hands. There was dirt under her fingernails from the excavation. "I heard footsteps and then he must have slammed my head into the display case over there. I don't remember anything after that until Anthony showed up."

Nadya pointed at a display case that housed a few examples of muskets and musket balls from the War of 1812 period. The thick museum glass was smashed, a spiderweb of fractures, but it had not been completely broken, and no shards could be seen on the floor.

"You think it was a man?" Bill asked, cutting a piece of bandage for Nadya's wound.

"I just assumed, but it could have been anyone," Nadya replied.

I immediately thought of Margaret. I'd only just been with her at her house. Could she have reached the fort before me and attacked Nadya? It seemed unlikely. I didn't drive very fast, and she might have known a shorter route, but it still wouldn't have given her much time to park her car and get across the grounds of the fort unseen to assault Nadya. How would she even know she'd find Nadya alone? It simply didn't make sense.

Marco, who had been silent, a shadowy presence hovering over Bill's shoulder until then, whispered: "Christopher wasn't at the excavation today."

He didn't say he thought Christopher was guilty of attacking Nadya, but he didn't need to. Had Evelyn's murderer attempted to harm Nadya or was this unrelated? Would Christopher have attacked her for some perceived slight or rejection of his advances? Or could Christopher be involved in both crimes? There was also the possibility he'd been sick that day and hadn't been at Fort York at all. The questions thundered in my head, and we were no closer to answering them.

Chapter 42

When Anthony returned to the blockhouse, he was sweating and out of breath. He must have run back from the pay phone.

"The ambulance is on the way," Anthony huffed. "The police said they'd meet us at the hospital."

"Thank you, Anthony," Bill said, packing up the first aid kit.

He had already placed a bandage over Nadya's injury and there was little more to do but wait for the paramedics to arrive.

"Did you see anybody leaving the blockhouse when you found Nadya?" I asked.

Anthony ran a hand over his hair and said: "I didn't see anyone, Mrs. Forster. I don't really know how long she'd been out cold though. Could have been some time, and someone could sneak out around behind the building and then leave through the east entrance without anybody noticing."

Anthony was right. It wouldn't be difficult to steal away when nobody was looking.

"What about upstairs? Did anybody look up there?" I asked, pointing at the stairs that led to the second floor.

Everyone, including Bill looked around at each other and shook their heads. Nadya's attacker could have been hiding upstairs, and nobody had gone to investigate.

"I'll go check, Mrs. Forster," Brian offered, though he looked nervous.

This was the first time he'd spoken since I arrived and I'd almost not noticed him; his large body pressed against a display case.

"Anthony and Marco, would you mind going with Brian," I gestured to the red-headed student as he walked toward the stairs. "Just pop up and have a look around, will you? It seems unlikely anybody is still here, but you never know. Just be careful. The culprit is probably unarmed given he pushed Nadya, but this building is full of old weapons."

Brian, Anthony, and Marco walked cautiously up the wooden staircase and out of sight.

"Nadya, what were you doing over here anyway?" I asked.

"We store a few tools over there in the corner," she gestured with her arm to a wooden chest with peeling grey paint that was tucked away behind some chairs. "There's no real storage shed here at the fort, so we make do with storing things wherever we can."

I'd forgotten that they also had a small coffee station in the blockhouse. I remembered that Anthony said he came here after Evelyn's lecture on the day of the murder.

"How long before you noticed she'd been gone too long?" I asked Bill.

"Hmm," he rubbed one side of his beard with the palm of his hand. "I'm not sure. It was Anthony who noticed she'd been gone awhile. We were all so focused on the work it could have been half an hour or longer, I'd say."

In that case, the attacker might have had plenty of time to exit the fort on the east side without anybody from the dig seeing him... or her.

I looked up when I heard footsteps on the staircase. Brian, Anthony, and Marco descended slowly, the creaky steps uneven from wear.

"Anything?" Bill asked.

"There's nobody up there," Anthony replied, running his hand over the banister as he walked.

Evidently, the attacker had gotten away without anyone the wiser as to their identity.

Chapter 43

At the hospital, Nadya sat with her legs hanging over the side of a bed while the doctor cleaned and dressed her wound. He had ruled out a concussion and said that she could go home once the injury was bandaged. Arthur and Mariana arrived shortly after Bill and I located where Nadya was being treated. Arthur asked her a series of questions, taking notes in his book as she spoke. His probing seemed to distress her, and I couldn't blame the poor girl. She was still young and had just been attacked by some unknown person. Wouldn't anybody be afraid?

Arthur motioned for us to step outside the room with him.

"We'll be back in a moment, Miss Shevchenko," Arthur said to Nadya, folding his notebook up and placing it in the pocket of his coat.

Out of earshot of Evelyn's graduate student, Arthur, shadowed closely by Mariana, tapped his pen to his lip.

"What the hell happened?" he asked. "How was she attacked without anybody seeing anything?"

I thought Nadya had explained that well enough herself, but apparently Arthur had not absorbed the information.

"Nadya went to get some tools from the blockhouse," Bill began, speaking calmly.

"That's not what I meant," Arthur interrupted, waving his hand at Bill. "Look, if there's a risk of people getting hurt at the excavation, we may have to shut the whole thing down. Suddenly we've got sitting ducks at Fort York. We don't have the resources to have a uniform down there all day."

"Do you think the attack was related to Evelyn's murder?" I asked.

"Of course, I do," Arthur said. "Unless there's something you're not telling me, Trixie. The way I see it, the girl saw something she wasn't supposed to, or knows something. She may not even be aware of it, but the killer thinks she knows something, for whatever reason. He probably just meant to send a warning. Let her know to keep her mouth shut. If he'd wanted her dead, from the description of the crime, sounds like it would have been easy enough. There was time, no witnesses, and once she was unconscious, she couldn't fight back."

"Well, there is something we didn't mention," I said, feeling ashamed of hiding things from the police. "Nadya told us, and Shirley confirmed it," I began, not knowing how much I should reveal. "One of the students has a history of violence and harassment against women."

"Which student is this?" Arthur asked, reaching into his pocket for the notebook.

"Christopher Pearson," Bill said. "Apparently there was an incident last year and his parents had the department cover it up. Christopher didn't show up to the excavation today."

"Ah, hah," Mariana interjected. "So, are you saying he could have attacked her and it had nothing to do with Professor Volk's death?"

Mariana pulled a chocolate bar from her pocket and opened the plastic wrapper. Arthur looked at her, his lips curling in disgust.

"What?" she asked, putting the half-unwrapped bar back into her pocket. "I haven't eaten all day. I'm starving."

"Is what Mariana said true?" Arthur asked, looking back to me. "Do you think Nadya was attacked by Christopher because of some altercation that had nothing to do with Evelyn?"

I glanced at Bill, and he shrugged, a deflation of his frame that made me realize he'd accepted defeat.

"I think you'd better tell him everything," Bill said.

Chapter 44

Bill was right. The attack on Nadya had changed things. I couldn't risk anybody else getting hurt by playing detective. The stakes were different now and I realized I'd have to confess what I knew to Arthur. I just hoped I wouldn't be putting others' lives and reputations in jeopardy.

"I'll tell you what I know, but I'll need some assurances," I said. "Perhaps we should discuss this over dinner. I'm sure Mariana could use a bite to eat."

Mariana smiled and held up her hands. "Can't say no to that offer, can we?"

When Nadya's mother arrived at the hospital to take her home, the rest of us headed to Bill's and my house. We drove separately so that nobody would have to go back to the hospital to retrieve a vehicle. It was dark when we left, the streetlights casting chilling shadows over the road ahead. I wondered if in the safety of her own home, Nadya would be able to sleep.

"I hope you agree that we need to share what we know with Arthur," Bill said, his hands gripping the wheel.

He sat slightly forward in his seat, almost hunched over the steering wheel, and I questioned whether he was struggling to see at night. Probably his eyes were as tired as mine were.

"I do," I said quietly. "I wish we didn't have to, but with what happened to Nadya I don't think we have a choice anymore. I can't play fast and loose with people's lives and wellbeing. I hope Arthur will accept my ultimatum. I'll tell him what we know, but he must assure me that he will only pursue criminal charges against the murderer, and he will be discrete regarding everyone's personal life. He'll get more from witnesses if he doesn't frighten them half to death. If they can't trust him, they'll clam up and he'll never get the full story."

"Better some honey than vinegar, as you always say," Bill agreed. "Since the case revolves around a homicide, I think he'll want to focus on what's important, which is solving Evelyn's death, not causing trouble for a few homosexual men."

"Gay men, dear," I corrected him. "Eduardo told me people prefer it these days. It feels less clinical."

"Gay, it is," Bill said, smiling at the gloomy road in front of him.

Chapter 45

Muffin greeted me and Bill at the front door, making a fuss as though she'd been left alone all day. I'd given Anthony my keys and asked him to drop her off so Bill and I could go to the hospital with Nadya. I wondered if he might be an option for dog sitting Muffin when Bill and I occasionally went away and couldn't take her with us. Graduate students were always glad of a little extra cash on the side, and he seemed to like her. I hustled into the kitchen and started boiling some vegetables and threw some chicken breasts in a frying pan. Bill answered the door when Arthur and Mariana knocked.

"Something to drink?" Bill asked, gesturing with his hand for them to sit at the kitchen table.

"What've you got, Bill?" Arthur asked, dropping his lumbering frame into one of the chairs.

"That's a good question," Bill muttered. "Beatrix, what do we have to drink?"

I turned away from the stove to look at him. "I think there's some beer left, and the regular non-alcoholic options.

Milk, juice, sparkling water, regular water. We don't often get to the liquor store, and when we do... well, you know the rules."

Toronto had been a temperance city and there were strict liquor laws in Ontario. Back in the 20s, after prohibition, Bill and I had been deemed moral enough to drink alcohol and allowed to have a permit book which was reviewed each time we went to purchase any beverages. Only one type could be purchased at a time and in limited quantities. The permit books had eventually been phased out, but there were still regulations regarding liquor purchase and consumption. I had always wondered how Evelyn managed to have a full supply of everything under the sun for his parties, but then again, the wealthy had ways around most rules.

"That we do," Arthur said, folding his hands over his round belly.

When Bill had set the table and I had placed the hot dishes on mats in the centre, we all migrated to the dining room. It was more spacious than the kitchen table for a group of four and added a layer of formality to the proceedings. Though I'd once held the position of a figure of authority in Arthur's life, his police training and career diminished my influence. He wasn't a little boy asking to play at the park anymore.

"So, tell me these assurances you need from me," Arthur said, cutting into the centre of the chicken breast.

I glanced at Bill, and he nodded supportively.

"There are some personal elements to this story about which I believe you and Mariana are likely not yet aware. Though I recognize the importance of divulging this information to the police, especially under the circumstances, I would ask that you and Mariana focus on the real crime here, the murder, and not any perceived crime. Additionally, for the sake of all involved, including Evelyn's children, I would ask that you be as discreet as possible. I think you will agree that the children are entirely innocent in this situation and should be protected at all costs from the often ugly glare of society. I know it will be difficult to agree to this without knowing what I'm about to tell you, but I need you, and Mariana, to provide this assurance. Then I can be transparent about what I know."

"I'm completely in agreement with Beatrix on this, Arthur," Bill added.

Arthur's shoulders slumped slightly. "Alright, I'll give you my word to be as discreet as possible with whatever information you're about to reveal, Trixie. Can she count on you, Mariana?"

"Sure thing, Beatrix," Mariana smiled. "I just want to hear what we've missed."

"Evelyn was gay," I said simply and waited for Arthur's reaction.

"Gay as in homosexual?" Arthur dropped his knife and fork onto the plate. The clanking noise made Muffin look up and twist her head at an angle.

"Yes, that's what I mean," I replied.

"Why would you keep something like this from me?" Arthur demanded, leaning forward and stabbing the table with his index finger. "And Jesus, Trixie, why would you protect a sex pervert?"

"Arthur," Bill warned, in a low voice.

Arthur leaned back in his chair and put his hands behind his head.

"Ok, I'd like to hear the rest of this," he said. "I'll keep my temper in check. I gave my word and despite my reservations, I intend to keep it."

I glanced at Mariana. She wore a blank, almost timid look on her face. I was surprised. She was anything but shy.

"What about you, Mariana?" I asked. "Do you have an opinion on the matter?"

"I do, Beatrix," Mariana said, looking down at the remaining chicken and vegetables on her plate. "My opinion and the law don't match unfortunately, but I feel strongly that what people do in the privacy of their own homes shouldn't be a matter for the police. We have enough to deal with in terms of serious crimes in this city."

"Well said," Bill added.

"Except they don't do it in the privacy of their own homes, do they Mariana?" Arthur spat. "Why do we have to have constables patrolling the parks and the alleyways? It's because they do it in public; that's why."

Mariana gripped the handle of her fork. "Who's there to see it at night?"

"That's enough," Arthur snapped. "We aren't here to discuss morality or what the law should and shouldn't be. I want to know how you found this out, Trixie. Did the widow tell you?"

I nodded. "Yes, she confirmed it once I'd tracked down Evelyn's lover. She couldn't really hide it once we knew the details."

"And how did you find the lover?" Arthur asked, the redness in his cheeks fading. "You'll be providing his name, I hope."

"I will," I said quietly, "since I think you'll have to speak with him. Though naturally, he would prefer not to talk to the police. I suppose he'll have no choice now. I got his name from a reliable source. You might consider, Arthur, that I gained all of this information by treating people with respect and a little bit of kindness. The police could learn a thing or two. A hard hand doesn't always get you what you want."

"You tell 'em, Beatrix," Mariana said. When Arthur gave her a harsh look, she covered her mouth. "Ooops, sorry. I'll be quiet."

"That's a fair assessment, Trixie," Arthur said. "However, not all criminals can be treated with kid gloves as you suggest."

"Of course," I said, running my fingers over the corner of the napkin on my lap. "We first learned that Evelyn might be gay when we spoke to Christopher Pearson, one of the students at Fort York. Nadya mentioned he'd had an argument with Evelyn last week and she thought it might have to do with inappropriate behaviour toward her and other female students at the university. There was an incident involving a young woman last year. However, when we spoke to him, he claimed he'd seen Evelyn cruising in Allan Gardens. We don't really know if that's true... everyone finds the story a bit fishy... but he was right about Evelyn's sexual orientation. With Chris, it's hard to know if he's telling the truth, trying to divert attention away from himself, or simply attempting to wreak havoc in Evelyn's life even after he is gone."

Bill bowed his head in agreement. He'd folded his fingers together, placed his elbows on the table, and rested his chin on his hands.

"You know what cruising is, Beatrix?" Mariana laughed. "Well, I'll be..."

A quick look from Arthur wiped the grin off her face.

"So, we have a lover, a wife, a student who may have had a grudge... is there anything else you want to share?" Arthur frowned at me.

"Well," I continued, "remember I said I'd seen a man in a yellow rain jacket the day after Evelyn was killed?"

"Yes." Arthur pierced a green bean with his fork. "We haven't been able to track him down."

"It turns out..." I began, smoothing a wrinkle in the lace tablecloth. "It was Evelyn's lover, Walter. He'd intended to visit Evelyn the day of his murder but didn't make it to Fort York because he missed the streetcar. Evelyn invited Walter on Sunday night to come see his latest publication in one of the archaeology journals the next morning. I would imagine that's why Evelyn asked Donna to bring the journals to Fort York. Walter went again the next day, but wasn't able to find him."

"So, he says he missed the streetcar," Arthur arched his eyebrows. "Convenient story."

I didn't like the way he'd said that, but things were out of my hands now. All I could do was call Margaret and Walter after dinner and warn them of the impending police visits they were about to receive.

Chapter 46

Arthur pulled his coat on in the front hall. He looked at me carefully and then gave me a hug and a kiss on the cheek.

"I'll keep my word, Trixie," he said, looking me in the eye. "But I need you to do something for me."

"What's that?" I asked, feeling that our family ties had made him more forgiving to my intrusions into a homicide investigation.

"You and Bill will go back to Fort York, back to your archaeology, and keep your noses out of our investigation."

It was disappointing, but what more could I do? Though it pained me to admit it, he was right. A murder investigation was no place for a couple of retirees who could barely stay awake through our evening crime shows on the television.

"We can do that," I said, looping my arm through Bill's. "We'll behave ourselves."

Arthur was turning to leave when I reached out to touch his arm.

"One more thing, Arthur," I said, as he turned to face me. "It's just out of curiosity. I was wondering if you'd tracked down the mothers of Evelyn's children."

"We did," Arthur sighed. I was surprised he didn't admonish me for asking. "No luck there, I'm afraid. The girl's mother died in a hit and run a little over a year ago. The boy's mother moved out west and has a family now. I checked with the local police, and they spoke to her. She hasn't been to Toronto since she left four years ago. It was a good lead, Trixie, but no dice. I know you hoped the murderer wouldn't be someone of your acquaintance, but it's not looking good."

"I see," I said, leaning against Bill. "Thank you for telling me."

"Trixie," Arthur said, reaching for the door handle. "Remember what happened to the cat."

He had obviously not forgotten the old proverb I taught him when he was an inquisitive little boy.

Chapter 47

I felt a sense of relief as Bill parked the car near Fort York, knowing Arthur would handle the investigation from here. Bill and I walked up the same path as we had before, Muffin slightly ahead, her tail rigid in anticipation of a new adventure. The difference was that I'd finally donned my archaeology garb: work blouse, khaki pants, leather boots, and a red, puffy down jacket to ward off the cold. I'd pulled a hand-knit hat over my hair and ears, and I had a pair of work gloves in my pocket. No longer an amateur sleuth, I would help out at the excavation since Bill and Nadya had agreed she would rest for a few days before returning. No doubt she would be afraid to return to the site after the attack. It was a Saturday, but it was typical for archaeology digs to carry on through the weekends, offering a day off here and there as needed, but the faster the artifacts were removed from the soil once they were exposed, the better. Oxidation was a speedy foe.

"Back to being a team, then," Bill said, marching between the soldiers' barracks at the west entrance.

"I suppose you could say that," I replied, wondering how much work I'd actually get done that day.

I'd woken up with back pain in the lumbar region and wasn't sure how much bending over or kneeling down I would be able to manage. I did have my drawing essentials to help sketch the burial outside the walls. I guessed it hadn't been done yet. When we arrived, Anthony, Brian, and Marco were waiting for us. Christopher, on the other hand, was still absent.

"Hello," Bill said, digging in his pocket and producing a handkerchief.

After the students had greeted him in turn, Bill blew his nose. The cold air always made it run.

"Professor Forster," Anthony said, clasping his hands behind his back. "I have good news, or maybe it's bad news. Depends on your view of it, I guess. I found some stone projectile points in the lower levels of the south-west corner of the excavation area."

I wasn't sure if that would be good news or bad news either. It meant that the students had probably reached pre-historic levels and were beginning to recover artifacts from the Indian tribes who lived and hunted here before the arrival of the Europeans. Many Indian warriors had joined the British in the War of 1812 to fight against the invasion of the Americans, hoping that, should they aid the British to victory, their allies would grant them an independent territory. The artifacts Anthony discovered were unlikely to belong to that period if they were located in the stratigraphy below early 19th century levels. Of course, when the War of 1812 ended in what can only be described as a draw, the British took no steps toward creating the territory so desired by the tribes who had helped prevent the annexation of land by the Americans, choosing conveniently instead to forget any promises made. That was easy enough with the Indian leader, the great Shawnee War Chief, Tecumseh, dead and buried after the Battle of the Thames. Though there were still streets named for him in cities across Canada, I felt certain that much of the population had forgotten or never even learned of his contributions to the nation.

"I would say that's excellent news," Bill said, looking over to the south-west corner of the trench as though he'd be able to spot a projectile point from where he stood. "I won't presume to try to identify the typology, nor do I know what the department will want to do about those levels, but I'll give Professor Blake a call later to find out if we can get a specialist down here to consult. As for the historic levels relating to the fort, this signifies we may be close to finishing, and that will be music to Professor Blake's ears, I assure you."

Anthony smiled, his teeth straight and shiny. "Glad to be the bearer of good news."

"We need it every once in a while," I said, opening my work bag and pulling a clipboard and sketching materials out.

"Since we may be drawing close to the lowest levels of what was mandated for this excavation," Bill began, "and we won't know about what comes next until I've spoken to Stephen, Beatrix why don't you go with Marco and start drawing the burial beyond the wall? I'll have a look at what Anthony's found here. Brian, you can stay here at the main excavation area with us."

Anthony was already heading back to work as Brian quickly stuffed a candy bar he'd been munching into his backpack and then tossed the bag to the ground. Marco said nothing, leading the way back to the entrance and out beyond the fort walls and the earthworks, constructed more than a century and a half earlier to defend the soldiers garrisoned at the fort. There were people beyond the flimsy fence that separated the fort from Garrison Common Park. Some walked dogs, others strolled across the grass, a few businessmen in suits carrying briefcases bustled down the hill to the walkway under the Gardiner Expressway, presumably late for a morning meeting.

At the excavation area, Marco pulled back a tarp to reveal that the original test pit had been much expanded. I knew to expect skeletons, but what I saw was a shock.

"Goodness," I said, standing at the edge of the burial and looking down at the remains of four individuals. "This doesn't look right at all."

Marco murmured something unintelligible. I knew Bill wanted to show me something at the fort, but I hadn't dreamed of this. I was surprised the singularity of this multiple burial had slipped his mind and he hadn't said anything before. I stood at the east edge of the excavation area, where the skeletons' feet rested, to examine the remains. There were four individuals in one grave. That was quite typical in war, given the interments had to be done quickly. In many cases, when the soldiers couldn't be transported to the closest military cemetery, the graves were dug directly on the battlefield and several individuals might be buried in the same pit. What was unusual in this case was that the three individuals on the south side of the grave were in a supine position and the individual on the north side of the grave was in a prone position. A supine burial was normal

– at the time of the war, European peoples were buried on their backs. Had the burial been of Indian peoples, who also participated in the Battle of York, they might have been buried in a crouched or flexed position on their side, as was traditional in many cultures of the Americas. Prone burials, on the other hand, meaning the individual was buried face-down, was unusual in most cultures. When people were buried on their stomach, rather than their back, you could often infer that the deceased persons in question had been viewed negatively by their community or the people who buried them. Was this simply a case of Americans and British buried in the same grave, the gravedigger getting creative with his sentiments toward the enemy, or was there something else afoot here?

"Did Bill, I mean, Professor Forster, say anything about this?" I asked Marco, waving a hand over the grave.

"He just hummed and hawed and said he wanted you to have a look at this," Marco said, placing his hands on his hips as we both surveyed the macabre scene.

Though I might have expected something disrespectful like this in some other conflict, I would not have guessed it of the War of 1812. From many accounts, the war, though still deadly and awful, had been more of a war amongst gentlemen, if you could say that of any bellicose conflict. Not what we'd experienced during the wars of our own century. In the early 19th century, captured combatants were paroled back to their country of origin and expected not to engage in war-time activities until they had been officially exchanged for a prisoner of the opposing side. Only then would they be able to rejoin the war effort in their home country. Unlike modern warfare, prisoners were not executed, tortured, or held in camps with terrible living conditions. Despite the general civility of the war, the British did not hesitate to threaten the Americans with leaving them in the hands of the Indian warriors. Being captured by the British meant life and a second chance, whereas being captured by warriors often meant certain death. In this way, the British had tricked the Americans into early surrender in several cases, the fear of slaughter at the hands of the tribes being widespread amongst the American regulars and militia.

In the case of the Battle of York and the grave before me, it was possible the Americans had been so angered by the explosion of the Grand Magazine, they'd buried a British soldier face down to symbolize their disgust over the circumstances of the capture of York. The British had, in fact, used the blast as a last-minute tactic to cover their retreat from the town and ensure their stores of gunpowder did not fall into the hands of the enemy. However, the largest explosion on Canadian soil until the Halifax Explosion a century later was considered by the Americans to be a trap. Their leader, Brigadier General Zebulon Pike, was killed by the explosion along with many other American officers and soldiers. The retribution against the citizens of York involved much looting and burning of both public and private property, though the terms of the capitulation of York allowed only for the confiscation of public property. The Americans even burned the parliamentary buildings which once stood at the corner of Parliament and Front streets. In the days of anger and revenge following the battle, it was possible that those responsible for the burial of the dead might have done something like this, but it would still have been unusual. It would also have been odd to bury the opposing sides in the same grave.

Marco's voice, piercing the heavy silence that had settled over us, startled me: "Professor Forster said we still need to clean things up a bit before the skeletons are ready to be exhumed, but that it was good enough for you to start drawing the burial."

Was he telling me to get started on my work? More likely he didn't quite know what to say and wondered why I'd been silent for so long. There was a lot to consider. I looked around and was relieved to find Muffin lying nearby chewing on a stick she must have found somewhere. I hadn't put her leash on, but at least today she hadn't run off.

"Yes, Marco," I said, digging in my bag to find a pencil. "We can get started on the drawing."

I looked over at the scruffy, quiet young man and realized he had tears in his eyes.

Chapter 48

"Are you alright, dear?" I asked Marco, taking a step closer to him. "It can sometimes be difficult to think of the dead and what they went through just before they succumbed."

I assumed he had been affected by the sight of the burial. The students working at Fort York would not have signed up to dig skeletons, thinking instead they would be focused entirely on early 19th century artifacts.

"It's not that, Mrs. Forster," Marco vigorously wiped at his eyes with a tightly balled fist. "I don't mind the skeletons. It's about Professor Volk. When the police talked to me, I was really nervous, and I didn't tell them everything. I didn't tell them much, to be honest. I've never been interviewed by the police before. I really liked Professor Volk, and I do want to help the police catch his killer. He was kind to us even though we were students. Not all the professors are like that. I've just been feeling guilty all this time because I could have said more. Maybe they would already have found the killer had I said something and Nadya wouldn't have gotten hurt."

I could imagine that being confronted with learning your professor had been murdered and being interviewed by the police on the same day might be disconcerting.

"What didn't you tell the police?"

"It was back at the beginning of September, on campus," Marco began slowly, "and I don't know if it was related, but I overheard Professor Blake and Professor Volk having an argument."

This did not surprise me at all. I knew very well, along with the rest of the department, that Evelyn and Stephen did not get on well. Their antagonistic relationship was surely well documented at every department meeting they'd attended together. Evelyn was lucky he'd been tenured, or I guessed that Stephen would have tried his best to get Evelyn unceremoniously booted from the department.

"Go on," I said, sticking my hands in my jacket pockets to keep them warm.

Marco nodded. "It was strange. Professor Blake said he knew what Professor Volk was doing, that he knew he was stealing. Professor Blake threatened to have Professor Volk thrown out of the university."

"Then what happened?" I asked.

"Professor Volk said, 'Let's talk about this in my office.' And they went inside and closed the door. I didn't hear any more than that, Mrs. Forster. I don't actually think Professor Volk was a thief. Do you? I thought Professor Blake was making things up."

"I don't think so either," I said, though my confidence in Evelyn had begun to waver. "But you didn't hear him deny the accusation?"

Marco shook his head. If Evelyn had family money, why would he need to steal? Was it a gambling addiction or had he lavished too much on Walter, Margaret, and the children? Had his family's money run out? And where or from whom was he stealing? The university, a person, a charity? I had only just taken a step back from the investigation to be pulled right back in.

Chapter 49

I had leaned over to fasten Muffin's leash to her collar when I noticed something that appeared to be metal between the arm and the ribs of the prone skeleton. It wasn't shiny, the way polished metal might look, or green the way a copper alloy would look after corroding in the burial environment, but rather it had a white patina, a dull, almost chalky surface. I wanted to speak to Bill about what Marco had just told me, but the object caught my eye and held me back.

"Marco," I said, righting myself and turning to face him. "What is that metal thing between the left arm and ribs of the northernmost skeleton?"

"Do you mean a button, Mrs. Forster?" he asked, stepping closer to the excavation area. "There's lots on the southern skeletons, but Professor Forster said the face-down individual would be lying on the buttons, if he had any, and we'd find them when we started removing the bones."

"It's not a button." I pointed at the object I'd spotted. "It looks like the edge of something. A corner perhaps. Do you mind brushing away some dirt so we can have a better look?"

Marco nodded and kneeled at the edge of the excavation area. He pushed some hair from in front of his eyes and with short, gentle strokes, he brushed soil from the mysterious object. After a few minutes, he looked up at me.

"I can't go much farther, Mrs. Forster," he said, squinting at me. "It carries on under the ribs. We'll have to remove bones before we'll be able to get at it."

I held Muffin's leash in my right hand and placed my left hand on Marco's shoulder for balance so I, too, could crouch down and get a better look.

"Well, let's have a quick peek anyway," I said, pushing my glasses up the bridge of my nose with my index finger.

There wasn't much to see, but with a little extra dirt removed from around the edges of the artifact, I could distinguish that the item looked like the corner of some kind of box. The white patina made me think the material was lead. I wondered what a soldier might have been carrying in a lead box. I believed in those days they'd carried gun powder in a cow's horn. It wasn't so much the box that captivated my imagination, but what could be contained within. What did this person, buried face-down in what was probably a War of 1812 grave, carry in a little, lead box?

Chapter 50

I left Marco at the burial excavation area and headed off to find Bill. My boots crunched over the gravelly, dirt path leading back into the fort. Muffin's padded paws made almost no noise as they skimmed the surface. I wondered how many times I'd pass through the gates of Fort York that day... or even that month. The toing and froing were wearing thin, the muscles in my thighs tight and irritated, my joints inflamed. Getting older was an exercise in patience, particularly with one's own body. Sometimes you had to forgive yourself for taking too long to get out of the armchair, or struggling to stand up once you'd crouched down, or thinking you might not be able to get out of bed that day. Everyone was different, but eventually, if we were lucky to live long enough, our bodies would break down, leaving nothing but bittersweet memories of the days when we climbed a mountain or paddled a canoe down the river without a care in the world.

What really ate at my self worth was that as I learned more about the War of 1812, I discovered that some of the soldiers who fought in the war were not young men at all, but ripe old vegetables my own age. How was that possible in the period before modern medicine or even in today's world? How did these men have the range of movement to be able to crouch, run, and shoot while my bones felt like they were crumbling away under my skin with every step I took? I saw Bill kneeling down in the excavation area and thought of him riding his bicycle to the university, still toiling away wherever he could. Would he have managed to fight in a war at his age?

"Bill," I said, inhaling deeply as I reached the edge of the pit. "I need to tell you something."

Bill said something to Anthony that I couldn't hear and climbed out of the excavation area. He stood next to me, pulling his dirt-stained gloves from his hands.

"What is it, Beatrix?"

"Marco's just told me something very interesting. He said Stephen accused Evelyn of stealing in early September."

"Which Stephen?" Bill asked, wrinkling his forehead.

"Stephen Blake," I clarified.

I wondered what other Stephen Bill thought it might be, but didn't ask.

"Oh, I see," Bill pursed his lips. "Who was Evelyn stealing from?"

"That's just it," I said, wrapping my fingers around my husband's forearm. "Why did he need the money in the first place, and where was he getting it from? Also, how did Stephen know about it, and if Evelyn really had been stealing, wouldn't Stephen have done something about it?"

"I need to speak to Stephen about the excavation anyway," Bill mused. "Should we pay him a visit this afternoon when we've wrapped up here?"

"Bill, you heard what Arthur said." I smiled, realizing he was just as curious about the case as I was. "And, it's a Saturday. Surely Stephen won't be in to discuss excavation matters on the weekend."

"Don't worry, we'll tell Arthur about this," Bill winked. "Doesn't mean we can't ask Stephen a few questions ourselves. I don't doubt he may just be in on a Saturday to avoid being at home. What do you think, Muffin?"

With surprising agility, Bill scooped the dog up in his arms. That didn't seem fair at all, I thought.

Chapter 51

Stephen Blake's office was chilly but had an inviting atmosphere. I wondered if they turned the heat off in the building on the weekends. The two armchairs pulled up to Stephen's desk were made of dark leather. The desk itself was large and made of a rich wood, while his office chair was a deep, oxblood red. The shelves were lined with books and despite the austere modern architecture of the building, Stephen's office had a classic old-world charm. I was surprised. I hadn't guessed Stephen would be one for concerning himself with décor. Bill's own office, when he worked at the university, had been a haphazard arrangement of furniture, papers, and books, without much thought to their organization or if the colour scheme was complementary.

"Have a seat," Stephen said, motioning to the overstuffed armchairs that might have been comfortable enough for a sizeable student, but threatened to swallow my body whole.

I sat awkwardly in the chair, my legs dangling over the edge like a ragdoll. Bill looked like a regular adult in his chair.

"What can I do for you, Bill?" Stephen asked, sitting down in his chair on the opposite side of the desk.

"I wanted to let you know that we've reached pre-historic levels at the excavation," Bill began, his arms relaxed on either side of the armchair. "I thought it would be best to check in with you to see if we could get someone down to consult. Someone with more expertise than I have."

"Fine, that's not a problem." Stephen had his elbows on the desk and his fingers laced together. "After the weekend, I'll have Michael or David swing by the site. I take it this means the excavation could be wrapped up soon?"

"The historic element, yes," Bill said. "There's one burial of four individuals also left to finish off, but it won't take long. Based on their location and potential injuries, I'd guess War of 1812, but I'll have Nadya check the buttons to see if we can get any useful information from them. The lettering and numbers may have been eroded but once we get them cleaned up, we can have a closer look. As for the Indian levels, in order to have a full chronology of occupations at the site, it would be valuable to excavate the artifacts from earlier periods as well."

"That's less of a concern, right now," Stephen said. "There's no money to waste, but we'll see what Michael says."

Stephen, a specialist in classical archaeology, had shown little care or interest in the archaeological sites here at home. He considered the country to be archaeologically poor, and excavations to be of little value to collective knowledge. Of course, recognition that much of what was used in daily life prior to the arrival of the Europeans would have been organic and therefore decomposed by the time archaeologists dug it up, was not Stephen's primary consideration. He was mostly concerned with yield from the archaeological record, especially of so-called treasures, less so with understanding cultures that came before. Perhaps that's why Stephen and Evelyn had clashed so frequently over academic matters.

"Fine," Bill conceded. He looked over at me and then back to Stephen. "There's something else I want to ask you. We were recently made aware of an accusation of theft you made against Evelyn a few months ago. From where was Evelyn stealing?"

Stephen's nostrils flared, like a horse sniffing at a carrot.

"I made no such accusation," Stephen snapped. "I may not have liked the man very much, professional differences as you know, but I would not have accused him of stealing. I don't know who told you that, but they're lying."

The vehemence with which Stephen responded to the suggestion made me wonder. Had Marco misheard the conversation or mistaken Stephen for someone else? Or was Stephen lying, and if so, why would he protect Evelyn now that he was dead? There was no love lost between the two of them. Could it be that Stephen wasn't protecting Evelyn at all, but himself?

Chapter 52

Bill and I walked slowly down the nearly empty hall, his pace matching mine. A student strolled by in silence, the building eerily quiet compared to the weekday rush of students madly hoping to get to their next class on time. I felt as though we were walking through water, my legs heavy with defeat, my neck and shoulders stiff. There were so many unanswered questions, and as the days ticked by, I wondered if Evelyn's case would have so many diverse lines of inquiry that the police would be overwhelmed and never work out who had killed a father, husband, lover, and friend. Even if Evelyn had been stealing, it wasn't a reason to end his life. The police could deal with such things. Or was the theft a red herring, meant to distract us from what was really going on? If so, why would Marco want to put us off the trail of the killer? In these cases, lies were plenty and most everyone had something they wished to hide.

"Do you want to stop by the police station on the way home?" Bill asked.

"Yes," I agreed, "but I'd like to keep Muffin with us. I'm sure it's fine but I don't like leaving her in the car in some of these neighbourhoods."

"I doubt anybody will notice a small dog with two senior citizens at the police station."

"We can always feign confusion if it comes to it," I said, reaching for Bill's hand.

Back at the car, we could see through the windows that Muffin was curled up in the back seat having a nap. She probably hadn't lifted her head since we left, but she leapt to attention the moment we opened the car door. If only I could go from sleeping to wide awake like that in the morning. Much to my vexation, a halo of mental fog always hung over me until I'd drunk at least half my morning tea.

* * *

The Toronto Metropolitan Police headquarters was located at 590 Jarvis Street in St. Jamestown. The building was constructed of brick with six stories of rectangular windows. There was nothing special about the place, just a large building with police cars parked all around. A young police constable escorted us to Arthur's desk. She glanced at Muffin, tucked tightly under Bill's arm, but said nothing. She probably thought we might make a fuss if she told us to leave the dog outside, and at that point in the day, though it wasn't normally my style, I confess I might have. Being elderly was an excuse for all kinds of behaviour.

Arthur was leaning back in his chair, smoking a cigarette. Likely embarrassed by his relaxed state, he quickly sat up straight and stubbed the cigarette into a glass ashtray on his desk.

"Glad to have caught you here," I said, smiling.

Arthur's cheeks flushed. "Caught me, indeed," Arthur said sheepishly. "I hope you've been behaving yourselves at Fort York."

"We did try, Arthur," I said, seating myself in the lone chair next to his desk. Bill stood slightly behind me and set Muffin down. She immediately started to sniff at Arthur's pants.

"Come here, Muffy," Arthur said, pulling Muffin up onto his lap. "That's a good girl." She sniffed at his fingers where he'd recently held his cigarette. "What does trying to behave mean exactly, Trixie?"

Bill squeezed my shoulder.

"Well, I was working with one of the students, Marco, and he was quite upset because he felt he hadn't been entirely forthcoming when you interviewed him. He's a nervous boy, you understand, and you can be intimidating, Arthur."

I looked at my cousin, who didn't look very intimidating at that moment, his face burrowed into Muffin's neck. Quite the opposite in fact, something more like a large teddy bear.

"Anyway," I continued, "he told me that back in September, near the beginning of the school year, he overheard a conversation between Evelyn and Stephen Blake, head of the Department of Anthropology at the university. Marco claims he heard Stephen accuse Evelyn of stealing. Marco says he only heard part of the conversation, because they moved into Evelyn's office. We did ask Stephen about the accusation, but he denied it."

Arthur pulled his face away from Muffin and sighed.

"How many times do I have to tell the two of you?" he asked, his voice reeking of exasperation, the way it would if you'd explained something to a naughty child for the umpteenth time. "Why did you talk to Stephen? Why didn't you come to me first?"

"Well," Bill said in our defence. "We needed to speak with him about another matter. An archaeological matter."

"That's no excuse," Arthur nearly squeaked. "Do I need to lock you two up?"

"I don't think that's quite necessary," I said, placing my hand on his desk. "We'll try to be good; I promise."

"I don't believe you for a second," Arthur shook his head. "However, this is interesting information. I'm still leaning toward the wife or the lover. Jealousy and money are powerful motivators. But I'll see if I can look into the professor's bank records. If he was stealing, hopefully there'll be a trail."

"You will let us know what you find out," I said, gathering myself and using Arthur's desk as support to stand up.

Arthur rolled his eyes. "Do I have a choice?"

"One other thing, Arthur," I paused, standing but not balanced enough to take my hand away from the desk. "Have you tracked down Christopher Pearson?"

"Ah, yes." Arthur pointed his pen at me over Muffin's head. "You'll never guess where he is."

I waited for Arthur to tell me, but it seemed he wanted me to take a stab at the location of a boy I barely knew.

"Hiding out at home?" I asked.

"Mexico!" Arthur hooted, dropping his pen onto the desk. "Can you believe it? His parents were none too pleased about it. Apparently, he's run off with an underage girl, saying he was in love and was going to get married to her down in Mexico. That takes the cake, doesn't it? He ran off in the middle of a murder investigation. Does he want to be the prime suspect? Foolish kids these days, not like we were. Anyway, I'm still trying to reach him at the hotel, but no such luck."

Perhaps Arthur had his reasons, but to me, if someone I needed to question in a murder investigation ran off to a foreign country, I'd view that as very suspicious. Very suspicious, indeed. Was there really a girl, or had Christopher decided that sunshine and beaches were preferable to further interviews with the police?

Chapter 53

Bill and I woke early on Sunday morning. I wondered what we would do with ourselves. No crime to investigate, no students to supervise. We'd given the students the day off after a very difficult week. How would we occupy our time now? In the past, I'd always looked forward to the weekend. Having the children around the house, Bill home from work, no illustrations or drawings to do unless I wanted to. Now, in retirement, weekends were less appealing than they had been. I would have suggested visiting Shirley and the grandchildren, but I knew they were away in Montreal for the weekend. I rolled onto my side in bed and looked at my husband.

"What do you want to do today?" I asked. It was still dark, but I could see his eyes were open.

No response.

"Bill," I tried again, nudging him in the arm. "What do you want to do today?"

"Hmm?" Bill slowly turned to look at me, his eyes wide. He focused on my face and said, "What do I want to do today?"

"Yes, Bill. That's what I said."

"Shirley's away?"

"She is, yes."

"Oh," he mumbled. "What can we do?"

"I suppose we can do almost anything we'd like to," I sighed. "Except shopping. We may be making progress in the areas of theatre and cinema, but you still can't shop on a Sunday."

"Yes, but what do we want to do?"

I nearly laughed. Had we run out of things to do? Did we not even know what we liked to do anymore?

"I'd like to solve this case," I said, rolling back so I could look at the ceiling. "But since that isn't an option, should we take Muffin for a walk in High Park and think on it?"

"That sounds like a good plan," Bill said. "What are your thoughts on the subject, Muffin?"

Chapter 54

The walk to High Park from our home in Roncesvalles was short, as we were just a few streets away. The neighbourhood had a distinct Polish presence and on occasion Bill and I would stop at a local restaurant for pierogi, the little dumplings stuffed with savoury ingredients, and cabbage rolls. The food was always hearty and had the same quality as a home-cooked meal. Those new to Toronto always struggled with the pronunciation of Roncesvalles, which Torontonians themselves pronounced quite differently from the origins of the name, a tiny village nestled in the Pyrenees mountains in Spain. It hadn't been very far from San Miguel, but Bill and I had not had time to visit. The Roncesvalles in Toronto was given its name by Colonel O'Hara, who fought in the Battle of Roncesvalles in 1813, the same year the Americans captured Fort York. Thus, our neighbourhood in Canada had a tenuous connection to a distant place in Navarre. I wondered if they even knew our Roncesvalles existed.

Once in High Park, Muffin strode off ahead of us, always the adventurer, while Bill and I, arm in arm, dawdled behind. We paused to look at the birds, or a squirrel that crossed our path, and commented on the coolness of the shade created by the magnificent trees that grew untamed at the margins of the largest park in the city. Once a farm, the land had been donated to the city under the condition that it remain in a natural state and be free for the citizens of Toronto to use. Use it, they did, with droves of people coming to the park to stroll, picnic, and benefit from a natural space in the city that each year lost more and more green space to developments. Bill and I had not discussed our route through the park, but Muffin had her own agenda, leading us directly to the animal display. There had been a small zoo at High Park as long a I could remember, but the animals that resided there changed over the years.

"Clever girl," Bill said, watching Muffin walk through the gates to the zoo as though she owned the place.

"We'll have to keep an eye on her," I said. "The last thing we need is for her to get into the bison or the ostrich enclosure."

"Then we'd really be in trouble," Bill quipped. "She'd scare the beasts half to death with her barking. Probably bite a few ankles here and there, too."

We meandered along amongst the paddocks, some animals at the fence, ready for interaction with humans, others standoffish, hoping to evade the piercing gaze and screams of children. Without having committed any crime, they'd ended up in a prison of their own. Near the bison display, Muffin stopped to sniff at two young children, their knitted mittens hanging at their wrists, supported by an invisible thread that went through their sleeves and across their shoulders. I knew of this magic trick because I'd knitted the same contraption for my grandchildren when they were young enough to lose their mittens. The children had sticky fingers, no doubt from eating a doughnut or cinnamon roll, and they laughed as Muffin licked their tiny digits with her smooth pink tongue. Disguised by the fur collars and knitted hats, I didn't recognize at first that the children were Sandra and Bobby, Evelyn's children. I assumed, therefore, that the woman with her back turned to us must be Margaret.

"Hello, Margaret," I said, realizing when she turned to look at me that it wasn't Margaret at all. "Sorry, I didn't know it was you, Abigail. Is Margaret here as well?"

I craned my neck, trying to find Margaret in the stream of people who walked by. Abigail smiled and shook her head.

"No, Mrs. Forster, she stayed home today. I thought a little fresh air and seeing the animals might brighten the children's day."

"Looks like it's done the trick," I said. The children were delighted taking turns as Muffin cleaned their hands.

"Goodness, you two," Abigail scolded them gently. "Always in trouble, Mrs. Forster. Can't take my eyes off them for a second."

She pulled a handkerchief from her purse and tried to wipe their hands. I had to admit, in this case, Muffin was more efficient than a dry hanky, the cloth sticking to the mess on their fingers. Abigail then helped them put their hands back in the mittens.

"How is she doing?" Bill asked. I remembered that he hadn't seen Margaret since before Evelyn died.

"Oh, some days are better than others," Abigail lamented. "I think she'll pull through. She's strong and she's got the children to keep her spirits up."

"And you," I said.

"And me?" Abigail smiled sadly.

"Abigail, forgive yet another impertinent question," I said, noting to myself that I'd made many nosy inquiries that week. "But one of Evelyn's students said another professor accused him of stealing. This would have been in early September."

Abigail frowned. "Stealing?"

"That's what the student overheard," Bill nodded. "We were surprised, too. The police said Evelyn had family money. Do you know if he was having financial troubles?"

Abigail rubbed the back of her neck with her gloved hand. "He came from a wealthy family. That's true. And everyone has passed, so he was the sole inheritor of the estate. I can say he was never late paying me, and he was more generous with my salary than some of our neighbours. The other nannies in the area often complain, saying their employers are late with their pay or stiff them, not paying the full amount, docking their pay for this or that. For some of the nannies, it's not just money they complain about; they have to take care around the husbands..."

Abigail looked down at the children. Fortunately, they were still engrossed by Muffin, not paying any attention to our very adult conversation.

"Did that ever happen to you?" I asked.

"Oh, no," Abigail said, waving her hand as though she could push the notion away. "Not me. Professor Volk was never like that."

It made sense. Evelyn hadn't been interested in Margaret or Abigail, at least not in that way. I guessed Abigail must have felt lucky not to have experienced the same tribulations as some of the other young women in her position. Had anything happened, both society and the courts would have accepted the word of the wealthy white man over the word of the mixed-race woman from the Caribbean. These women never stood a chance, and thus, there was little protection for them in these grand homes. Not when it came to their pay, and not when it came to themselves.

"Did you notice anything strange relating to Evelyn's finances, perhaps starting in September?" Bill interjected, placing a hand on the fence that separated us from the woolly, horned creatures on the other side.

Abigail began to shake her head, but then paused. Her lips were parted as though she was about to say something, but she changed her mind.

After a few moments, she said, "Yes, I had almost forgotten, but around that time I saw Professor Volk put a lot of bills into an envelope and then put it into his briefcase. I only saw him do this twice, but it did seem strange. He'd never done it before. What would he need so much money for?"

Chapter 55

After bumping into Abigail and the children at High Park Zoo, Bill and I walked home slowly, with Muffin just ahead. She was entirely oblivious to the turmoil of Evelyn's murder investigation, her tail and ears perky, ready for the next squirrel to dart across the path.

"The envelopes of money suggest Evelyn was up to something," Bill said, unbuttoning the collar of his coat.

We'd walked enough that it felt warmer than it had when we left the house.

"I would agree with that," I said. "There's something fishy about having large sums of cash. The question is: who would know what he was doing with it? Would Margaret know? And if she does, would she tell us?"

"What about the man Evelyn was seeing? What was his name?

"Walter," I reminded Bill. "It's possible he knew something, and it's also possible he was in the dark. If only we knew why Evelyn needed the money. Whenever someone has money trouble, I can't help but think of gambling. Do you think Evelyn was gambling the family fortune away or are we grasping at straws here?"

"Your guess is as good as mine, Beatrix."

"I suppose Arthur will be able to determine the state of Evelyn's finances soon enough," I said, glancing around at the large Victorian and Edwardian homes typical of our neighbourhood. "He said before that Evelyn had plenty of money, that it was a motive for Margaret to murder him. If there was so much, then what was Evelyn up to?"

Soon enough felt very far away as we arrived home. Bill pushed the key into our front door and turned it. He nudged the door open, Muffin running across the threshold first. I could hear the phone was ringing.

"I'll get it," Bill said, rushing after the dog.

"Hello?" I heard him say from the kitchen as I took my shoes off at the front door. "Yes, she's here; we just came through the front door... Oh, yes, she did... Well, that's very kind of you, we'd be happy to come over this afternoon. Can we bring anything? Oh, she's invited, as well? You're sure you don't mind? Alright, we'll see you later then."

"Who was that?" I asked, sticking my head into the kitchen as Bill hung up the phone.

"You'll never guess," Bill smiled.

"Yes, that's why I asked who it was? It can't have been Shirley, surely."

Bill laughed as he always did when I said Shirley, surely.

"You're correct," he said. "It was Walter. He'd like us to come for tea this afternoon, and Muffin is invited, as well."

"Oh," I said. holding onto the door frame as a muscle spasm twitched its way through my posterior after such a long walk. "That's unexpected, but entirely welcome."

I waited in the doorway as the ripple of involuntary gluteal contractions dissipated. Perhaps, next time, we should not walk quite so far.

Chapter 56

On the way to Walter's house that afternoon, Bill stopped the car briefly and I popped out to buy some flowers at a corner shop. Walter had said not to bring anything, but under the circumstances, a nice bouquet seemed appropriate. Though Bill and I could lose ourselves in Evelyn's case, pushing aside the sorrow of his death temporarily as we focused on the pressing matter of who killed him, Evelyn's loved ones could not do the same. They simply mourned his loss and prepared for a future without him. Grief was different for everyone, but nobody could escape unscathed when someone they cared for deeply was suddenly gone forever.

Walter greeted us at the door, as he had the day I visited with Eduardo, though this time he was dressed in a black turtleneck and loose pants.

"You must be Bill," he said, reaching out to shake my husband's hand.

"It's a pleasure to meet you," Bill said. "I only wish it could be under happier circumstances."

Walter nodded and then smiled as he looked down at Muffin. I'd put her on her leash to keep her from running wild in Walter's house.

"And you must be Muffin," he said, kneeling down to pat the little terrier.

"These are for you, Walter," I said, handing him the bouquet of flowers when he stood up again.

"They're beautiful, Beatrix," Walter said, taking the flowers in one hand and embracing me tightly with the other. He made it feel as though we'd known each other for years.

"Come in, come in," he said. "Make yourselves comfortable while I put these lovely flowers in a vase."

Walter disappeared into the kitchen, while Bill and I seated ourselves on the velvet sofa, where Eduardo and I had sat just a few days before.

"Can I help you with anything, Walter?" I called out.

"Nothing much to do here, Beatrix, but thank you."

As Walter had said himself, he seemed much older than he was. What other young man of university age had perfected the art of hosting, keeping his house immaculate, and would even consider inviting two elderly people over for tea. Though I was starting to wonder if young people thought that's all older people did these days. As much as I enjoyed a nice cup of tea, it wasn't my only hobby. However, I couldn't imagine my eldest granddaughter inviting me and Bill over to drink an infusion, though she couldn't have been much younger than Walter.

Walter returned with the flowers in a vase and placed it on the coffee table. His movements were smooth and graceful, and I wondered if, in addition to being a gymnast, he might also have training in ballet. One was not simply born with the ability to glide through a room with elegance and poise. He went back into the kitchen and appeared with the tea service.

"How are you doing, Walter?" I asked seriously when he sat down.

"I miss him," he said simply. "But I think that will last the rest of my life."

"I imagine you're right about that," I said. "You'll let us know if we can do anything to help you."

"I appreciate the offer," Walter smiled sadly. "It's nice to know people care."

We sat silently for a few moments. Walter scratched Muffin's head, and I was reminded of the healing powers of animals. They seemed to lighten the burden of being human with nothing more than their presence.

"I must admit I asked you here under false pretences," Walter broke the stifling silence. "Well, not exactly false pretences, but I do have a favour to ask of you and I might as well come out with it now."

"Of course," I said, placing a cookie on a small plate. "What can we do for you?"

"This comes with a small confession," he said. "I've already shared this with the police, so I don't think there's any harm in telling you."

Walter leaned back in his chair and took a sip of tea.

"The police have already interviewed you, then?" I asked.

"They did," he nodded. "I spoke to your cousin, Arthur. He was very efficient and respectful, and I imagine I have you to thank for that."

I could feel myself blushing, which at my age only embarrassed me more.

"Beatrix was concerned," Bill said, placing a hand on my arm. "Eduardo told her about police treatment of gay men in Toronto while we were away this summer."

"Until they change the laws…" Walter began, leaning forward to place his teacup and saucer on the coffee table. "This is the risk of existing."

"What did you want to ask us, Walter?" I said, drawing us back to the topic at hand.

"Yes, that's right," he said, looking over at me. "Before he died, Evelyn had wanted to show me a copy of his latest article. When I was in Evelyn's office on Tuesday, the one at Fort York, not at the university, I saw the copy of Historical Archaeology on his desk. When he didn't come to his office and I didn't have the chance to see him, I decided to take the journal with me and read the article at home. I'd come all the way across the city since I don't have a car, you see. I knew Evelyn wouldn't mind. Only, the thing is, when I got home and tried to read the article, it was missing. Someone had ripped it out of the journal. It was obvious as there were missing page numbers and a bit of torn paper. Anyway, I gave the journal to the police when they came. They said they would look into it, but I don't know that they'll fill me in if they learn anything. Either way, I realized, I don't actually know how to get my hands on an archaeology journal, and I was wondering if you and Bill could help me get a copy.

One last piece of Evelyn for me to keep. I really would like to read the article even if I won't understand it all."

When Walter mentioned the missing pages of the journal, I remembered the burnt article in the fireplace in Evelyn's office. Had Evelyn burned the article himself? Why would he if he'd been excited about it and wanted to show Walter? If not Evelyn, then who? And did it have anything to do with Evelyn's death or was it pure coincidence?

Chapter 57

Before we left Walter, Bill and I promised we would find a copy of Historical Archaeology for him. It was the least we could do.

"I think we should visit Nadya," I said, as Bill and I walked back to our car.

"To see how she's doing?" Bill asked, pulling slightly on Muffin's leash as she buried her head in the dead flowers in someone's front yard. "Come on, Muffy. Let's go."

"Well, yes," I said, slowing my pace so as not to run into the leash that crossed my path. "That, and to ask her about the article."

"Ah, I see," Bill said. "It's not rude to just drop by?"

"We could take something," I said, wondering if she'd enjoy some baked goods. "Do you know her address?"

"Lucky for you, Beatrix," Bill smiled, "she had to stop at her house before dropping me off the other day. I felt sorry for her, as it was out of the way to go to Bloor West Village and then back to Roncesvalles, but she needed to give me some field notes she had at home. I don't know the number of the house, but I'll remember what it looked like. It's a brick semi like any other, but her mother keeps some Ukrainian embroidery in the front window."

That was convenient. I didn't know whom we could ask for Nadya's address on a Sunday.

"Shall we then?" I asked Bill, as we reached the car. "There are plenty of bakeries on the way."

Bill shook his head as he opened the car door for me, but said nothing. I knew exactly what he was thinking, but Arthur would eventually forgive me.

Chapter 58

Nadya lived in a small house west of High Park with her mother. Her father died just a few years after they'd moved to Canada, leaving Nadya and her mother to fend for themselves in a new country. I was sure it hadn't been easy, but Nadya was intelligent and resourceful, and despite a difficult start, she'd enjoyed academic success and was well on her way to receiving her PhD.

We left Muffin in the car with the windows partially open. It was an excuse not to stay long. Bill knocked on the front door. Mrs. Shevchenko answered, wearing a floral apron with traces of flour across one cheek.

"Hello," she said smiling. Her accent was thick. "You are here to see, Nadya, yes?"

She must have recognized us from the hospital, though we had only just crossed paths.

"Yes. How is she?" Bill asked.

Mrs. Shevchenko pushed the door open wider and motioned for us to step inside.

"Come in, come in," she said, stepping back so Bill and I could squeeze inside. "She's good; she's strong girl, you know?"

I nodded. Nadya obviously had the physical strength to work in field archaeology, but it was the other kind of strength that would get her through this kind of attack.

"Would she be up for a quick visit?" I asked. "We won't stay long."

"Yes, of course," Mrs. Shevchenko said, brushing her hands on her apron. "I get her. You sit, wherever you like."

The living room at the front of the house, just beyond the foyer, was narrow and cozy. It was obvious Mrs. Shevchenko was a prolific knitter. There were afghans of various colours neatly folded on each arm of the sofa and chairs. As we had at Walter's house, we sat on the sofa together.

Nadya came in, her face still bandaged. There was a purplish yellow bruise in the shape of a sunburst around the edges of the white bandage. I couldn't help but grimace at the sight of her.

"It doesn't hurt very much," she said, likely in response to my reaction at seeing her.

"I'm glad," I said. I handed her the box of pastries we'd picked up on the way over. "I hope you have a sweet tooth."

Nadya smiled. "I do, thank you."

Nadya's mother appeared with juice and sweet poppy seed rolls, then disappeared back into the kitchen.

"We won't stay long," Bill promised, reaching for a roll. "Are you feeling any better?"

Nadya fidgeted in her chair and glanced down at the carpet.

"I'm doing fine," she said. "I'm already healing. I can come back to Fort York tomorrow, if you like."

"I think you'd better give it a few more days," Bill said, brushing a crumb away from his moustache. "You'll want to make sure you don't get dirt in the wound. There's no rush. We've reached pre-historic levels in the main excavation area already, and the weather seems to be holding for now."

"Oh," Nadya sounded disappointed. "Already?"

Bill nodded. "There's still plenty of work to do, though."

Bill and Nadya discussed the work to be done the following week. When the archaeological discussion died out, I asked her about the article.

"Nadya, we were wondering about an article of Evelyn's that came out recently."

Nadya looked at me, but said nothing.

"The one in Historical Archaeology," I clarified.

She pushed some hair over her shoulder. "Yes. I read it when the journal came out. What do you want to know?"

"Evelyn seemed to be quite excited about it," I mentioned. "Do you know why?"

"Probably because it was the first publication after a dry spell," Nadya shrugged.

"You mean Evelyn hadn't been publishing much?" Bill asked.

"Yes," Nadya said, but didn't elaborate.

"He was struggling with his research, then?" I wondered aloud, placing my hand on the afghan next to me.

"I don't know much," Nadya reached over and grabbed a glass of juice. "He rarely talked about it, at least not with me, but I could tell he was worried about not publishing enough. He complained about the journals not accepting his work when he submitted it."

"Do you know why it wasn't getting accepted?" Bill leaned forward and took another poppyseed roll.

"I don't," she shook her head. "Sorry, Professor Forster. Does this have something to do with why he was killed?"

I folded my hands in my lap. I didn't know the answer to that. Certainly, everyone in the academic world knew the adage: publish or perish. Though Evelyn might not have been fired for lack of publications, it would have affected his reputation and prospects for advancement in the field. Had his professional struggles led to his death? That, I could not say.

"We don't know anything," I told her. "I'm sure the police will work it out, though, dear."

I said it, but I wasn't sure if I meant it. Evelyn's life grew more complex with each passing day. What he had appeared to be on the surface, all these years we'd known him, was proving to be less and less accurate.

Chapter 59

At home, I prepared dinner while Bill set the table. Muffin got under my feet with every trip to the refrigerator, ever present when there was begging to be done. After visiting Nadya, we were late arriving home, and I wanted to make something that was quick and not too fussy. As I was unwrapping some thin pork chops from the butcher, the phone rang. Bill and I looked at each other.

"It's probably for me," I said, rinsing my hands under the tap and then drying them on my apron. "I'll get it. Could you please keep things moving here?"

Bill assented and we swapped places. I hit my hand on one of the kitchen chairs as I maneuvered through the tight space to get to the phone. It sent a shockwave of pain through my nerves. I cursed quietly and picked up the receiver.

"Hello?" I said, squeezing the receiver between my ear and my shoulder.

"Trixie, it's me," Arthur said.

"Oh, hello, you," I replied, rubbing the injured part of my hand. "I wasn't expecting to hear from you today."

"Well, I shouldn't be telling you this," he said quietly, "but since you've been involved and somewhat helpful with this case, I wanted to share this news with you."

"Sorry, I've been what?" I pestered him. "I couldn't quite hear you."

"Oh, come off it, Trixie," Arthur growled. "You're too old for that."

"Get on with it then," I said. "I'm a busy woman, mother to a three-year-old fox terrier. You know that's not an easy job."

"I won't take too much of your precious time," Arthur replied. "I wanted you to know that we looked into Volk's finances. I can assure you, as I said in the beginning, the professor had anything but money troubles. His widow and children won't be suffering; they've got enough to live on for several generations if you ask me."

"So why would Evelyn steal?" I asked. "If he had plenty of money, it doesn't make any sense. Maybe Marco was lying."

"There's another thing," Arthur said. I could hear him breathing directly into the receiver. "The constable who looked at Volk's statements at the beginning of the case only looked at the total balance, not the individual transactions. So, we only knew he was wealthy. However, upon closer inspection, there were three withdrawals of large sums of money in cash."

I straightened up, grabbing the receiver so it didn't crash to the floor.

"Withdrawals in cash?" I asked.

"Yes, he was making some kind of cash payment monthly. The withdrawals were for fifteen hundred dollars each time."

"Goodness," I said, glancing over at Bill who was pushing things around the frying pan. "That's a lot of money."

"It sure is," Arthur said. "That's a year's income for some folks."

"It's my turn to tell you something," I said. "I bumped into Abigail and the children at High Park today. I mentioned financial troubles to her, and she didn't know anything. However, talking about money seemed to jog her memory because she told me she'd seen Evelyn with envelopes of cash on two occasions. She didn't know what the money was for, of course, but obviously he needed cash for something."

"That's interesting," Arthur said. "It's starting to sound like that Marco kid is lying to you. The question is, why?"

"I can't imagine," I said. "What would be his motive? Yet, Stephen says he did not accuse Evelyn of stealing, and it appears that Evelyn wasn't short of money. Why would Marco make something like that up?"

"I don't know," Arthur said. "But it did get us to take a second look at Professor Volk's bank records. I'll be honest, Trixie. Usually if someone is running around with that kind of cash in an envelope, they are paying someone off. We just need to know whom he was paying off and for what. My guess is someone found out about his relationship with Walter, and they were willing to take cash instead of going public about it."

"Oh, I see," I mumbled. "Well, that would certainly be one rather significant reason why Evelyn might grease someone's palm."

"Exactly," Arthur agreed. "I need to talk to that Christopher kid pronto. Another possibility is he was blackmailing the professor because of the Allan Gardens thing. That'd be a damned good reason for Volk to pay him off."

Chapter 60

The next day, Bill and I dressed in our warmest dig-appropriate clothing, tied a red handkerchief around Muffin's collar, and stepped outside. I shivered when I saw my breath form a wisp of cloud as I exhaled warm air into the frigid morning atmosphere. Each day the weather grew a little colder, as November took hold and propelled us against our will toward December. There was no imminent sign of snow just yet, but the sooner the skeletons came out of the ground the better. The bones would benefit from a swift removal, and I could tell Bill was anxious to start analyzing the remains and the grave goods found amongst the bodies. Especially after I'd told him about the lead box in the grave.

"Why is it that we aren't staying home with a nice hot beverage?" I asked Bill as we got into the car to drive to Fort York.

"Being retired doesn't mean being boring," Bill said, turning the key in the ignition. "There's still life in us yet."

"Speak for yourself," I said, closing my eyes in the passenger seat and wondering how long exactly it would take for me to become a human icicle.

All we needed was a nasty wind coming off the lake to send us running home to the warmth of our house. Even Muffin, who particularly liked the cold and snow, suffered when Lake Ontario sent tidings of winter through the city streets. With my eyes closed I thought of Mexico, palm trees, iguanas, and most importantly, the sun.

Before I knew it, we had arrived at Fort York, and it was time to leave the car. I considered napping inside the vehicle while Bill worked, but he insisted I should come to draw the skeletons while he recorded every last detail and photographed them before they could be removed from the ground for analysis. Muffin led the way, ignoring the other dogs in the park. She was on a mission.

At the grave excavation area, Bill peeled back the canvas tarp. I helped him fold it and set it aside. Then I pulled my clipboard and pencils out for drawing, along with two tape measures and a weighted pendulum attached to a string we used for measuring distances to ensure the excavation drawing was to scale. We'd arrived before the students and Nadya wouldn't be coming to the site that day.

"You'll have to help me get these measurements," I said to Bill, watching Muffin roll around on her back in the grass.

She'd likely found some bird excrement and was attempting to hide her scent. Not that she needed to hunt for her food, but she'd certainly give it a try if she sniffed out a small rodent on the grounds of the fort. When I looked back at Bill, he was already kneeling at the edge of the excavation area, picking at some dirt around the lead box with a dental tool.

"Bill," I said. "Did you hear me?"

No response.

"Bill," I repeated, nudging him lightly with my foot since my hands were full of drawing materials.

"Did you say something, Beatrix?" He turned to look at me, shoving his glasses back up his nose.

"Yes," I said. "I need you to help me with the measurements for the drawing before you get too involved with other things."

"Oh, yes," he mumbled. "Sorry, Beatrix. I got distracted by the box."

"I noticed," I said, handing him the first tape measure.

He extended the tape measure along the south side of the excavation area, holding each end in place with a rock. Once the baseline was set, I gave him the other tape measure and the plumb bob. He would use the plumb bob to mark the vertical position of the object and the second measuring tape to determine the distance from the baseline. I kneeled at the baseline, my knees cracking as I got down, and held one end of the free measuring tape in my hand and my pencil in the other. I laid the clipboard on the grass beside me. This was a job best done with three people, but we'd have to make do unless we wanted to wait for the students. Bill held the plumb bob above each point of reference, top of the skull, pelvis, tips of the toes, letting the pendulum come to a rest and then lining up the measuring tape with the string. I slid my end of the measuring tape along the baseline until we'd created a right angle and then I took note of the x and y axis measurements on the transparent drawing paper, laid carefully over graph paper, and held in place by my clipboard.

When I was a young woman studying art in Europe, doing oil paintings and water colours of flowers and landscapes, I'd never dreamed I'd one day use my skills to make scale drawings of skeletons in their graves. It seemed morbid at first, until I learned the value the study of human remains brought to the field of archaeology. Now, in my late 60s, skeletons never gave me the willies the way they had when I first started working alongside Bill in the mid 1920s. The field of archaeology had been quite different then. Mostly men, of course, but the few women who participated still wore long skirts, even to excavate. Of course, now in 1967, women in pants, especially older women like myself, shocked a few, but I'd say if they were concerned about rebellious women, they had more to worry about with the mini dress than women in masculine clothing.

Once we'd taken all the necessary measurements and I'd made little dots for each point on my transparent paper, Bill returned to his work and I stood at the side of the excavation, referencing the four skeletons and the few artifacts in the grave that had been uncovered, which were mostly buttons, but also the mysterious box. As I sketched the tiny details onto the page, I wondered about these men. Had they died in the explosion? Or had it been a musket ball or artillery fire that had killed them on the battlefield? And why was one of them buried facing down? What shame had this person caused to be treated in such a manner? And, of course, what was in the box, if anything?

I was allowing my imagination to run wild, coming up with all kinds of treasures the box might contain, when a shadow fell over my clipboard and I let out a small shriek.

Chapter 61

"Why so jumpy, Mrs. Forster?" Christopher sneered, staring at my drawing.

"Goodness," I said, clutching my pencil to my heart. "Are you trying to frighten an old woman half to death? Where have you been?"

Suddenly Bill was beside me, with Muffin under his arm, and I felt more secure. Surely, Christopher would not hurt me with Bill here.

"Jetted off to Mexico to get married," he said, as though it was a normal thing to do.

"Many congratulations," I said, not really meaning it. I wondered how young his new bride was. "The police have been trying to find you. They have a lot of questions."

"I heard," Christopher said, his voice lower than when we first started talking.

"Were you blackmailing Professor Volk?" I blurted, before I could stop myself. I felt Bill squeeze my arm.

"What? No," Christopher gasped. "Why would I do that? Is that what the police think?"

"You saw Professor Volk in Allan Gardens," I began, holding my clipboard tight to my body. "And then decided to blackmail him to keep it quiet."

Christopher looked surprised, his mouth open and eyebrows arched. It took him a few moments to find his words.

"I made that up," he confessed, hanging his head. "I didn't see the professor at Allan Gardens. I was angry and even though he was dead I still wanted him to suffer. He was so arrogant and righteous about things, threatening my place at the university. It was stupid, I see that now, but I hated him."

I was shocked. Christopher was the first person to admit he hated Evelyn. Yet, if he'd invented the story about Allan Gardens, why had Evelyn threatened to have him removed from the university?

"Christopher, this is important," Bill said firmly without raising his voice. "The police are serious and it's time for you to start telling the truth. Why did you tell us you saw Professor Volk in Allan Gardens?"

"It was payback," Christopher said flatly. "What's the worst thing someone could think about you after you're dead? That you were a queer. Everyone would have been scandalized."

I looked up at Bill, realizing that Christopher had no idea Evelyn really was gay.

"Why did you want to hurt his reputation?" I asked, trying to keep my voice from showing the anger I felt. What a horrible young man to say such things.

"He caught me," Christopher said, looking at me and then down at the laces on his boots.

"Caught you doing what?" Bill pressed.

Christopher shrugged his shoulders. "I pinched Nadya's backside one day at the excavation and Professor Volk saw me. It wasn't a big deal. I do it all the time. The girls like it, you know? They crave the attention, especially from a guy like me. But Professor Volk lost it on me later that day. Said he'd have me kicked out and he didn't care who my parents were. He acted like it was the end of the world. Nadya didn't complain, so why should he? Anyway, I was not blackmailing the professor. I had no reason to. He didn't have as much power as he thought."

"Good Lord!" Bill exclaimed. "I may not have the authority to kick you out the university, Christopher, but I will exercise my right to tell you to leave the premises at once and never return to this excavation. You can be rude all you like, but interfering with other students is unacceptable. Do I make myself clear? We'll let the police know they can find you anywhere but here."

"You'll be hearing from the department," he spat, his eyes narrowed into slits. "You can't do this to me. You'll regret it."

With that, Christopher turned and walked away, hands shoved into his pockets.

Chapter 62

At the end of a long day in the field, I slumped, exhausted into my armchair at home. Even Bill looked tired, his shoulders hunched more than usual and the wrinkles under his eyes more pronounced. Muffin, the model of youthful energy, had curled herself into a tight ball near the empty fireplace. All three of us had nothing left to give.

"It seems the police haven't made much more progress than we have," I sighed, my eyes shut, and my head slumped against my chest. "They've only managed to confirm Brian's alibi. It seems he was indeed at the gas station, as he claimed."

"Yes," Bill mumbled. "He certainly made sure to remind everyone of the fact."

"Repeatedly," I agreed as we both sat, nearly incapacitated in our armchairs. "I think we should get delivery. I won't be cooking anything tonight."

"Chinese or pizza?" Bill asked. "I'll make the call."

"Pizza," I replied, suddenly craving hot melted cheese and chewy dough the moment Bill uttered the word.

"Ham and pineapple?"

I nodded. Hawaiian pizza had become a staple in our house since our grandchildren had asked to try it one night. Shirley and her husband were out of town and the children stayed with us. They'd heard about ham and pineapple pizza from friends who sampled the dish at a restaurant run by a Greek Canadian in a small southern Ontario town. The unusual flavour combination had taken off from there and was a standard item on pizza menus in Toronto. At first, Bill and I had questioned the logic of mixing sweet and savoury, but after we'd tried it, we were hooked. We didn't often agree on flavour combinations with our grandchildren, but this was one that pleased all the generations.

While Bill was calling, I turned my attention to the television. A journalist was reporting from Quebec, where thousands of litres of maple syrup had been stolen overnight. They were calling it a maple syrup heist. As I chuckled to myself and prepared to tell Bill the story when he returned from the kitchen, I realized something we had overlooked in Evelyn's case. People steal money, of course, but they can steal other things, too.

Chapter 63

"Bill," I said as he returned from ordering the pizza. "I've just realized something."

"What is it?" Bill asked, settling back into his armchair.

"I just saw something on the news about a maple syrup heist."

"What does that have to do with anything?" He raised his eyebrows.

"Well, it made me think," I said, twisting in my chair to look at my husband. "What if Evelyn were stealing? Maybe Marco isn't the one who is lying. What if Stephen is lying?"

"Why would Stephen lie?"

"If Stephen knew Evelyn was stealing," I began, "let's say artifacts from the collection in storage, for example, and he threatened Evelyn with going to the police, what would Evelyn do to keep his job?"

Bill scratched at his beard. "You mean you think Stephen might have been blackmailing Evelyn?"

"It makes sense, don't you think? Christopher may not have been the one doing it, but someone was. Whatever Evelyn was stealing might have cost him his job, which he valued. He didn't need to work, but I think he genuinely enjoyed it."

Bill nodded in agreement.

"When Stephen caught him and threatened him," I carried on, "he used his wealth to deal with the situation. Evelyn was giving Stephen cash each month to keep him quiet."

"So, you think Stephen lied to us to cover up the fact he was extorting money from Evelyn?" Bill asked.

"That's exactly what I think," I said, pushing myself out of my chair and onto my feet.

"Where are you going, Beatrix?" Bill asked, also standing up. "And what about the murder? Do you think Stephen killed Evelyn?"

"That I'm not so sure about," I said, walking toward the kitchen.

"It doesn't make sense for him to kill a cash cow," Bill said, following me. "If Evelyn were giving him fifteen hundred dollars a month, why would he kill him?"

"Maybe Evelyn threatened to stop paying him?" I suggested.

"Then Stephen could go to the police," Bill replied, entering the kitchen after me.

I heard a thump from the other room and suddenly Muffin was standing in the kitchen with us.

"What if Evelyn found a way to cover up his crime?" I asked, holding onto the back of a chair. "If he were stealing artifacts he could put them back, assuming he hadn't sold them."

"But why steal artifacts at all?" Bill asked, pulling out a chair and sitting down. "If he didn't need money, why steal and sell artifacts?"

I shook my head. I didn't really know.

"It may not have been about money," I said, noticing how much my feet hurt now that I was standing. "Some people have a strong urge to possess things they aren't supposed to have. The black market is full of these things. People want what they can't have."

Bill put his elbows on the table and his head in his hands.

"What about Stephen?" I continued. "Why get involved in blackmail? Surely, his salary was enough to live on."

"Greed," Bill said. He paused a moment and then his head shot up. "Greed and something else."

"What else?" I asked.

"I'll show you," Bill said, pushing his chair back. "Get your coat, Beatrix."

"What about the pizza?"

"Don't worry about that," he said hurriedly. "I'll leave some money and it will be here when we get back."

Bill grabbed his wallet from near the phone and started pulling a few small bills out. I had come to the kitchen to call Arthur, but I could do that when we returned. What did Bill want to show me that couldn't wait?

Chapter 64

"Where are we going, Bill" I asked from the passenger seat as we drove along darkened roads illuminated by the soft glow of the streetlights and the yellow radiance that shone from the windows of some of the houses.

"You'll see," Bill said, not taking his eyes off the road.

I huffed my disapproval and scratched Muffin's ears as she slept on my lap.

We had only driven for about ten minutes when Bill slowed the vehicle to a crawl and finally a full stop in front of a drab middle class, semi-detached abode built of brick. The front garden was untidy, and not just because of the season. Its dishevelled appearance made me think nobody had tended it for years and come spring, only a few stubborn perennials would blossom out of the overgrown tangle of vines and leaves that protruded every which way.

"Whose house is this?" I asked, shifting Muffin's weight on my lap. My hip had started to ache beneath the pressure of her small body. "The garden's a disaster."

"Don't you remember coming here?" Bill leaned closer to me to see out my window. "It's Stephen's house."

"Is it?" I couldn't believe it. Maybe it was the dark, but it didn't seem familiar to me. "Nobody looks after the garden?"

There was a light on in the front window of the house, but I couldn't see anybody inside.

"Stephen's wife left him," Bill said. "I thought I told you, but maybe I forgot. It must have been a year or two ago. And I think we both know Stephen wouldn't think gardening was a job for him unless there were some Roman sculptures or Greek ceramics to be found under the weeds."

"What about the children?" I shook my head, peering through the gloom at the melancholy plants that had probably once been tended with care and now grew neglected and wild. "They can't help him?"

"I couldn't say," Bill replied, sitting back in his seat. "I don't think they visit much, especially now with Gladys gone. Anyway, I didn't bring you here to look at the garden, Beatrix."

"Oh," I said, taking my glasses off and polishing them with the loose corner of my silk scarf. "What is it then that I'm supposed to be looking at?"

"Have a look at what's in the drive." Bill pointed through the windshield to the inanimate car that sat on the paved driveway of Stephen's house.

The vehicle gleamed in the low light reflecting off the shiny cherry red paint job.

"Goodness, Bill," I said, realizing what he was getting at. "That car looks brand new."

"Exactly," he said triumphantly. "Obviously we can't prove it, but I'd bet that if Arthur looks into it, Stephen probably bought it with cash. You can do a lot with forty-five hundred dollars."

"How did you know he had a new car?" I asked. "Had you seen it?"

"No, this is the first time I'm seeing it, but I recall his mentioning a new car recently. He said something about picking up his Mustang. I don't remember exactly when he told me, the week before last maybe, but I know I thought at the time that his other car wasn't that old, and I was surprised he needed to replace it so soon. Now, I think maybe he wasn't replacing the old car at all."

"Oh, I see," I said, peering at Stephen's glossy new toy. "Yes, it's always a little suspicious when someone makes an expensive purchase of something they don't really need. I'd say that car looks a little too sporty for it to have been a necessity. And the red colour certainly begs to be noticed. That's a young person's car if I ever saw one."

"What was it they called that?" Bill asked, squeezing his eyes shut and scrunching his face.

"You mean the purchase of a flashy, unnecessary item for show?"

"Yes, but in relation to the effort to stay young as death looms ever closer."

I knew then what Bill was getting at. The psychological concept had only recently been introduced to the public, but it had captured the collective imagination and flourished. It was entirely relatable.

"The midlife crisis?" I asked.

"That's the one," Bill hit the wheel with his palm. "This looks exactly like a midlife crisis."

"He might be a bit old for that," I replied, "but if it is, it could very well be a midlife crisis funded by Evelyn Volk."

I sat silently for a moment, staring at the ill-gotten vehicle. Blackmail certainly paid well. Had things gone sour with the arrangement and Stephen killed Evelyn? And what was it that Stephen held over his younger colleague? What had Evelyn done that he was willing to pay to cover it up? Had Stephen found out about Walter and threatened to out Evelyn publicly? It could have ruined Evelyn's career if anybody knew, not to mention potential problems with the police. It seemed plausible, but then why had Marco overheard them arguing about theft?

Chapter 65

As we pulled into the driveway at home, we could see there was a cardboard pizza box resting on the front door mat. I opened the door and Muffin jumped out, racing up to the box to sniff the alien object. She wagged her tail enthusiastically, nudging the pizza with her nose.

"I told you they'd leave the pizza," Bill said, sliding out from behind the steering wheel.

"We're just lucky a raccoon didn't beat us to it," I replied, using the door handle to support my exit from the vehicle.

"Let's eat first and then we can call Arthur." Bill bent over and picked up the box, balancing it in one hand as he found the correct key with the other.

I heard my stomach growl.

"That sounds like an excellent idea," I said.

After we'd scarfed down a sufficient quantity of ham, pineapple, and melted mozzarella cheese, we sat back in our chairs and stared in satisfied silence at the two slices that remained in the box. Bill closed the lid and I collected myself, wondering if Arthur would scold me for going to Stephen's house. My excuse would be that this time, at least, we hadn't actually spoken to him. I walked to the phone and thinking better of standing to make the call, I pulled out a chair and sat down, lifting the receiver and pressing the numbered buttons.

"Hello?" Arthur answered the phone.

"It's me," I said.

"Lord, Trixie," Arthur said, exasperated. "What have you and Bill done now?"

"Not much this time," I replied defensively. "It was more of a revelation. We didn't actually talk to anybody involved in the case."

"Out with it then," Arthur said curtly.

"On second thought, that might be a bit of a fib," I said. "I just recalled that we did speak with Christopher this morning when he came to the site. He's back from Mexico, married now. However, as much as I'd like to see that boy in jail, I don't think he was blackmailing Evelyn. Apparently, he made up the story about Allan Gardens as some form of twisted revenge against him because Evelyn caught him pinching Nadya's derriere and scolded him for it. Well, it was a bit more than scolding; he said he would have the university expel him."

"You didn't think to tell me this sooner?" Arthur asked.

"The mind isn't what it used to be, Arthur," I reminded him. "Just wait, you'll be there soon enough.

"Don't I know it!" Arthur mumbled.

"Anyway, that's not the real reason I called you; there's more," I said.

"Go on."

"Well, I saw that news report about the maple syrup heist," I began, glancing at the clock on the kitchen wall, the second hand ticking rhythmically. It was nine at night. "And it got me thinking. Maybe Evelyn wasn't stealing money. He was wealthy and didn't need it, but what if he was stealing something else?"

"That sounds plausible," Arthur said slowly. I imagined him mulling it over in his mind. "Is that it? That's why you called?"

"No, there's more," I said. "Be patient."

"Go on."

"Bill and I started talking about it and we don't know what he could have been stealing, but we thought he might have been paying Stephen Blake, the department head, to keep it quiet."

"Go on."

"Bill and I took a drive past Stephen's house," I explained, "and there's a brand-new, red Ford Mustang in the driveway."

There was a long pause on the other end of the line.

"Hmm," Arthur began. "It's not much, but it is interesting. I can look into the car and ask him about it. If we squeeze him hard enough, I think he'll tell us about the blackmail. That is, he'll tell us if he didn't kill the professor. Of course, if he did murder Volk, he'll be tight lipped about the whole thing. Blackmail doesn't seem like such a bad thing when compared to murder, but if he's guilty of both, he'll hold out and lawyer up. Of that I'm certain. Blake sounds sleazy to me, but you don't kill an easy source of income unless something goes wrong."

Chapter 66

On Tuesday morning, Bill and I dressed for Fort York once more. We'd finished recording the burial the day before and it was time for the students to remove the bones and artifacts from the grave. Bill was excited to start analyzing the remains, but even more than that, we all wanted to know what the lead box contained. Even I felt the tingle of anticipation as we drove to the fort, hoping with every bone and muscle in my body that it wouldn't be empty, or contain trivial items like musket balls or buttons. It seemed likely that it would not be a spectacular find, but every now and then you could win the archaeological lottery and discover something of note. There was also the issue of why the individual had been buried face down. It was a mystery we might never solve with certainty, but it didn't mean we couldn't speculate. Nadya would be back at the site, and I anticipated that once the skeletons were exhumed, there would be a heavy load of historical research for her to do. Matching buttons to regiments, and looking at the registry of deaths and contemporary accounts of the Battle of York.

Bill, Nadya, and the students, with the exception of Christopher, of course, set to work on the remains while I took Muffin walking around the grounds of the fort. We ambled past the soldier's barracks that framed either side of the entrance gates and headed toward the officers' quarters. I noticed the police tape had been removed. I did a quick turn to see if anybody was around. With not a soul to see us, I walked into the building with Muffin at my side.

Without thinking about it, I turned right and went through to the officers' mess. The day I'd found Evelyn's body, I hadn't stopped in the room, hadn't noticed any blood, or scuff marks from where the perpetrator dragged the body out of the room and down the hallway to push the corpse down the stairs into the cellar. I tried to imagine the events of the morning Evelyn was killed. After his morning lecture, he came back to his office to put the replica musket away and Donna left the journals, including the copy of Historical Archaeology on his desk. According to the interviews with Nadya and the students, the musket was still loaded and ready to be fired when he left them at the excavation. Donna confirmed he had not unloaded the musket in her presence. Thus, no special knowledge of how to prepare the antiquated weapon was needed for the murderer to commit the crime. Anybody could have pulled the trigger and ended Evelyn's life.

Donna said she didn't notice anybody else in the officers' barracks while she was there. Unless she herself had killed Evelyn, the murderer must have entered after she left. I thought about what motive she might have had to want

Evelyn dead, but nothing sprang to mind. However, the simple fact she was the last person to see Evelyn alive made her a potential suspect. Murder wasn't always as clear cut as we would like it to be, although I had got the impression when we spoke to her that she genuinely liked Evelyn.

Then I wondered about Walter. As much as I admired the young man, there was always the chance he was lying to us. Had he in fact been at Fort York the day Evelyn died? That begged the question, however: why return to the scene of the crime the next day? Had he left some evidence behind and needed to recover or hide it? That was a possibility. But what was his motive? Jealousy? Money? Christopher admitted he lied about Allan Gardens and Evelyn wasn't out cruising for other men. Why would Walter want to kill someone for whom he cared deeply? It hardly seemed likely Walter would have been named in the will. The inheritance would go to Margaret and the children.

Of course, that raised the question of Evelyn's wife. Margaret wouldn't have been surprised by Evelyn's extra-marital activities. She had agreed to the arrangement. She had, however, inherited a large sum of money as a result of Evelyn's death. From our conversations, though she may not have loved her husband in the way that most husbands and wives love each other, she did care about him as her partner and father of her children. Would she have come all the way down here and, in a burst of anger, killed her husband? It was clear that the murder was not pre-meditated. It was improbable the criminal could have known Evelyn would be carrying around a loaded musket.

Stephen was another possibility. The department head was blackmailing Evelyn over the theft of something unlikely to be money, or perhaps over Walter. That was still to be determined. Whatever Evelyn had done, he was willing to part with a large sum of cash each month to keep Stephen quiet. Had he decided to come clean and end Stephen's blackmail? If Evelyn had decided to go to the police, Stephen might have faced time in prison for his crime. The thought of the consequences of his actions might have pushed Stephen to kill the source of his extra income.

That left the students and Nadya. Had Christopher lied yet again and his spat with Evelyn was significant enough for him to want his professor dead? What about the others? Would Nadya benefit if her supervisor were out of the picture? It seemed less probable. She'd have to find someone new and potentially start over. Evelyn certainly hadn't been engaged in an inappropriate relationship with her, as Arthur suggested early in the case. Marco and Anthony could each be hiding some motive, of which I was completely oblivious. They claimed to like him, as much as students liked professors, and none had confessed to any motive for wanting him dead. Arthur had confirmed Brian's alibi, but if Alfred Hitchcock had taught us anything, it was that a clever criminal could find a way to have an alibi and still commit a crime. I didn't really get the impression from Brian, though, that he was capable of plotting a murder for which he would not be a suspect.

I tried to think if there were any other potential culprits I had overlooked in my haste to assign blame to someone for the terrible tragedy. I looked around the room again, the furniture placed to create a sense of how things would have been for officers in the British army in the early

19th century. As I took stock of the objects representing lives long gone, I realized Muffin had wandered off.

"Muffin," I called out. "Muffin, where did you go?"

I turned my back on the large dining table in the middle of the room and went back the way I'd come. From the hallway, I could hear scratching coming from Evelyn's office. I rushed over, hoping Muffin hadn't decided to damage the walls or floors of the historic site in an effort to catch a mouse. When I walked in, I saw exactly what I'd expected. Muffin turned to me, a lifeless mouse clamped in her deadly jaws. She looked at me innocently, and sat down, probably expecting me to praise her. I did think I would have been quite happy if she'd taken care of a rodent in my own home. Having a mouse-catcher wasn't the worst thing, even if I did feel a little sorry for the poor creature.

"Come on, Muffy," I said to her, pointing at the door. "Let's take that outside."

I was turning to leave the room when something caught my eye. It was then that I realized what Evelyn had been stealing.

Chapter 67

Muffin followed me out of the officers' barracks and then overtook me as I trudged across the grass as fast as my little legs could carry me. She trotted proudly, the mouse still firmly clenched in her mouth. I'd have to deal with that later, but I urgently needed to talk to Bill alone.

I barely had any breath left in me as I approached the burial excavation area.

"Bill," I shouted, once I felt I was within hearing distance.

Nadya and the students looked up from the trench, but Bill kept his head down.

"Could you nudge him, please" I gasped.

Brian nodded.

"Professor Forster," I heard Brian say. "Mrs. Forster wants to speak with you."

Bill popped his head up, looked at me, and then quickly stood and walked away from the excavation area.

"What's wrong, Beatrix?" he asked, wrinkling his brow. "Are you alright?"

I was sweating despite the cool weather, and I pulled at my scarf, hoping to feel a refreshing breeze on my neck which was hot and itchy.

"Nothing wrong," I said. "I need to talk to you."

I started walking away from the burial, Nadya and the students staring after us. Bill looked back at them.

"Back to work, please," Bill said firmly. "We have a lot to do today."

We walked across the path leading to the entrance gates of the fort and stood near the sharpened spikes of the fraise, jutting ominously from the earthworks.

"What is it, Beatrix?" Bill asked again, when we were far enough from the students.

"I've just realized what it was that Evelyn was stealing," I said.

"What's that?" Bill leaned closer to me.

"Work," I said.

"Work?" Bill raised his eyebrows.

"Yes," I said emphatically. "Research, ideas, intellectual property. That's what he was stealing. We just need to find out from whom."

Chapter 68

"Of course," Bill said, throwing his hands in the air. "He didn't need money, but you can steal all kinds of things. Nadya said he'd been struggling with his research and getting published. I just wonder why he would be so excited to publish an article if it weren't genuinely his work."

"People don't always get fulfillment from the same things," I sighed. "Some need the discovery, some need the process, and others want the recognition regardless of whether they did the work themselves or not. Maybe that's how Evelyn felt. He'd not done the work himself, but he needed others to congratulate him for the accomplishment."

"Vanity comes before the fall," Bill said quietly.

"Indeed," I said, shaking my head. "Now we need to find out whose work he was stealing?"

Bill looked over at the students in the distance and scratched his beard.

"One of them?" He asked.

"Possibly," I said. "They are all conducting graduate-level research that could be published at some point, or already has been if we consider Evelyn's paper. However, it could be another one of Evelyn's graduate students or a professor."

"True..." Bill mumbled.

I ran my hand over my short curls, trying to make sense of it all. "If someone's work was stolen, though, why wouldn't they speak up? It couldn't be that hard to demonstrate the work was theirs, could it?"

"Perhaps Evelyn had something to hold over them," Bill suggested, "but we do know someone who can tell us what work was stolen."

"Stephen?"

"Exactly."

Chapter 69

Bill and I plodded back to where the students were still pulling bones from the grave and wrapping them carefully in newspaper.

"Professor Forster," Nadya called as we approached. "We're ready to remove the box."

"Oh," Bill said, his eyes growing wide. "Excellent."

Bill and I stepped close to the edge of the excavation area to watch Anthony clear the last bits of dirt from around the box. There were few bones left in the grave that belonged to the individual who had the lead artifact tucked under his arm. Once the box was loose, Anthony pulled it from the earth and held up the mysterious object. Bill took it with both hands and examined it.

"Nothing special, really," Bill said, holding it close to his eyes. "Just a lead box. Who wants to do the honours?"

Bill looked around. Everyone was silent.

"Whatever is in here won't bite after all this time," Bill said smiling. "Nadya, you've been running the show. Please open this up for us."

Nadya nodded solemnly and reached for the box. It felt like a ceremony of sorts. I hoped it wouldn't be empty after all this fuss. There was a small latch on one side of the box, all crusted over with the same white patina that covered the entire artifact. She gasped when she went to open the catch and it simply fell off, landing somewhere in the grass at her feet.

"I'm so sorry, Professor Forster," she mumbled, glancing at Bill. "I thought I was being careful."

Brian kneeled down and recovered the broken latch, holding it gingerly in his palm.

"It's no matter," Bill said, folding his work gloves and shoving them in his pocket. "These things happen. Nothing to be done. Keep going, Nadya."

Nadya balanced the box in the palm of her hand and used the other to slowly open the lid. Her mouth fell open as she saw what it contained, and we all instinctively moved forward to have a look.

Chapter 70

"What is it?" Brian demanded, peering over Nadya's shoulder at what the box contained.

Even on tiptoes, I couldn't quite see into the box myself. I stood back patiently and waited for Bill to remove the item from the box so we could all have a look. Bill peered at the contents, and I watched his mouth form a small "o" of surprise, but he said nothing. He began patting his pockets and looking around.

"Could someone please hand me a set of tweezers?" He asked.

Marco dug through the small tools in a green metal toolbox nearby, the sound of metal scraping against metal clanging in our ears. Muffin stuck her head into the box as well, thinking there might be something for her to play with. She seemed to have abandoned the mouse for now.

"Here, Professor Forster." Marco handed Bill a large set of tweezers.

"Thank you," Bill said, hunching his shoulders as he leaned over the box.

"What is it?" Brian demanded again.

"I'm not entirely sure," Bill said. "It looks like hair."

"Why would someone carry hair around in a box?" Brian asked.

"Hair?" I asked. "Like a lock of hair?"

Bill shook his head. "No, it's much more than just a lock."

I was shocked. I agreed with Brian's question. In a time of war, when speed and agility were of the essence, why would someone carry around an unnecessary item? Was it a talisman of sorts? The people of that time period had often been superstitious. Yet, if it were an object believed to have magical properties, would a lock of hair not have been sufficient?

Bill carefully squeezed the hair between the tweezers and removed it from the box. We were lucky it wasn't windy that day, or the whole thing might have been carried away on the breeze. I could see more clearly now. The hair was a medium brown and slightly wavy in texture. As Bill had said, it was definitely more than a lock of hair someone might carry in memory of a loved one.

"How did something organic like that even survive the burial environment?" Anthony asked.

"Good question, Anthony," Bill said, still holding the hair up and examining it closely. "The lead box likely provided some protection from acids in the earth, but there are cases where, given the right soil conditions or burial environment, organic elements can be relatively well preserved. I would say in this case it was likely the box that

265

did the trick, but I've seen brain matter survive 80 years and hair can survive in environments like bogs or desert caves for thousands of years. Not all organic matter decomposes given enough time. The archaeological record taketh away, but sometimes it giveth."

The students chuckled.

"Beatrix, look at this," Bill said, stepping closer to me. "What do you see?"

He held the hair up in my face.

"Not so close, Bill," I said, stepping back.

"Oh, sorry," Bill said.

The hair undulated as Bill's hand moved slightly.

"Stay still," I commanded, examining what appeared to be simply a mass of human hair.

Then I saw that the hair was being held together with something dark and wrinkled, like a prune.

"Goodness," I said, moving away slightly as my stomach lurched with revulsion. "Is that skin?"

Chapter 71

"Jesus, Mary, and Joseph!" Brian exclaimed. "Does that mean what I think it means?"

Bill looked hesitantly at me and then returned the hair to the box. Nadya closed the lid. I knew Bill didn't like sensationalism, but what he was about to say would certainly raise some eyebrows.

"Yes," Bill said quietly. "I believe it may well be what you think it is, Brian. It looks to be a human scalp."

Marco quickly crossed himself. I wouldn't have expected an archaeologist to be susceptible to the influence of religion, but perhaps it was force of habit from when he was a child. It certainly wasn't everyday either that one was confronted with a scalp from over 150 years ago.

I noticed Nadya bite her lip.

"What is it, Nadya?" I asked her. "Did you want to say something?"

Prompted, she said: "Oh, maybe it's nothing, Mrs. Forster. I think I remember reading some mention about a scalp or scalping when I was researching the site. I just don't recall the details. I need my books, but they're back at the university. I swear this head injury has made my memory go mushy."

She carefully touched her temple, where there was still bruising, but she no longer wore a bandage. The wound had scabbed over and it was now just a ragged area of dark red, crusty skin.

"We'll have to take the remains to the university today, anyway," Bill interjected. "You can have a look then."

"Do you think an Indian took the scalp?" Brian asked.

"It's possible," Bill said. "Though both Indian tribes and European settlers scalped in the past. Remember, culture is learned not intrinsic. Cultural practices have always and will always be exchanged and adopted."

"It's a savage practice," Marco murmured.

Bill glanced at me and sighed. "Let's not forget we are anthropologists, here. We approach past and present cultures objectively, not subjectively. Ethnocentrism leads to judgement, not understanding. It's our objective here to understand cultures of the past."

Bill's statement was met with silence and much staring at the grass. It was occasionally necessary, even amongst anthropologists, to remind practitioners of the principles of the field and the need to leave our own learned, cultural biases behind.

"Beatrix," Bill stepped close to me and leaned in. "Do you mind going to see Arthur about you know who while I wrap things up with the students?"

I nodded and snapped my fingers to get Muffin's attention. There was little I could add to the discussion of the scalp, and perhaps Stephen could enlighten us as to whose work Evelyn had stolen for his article in Historical Archaeology.

Chapter 72

When I arrived at Arthur's desk at the police station, Muffin tethered to me on her leash, he was just putting on his coat.

"Trixie," he said, smiling. "Am I glad to see you or not glad to see you?"

"I would say glad to see me," I replied. "Looks like you're on your way out."

"I am," Arthur grabbed some keys off this desk. "Going to see your friend, Blake. We intend on asking about the car. What I wouldn't give to get a brand-new Mustang. Though I don't know I'd resort to blackmail."

"That's exactly the person I wanted to speak with you about."

"No Bill, today?" Arthur looked around.

"No," I shrugged. "It's just me and Muffin. Bill stayed at Fort York."

Arthur crouched down to greet Muffin. She stood on her back legs and sniffed at the collar of his coat.

"That smelly, huh, Muffy?" Arthur asked. "Guess I should ask my wife to wash it."

I was about to make a quip about him being fully capable of washing it himself, when I heard a woman's voice behind me.

"Hello, Beatrix."

I swivelled to look at her and felt a slight twinge in my back.

"Oh, hello, Mariana," I said, wincing. "It's nice to see you."

"Are you alright?" she asked, putting her hand on my arm.

"I'm fine, thank you," I said. "Just a little pinch in my spine. Be glad you're still young and healthy."

"Back to the subject at hand," Arthur cut in, obviously forgetting that he had changed the topic in the first place. "Trixie, what is it you want to tell me?"

"Why don't you take me with you to see Stephen?" I suggested. "I can tell you everything on the way."

Arthur and Mariana exchanged a look.

"Oh, alright, fine," Arthur conceded. He motioned with his chin toward the hall. "Let's get on with it then. You can stay in the car when we interview him."

I said nothing, but I didn't plan to stay in the car.

Muffin and I sat in the back seat of the unmarked police vehicle as Mariana drove us and Arthur to the university.

"I was back at the crime scene this morning," I said.

Arthur jerked around in the passenger seat to look at me meaningfully. I held my hands up.

"They removed the police tape," I said. "I didn't cross any lines."

"Did I or did I not tell you to stay out of the investigation?" Arthur asked.

"You can't very well tell her to stay out of it and then take her along for an interview," Mariana interrupted. "That's not fair. You're sending mixed signals, Arthur. Plus, she's helped a lot with the investigation. Beatrix has a lot of insightful information, don't you think?"

"I said she was going to stay in the car," Arthur huffed.

"She can't stay in the car," Mariana said, lifting her fingers off the wheel. "She's not a dog."

"Fine, what is it you saw at the crime scene, Trixie?" Arthur ignored the junior detective.

"I remembered that shred of the article that was in the fireplace," I began. "It had mostly been burned. I imagine you have it amongst the evidence at the station. Your investigators will have collected it, I'm sure. Well, I realized then that we were right. Evelyn didn't need money. That wasn't what he was stealing. Nadya, told us the other day when we saw her that Evelyn was struggling to get his work published. At the university, publications are essential to one's career advancement. Not keeping up with the other professors in the department, in terms of publishing, would have tarnished his reputation. He was generally considered to be up-and-coming, but this would have made things difficult for him, a sitting duck for critiques at academic conferences, too."

"So, you think he was stealing research and passing it off as his own," Arthur said, nodding as though putting the pieces of the puzzle together. "And Stephen found out and was blackmailing him for it."

"Exactly," I replied, bracing myself against the back of Mariana's seat as she made a quick turn.

"Whose work?" Arthur asked the burning question.

"We don't know," I sighed. "It could be the students, or other professors. Bill and I thought that Stephen would know."

Arthur nodded. "And you think the person he was stealing from killed him and likely also attacked Nadya?"

"Not necessarily," I said, "but it's possible. It seems extreme to resort to killing him over theft of intellectual property, but people can get desperate or overreact in certain situations."

"Hmm," Arthur murmured, turning back around in his seat to face the front. He rubbed his neck. "You should have been a police detective, Trixie."

I blushed. "A little late for that now."

Chapter 73

Mariana, Arthur, and I stood awkwardly around Stephen's desk while Muffin slept in the car a few blocks from campus.

"Sit," Arthur commanded, and Mariana and I did what we were told.

I didn't want to be seated in the horrible leather chair that I already knew would consume me into its depths, but it was better than standing if this interview happened to become lengthy.

"We have some follow up questions, Professor Blake," Arthur said, perching on the arm of Mariana's chair.

Despite the unnatural position, he looked to be in his element. An eagle who had just spotted its prey in the field below.

"I understand you are in possession of a brand-new vehicle," Arthur said.

Stephen blinked. "I am. What's that got to do with anything?"

"How did you pay for the car, Professor Blake?" Arthur asked, ignoring Stephen's question. "Cash, credit, a loan?"

"I paid in cash," Stephen frowned. "Not that it's any business of the police."

He clasped his hands in front of him on his desk and twisted his fingers so the skin on the backs of his hands wrinkled.

"It's our business if you obtained that money unlawfully," Arthur stated, never taking his eyes off Stephen.

"Of course, it was obtained lawfully, as you say," Stephen squeezed his fingers even tighter. "How else would I have got it?"

"I think we both know that you received a cash payment from Professor Volk each month."

Stephen blanched. I realized he had believed he would get away with his crime now that Evelyn was dead.

"You were blackmailing him, weren't you?" Arthur continued. He tapped his pen on his notepad but wrote nothing.

Stephen shook his head vigorously. "I did no such thing, Detective. Why would I blackmail Evelyn?"

"He was stealing," Arthur said. "You knew it, but instead of putting a stop to it and reporting him, you decided to take advantage of the situation."

Stephen shot me a withering look.

"I don't know what ugly rumours Beatrix has been telling you," Stephen said, looking back at Arthur. "But I can assure you I have not been blackmailing my colleague."

"We've seen Volk's bank statements." Arthur stood up and set his notepad on the desk. "We know he withdrew fifteen hundred dollars each month since September. That money went to you, Professor Blake. To keep you quiet about the theft."

Stephen laughed. "Why would Evelyn steal? He had plenty of money."

"People steal more than just money." Arthur folded his arms over his chest, his pen sticking out above his elbow. "This would be a good time for you to tell us the truth. As of right now, we don't think you murdered Evelyn, but we could add that charge to the list and see what sticks. Prison time for murder is a lot more than prison time for blackmail. I'm sure you know that."

Stephen scanned the three of us. I thought he might break one of his fingers he was twisting them so hard.

"You meddling old witch," Stephen spewed, glaring at me. "You've never known when to mind your own business."

"Professor Blake, you might care to watch what you say to my cousin," Arthur said, smiling in a cruel sort of way. "I can always drop the rumour that you assaulted a young woman. You know what they do to people like that in prison, don't you?"

That was the last straw. Stephen hung his head in shame.

"I'm sorry," he babbled, reduced to a whimpering child behind his imposing desk. "I shouldn't have done it, but after Gladys left me, life was bleak. My own children won't even speak to me except when they need something. I had nothing in my life, and I thought if I could spiff up my look a little it might make me more appealing to some sad, pathetic divorcée out there. What else could I hope for?"

I wondered what divorcée would be so miserable she'd want Stephen after escaping a loveless marriage. I would have felt sorry for him, but he was a scheming criminal.

"Go on," Arthur prompted him, returning to the arm of Mariana's chair with his notebook. He scrawled some notes onto the page, the pen scratching over the paper in the silence of the room.

"I... I know what I did was wrong," Stephen said.

"How did you know he was stealing?" Arthur asked.

"One of the students came to see me, saying that Evelyn was taking his ideas and planning to pass them off as his own."

"Which student?" I blurted.

Arthur shot me a warning look. I'd promised I would stay quiet.

"Anthony," he said.

I gasped inadvertently and Stephen's head shot up, his eyes flickering over each of us in turn.

"Does this mean you think Anthony killed Evelyn?" he asked. "I swear it wasn't me who did it. Why would I kill him when he was giving me all that money to keep me quiet?"

"We can't disclose that right now," Arthur said flatly.

I was shocked. Had Anthony, usually so polite and mild mannered, killed Evelyn in a fit of rage over the theft of his work and then attacked Nadya because he feared she knew something? He had been the one to find Nadya in the blockhouse. Perhaps it wasn't coincidence at all if he'd been the one to shove her into the glass display case. With horror, I remembered Nadya saying that Anthony was the one to ask Evelyn to demonstrate how to load a musket. I had always believed this was a crime of passion and the musket had been an opportunistic weapon for the murderer. Had Anthony plotted the entire crime?

Chapter 74

Arthur insisted on dropping me and Muffin off at home before he went to find Anthony at Fort York.

"It's time for you to stay home," he said as I stepped out of the backseat of the vehicle. "Let the professionals handle it from here."

I wished I could call Bill and tell him what happened, but it would be difficult to reach him at Fort York without driving down in person. I knew Arthur was right and that I should stay out of the investigation. While I waited for Bill to come home, I started to chop vegetables and meat for a stew. There was little I could do, and I felt helpless. Keeping myself busy was the best way to manage the situation as it stood. If Anthony had killed Evelyn, then he would rightly find himself in prison. Even though Stephen had decided not to help Anthony with the theft of his work, there were better options than murder. The problem was Evelyn had preyed on someone he knew society could overlook, even though he himself could just as easily have fallen victim to the same kinds of prejudice had people known the truth. Evelyn could hide behind Margaret, but Anthony couldn't pretend to be something he wasn't. If he were innocent, he would have to work a lot harder to prove it than any of the other students.

As I stood at the counter, slicing the vegetables with a butcher's knife, and tossing Muffin a small piece of carrot here and there, I wondered why, as humans, we were often incapable of recognizing that our similarities outweighed our differences.

Chapter 75

"Beatrix?" Bill called out as soon as he opened the front door.

I rushed from the kitchen into the front hall, Muffin beating me by several seconds. I watched Bill lean over to pick her up.

"What is it?" I asked.

"They took Anthony to the station to question him," Bill said.

I covered my mouth and then let out a sigh.

"Oh, my," I said. "I hoped it wouldn't come to this, but if he's guilty I suppose it must be done."

"Do you think he killed Evelyn?" Bill asked, kicking his shoes off and stepping toward me.

"I don't know what to think," I said quietly. "I wouldn't want to believe it of such a nice young man, but he certainly had the opportunity and if Evelyn had been stealing from him and he felt he couldn't do anything to defend himself, especially after Stephen decided to take advantage of the situation instead of helping, I suppose he could have. Do you think he did it?"

We stood there looking at each other.

"I don't know either," Bill said, running his free hand through his hair. "He's young, but I'm sure he has enough sense to ask for a lawyer."

"At this point," I said, moving close to Bill, "all we can do is wait and see what happens. I know Arthur won't want to arrest someone who is innocent, but the police sometimes get things wrong."

Bill wrapped his arm around me and pressed his cheek to the top of my head.

Chapter 76

After a sleepless night, Bill and I shuffled around the kitchen like the walking dead, mumbling to each other and clumsily preparing toast with jam and tea. I almost forgot to feed Muffin, but she'd never let me get away with such blasphemous behaviour. She bounced around whining and staring at her food bowl until I got the message, loud and clear.

"What should we do?" I asked, slumping over my toast.

"About the investigation?" Bill asked, spreading butter over the crusty surface of the bread.

"Yes."

"Give Arthur some time to sort this out," he said. "There's little reason for us to stay involved."

I said nothing and took a small bite of my toast.

Bill looked at me. "Why don't you come to the lab with me today? We can have an initial look at the skeletons. It will take our minds off the case."

I didn't know if that were true, but I decided to go with Bill. We left Muffin at home and drove to the university.

In the lab, Bill and the students had already laid out the four skeletons in anatomical position on the tables. Each individual also had a tray with the artifacts that could be associated to the body. They were mostly buttons, but there were other bits of unidentifiable metal, clay pipes, and a few coins that were probably missed by those who buried them. There wasn't much, though, since anything of use would not normally have gone into the grave.

"Where are the students?" I asked Bill. "Are they not coming to the lab today?"

"They'll come by later," he said, not looking up from a bone he held. "They're at Fort York with Nadya. There's still work to be done on the main excavation area."

I settled into a chair in the corner of the lab and drifted off to sleep. After a wakeful night, I needed the shuteye. When I was startled awake by Bill's voice, I couldn't be sure how much time had passed.

"Beatrix," he nearly shouted. "I've had an epiphany!"

"About the murderer?" I asked, rubbing my eyes.

"No," Bill said, striding over to me. "About the skeletons. Come look at this."

He took my hand and helped me to my feet, leading the way to the first individual.

"Look at the fracture patterns on this individual," Bill said, pointing to various sites on the skeleton.

The preservation of the remains was not excellent, and I wasn't certain if I was correctly distinguishing peri-mortem from post-mortem injuries, peri being from the time of death and post occurring in the burial environment.

"I'm afraid, dear," I said, adjusting my glasses, "I don't know what you're getting at."

Bill launched into a lengthy explanation. "There are many highly comminuted fractures in the limbs, fractures of the ribs, and for one individual, there's also blunt force trauma to the head. The three individuals who were supine, have similar, though not identical injuries. Almost certainly, these three individuals were killed in the explosion from the blast itself or from flying debris from the magazine. The blunt force trauma to the head was probably caused by a chunk of rock or metal propelled from the magazine. The other injuries look like they may have been caused by the force of the blast. Of course, there's not much literature on the subject so it's difficult to know for sure. And without blowing up a few pig carcasses, which we'd never receive permission to do, it's speculation based on experience more than anything. However, the reports of the explosion indicate that the radius of the blast was extensive, reaching a great distance from where the magazine actually stood. Casualties due to the blast were minor on the British side, because of the direction of the explosion, but 250 Americans were killed or wounded when they detonated the magazine."

"Goodness," I said, looking over the remains with fresh eyes. "And the one who was buried face down?"

"That's just it, Beatrix," Bill said waving me over to have a look at the remains. "No signs of trauma."

"Nothing at all?" I asked.

"I'll have another look, but I didn't see anything obvious right off the bat. Whatever killed him only affected the soft tissue, be that disease or injury."

"What about nationality?" I asked.

"American," Bill said. "Nadya confirmed they each wore American regimental uniforms by matching the buttons to the military records. This makes sense why they were all buried together. It wasn't typical to have the opposing sides in the same grave under ideal circumstances. Nobody wanted to spend eternity with the side that killed them. Once the British abandoned Fort York and went to Kingston, the Americans had time to bury their dead unimpeded."

"I see," I said, running my finger over the smooth shaft of a tibia. "In theory they were buried by their own, thus, the prone burial fails to make much sense. Do you think he might have been a deserter?"

"Possibly. I'd have to look into the historical records, but I'm not sure that deserters were executed in those days. Punished, yes, but executed? I don't know about that. Maybe Nadya will know."

I was about to respond to Bill when there was a knock, and Donna slowly opened the door. Her silvery-grey hair, which she normally wore straight, was pulled back into a French twist.

"Hello, Donna," Bill said, straightening up and taking a step away from the table. "What brings you down here today?"

"Hello Professor Forster, Beatrix," she breathed. Her chest heaved and I could tell she was out of breath from the journey to the basement of the building where the labs were located. "I just received a phone call from the police station. I came down as quickly as I could. It sounded urgent. It was Detective Campbell. He asked that you both go over as soon as possible."

"Thank you for letting us know, Donna," Bill said. "We'll head there now."

"Do you know anything more about what happened to Professor Volk?" she asked, blushing. "He was such a charming young man; I still can't believe what happened. Nobody tells us anything. We're completely in the dark."

I shook my head sadly and said, "Unfortunately, not. The police are still working on it."

I could have said more, but the last thing anybody needed in this situation was for the rumour mill at the university to run rampant.

"I understand," Donna answered and disappeared back into the hallway.

Chapter 77

Arthur looked angrier than usual when we arrived at the police station. He was pacing back and forth outside an interrogation room, a scowl on his face.

"We came as soon as we could, Arthur," I said. "What happened?"

"That stupid kid won't talk unless you're here," Arthur's nostrils flared as he spoke.

"You mean Anthony?" Bill asked.

"Yes, I mean Anthony," Arthur said, squeezing his hands into fists.

"How long have you had him in there?" I asked. I couldn't see Anthony, but I guessed he was behind the closed door. "All night?"

"I tossed him in a cell overnight," Arthur said matter-of-factly. "To help him think. The young ones usually crack pretty quickly."

I crossed my arms over my chest. "Are you allowed to do that?"

"Trixie," Arthur stopped in his tracks, "we don't go soft on murderers here. The kid killed Volk in cold blood, and you're worried about his spending the night in a jail cell? He'll be spending years in prison if he's convicted."

I still didn't like to think that Anthony had committed the crime.

"Why didn't he ask for a lawyer?" Bill asked. "He should have done that."

"Don't remind him," Arthur said pointing a finger at Bill. "The only reason I brought you down here is because he said he'd talk if he could have someone he trusted present to hear what he had to say. He claimed he didn't need a lawyer because he wasn't guilty of anything."

I wasn't sure what Anthony thought we could do, but he must have believed we would help in some way.

When Arthur led us into the room, Anthony was sitting across the table from Mariana. He looked tired, his skin grey and dull, eyelids droopy, and shoulders slumped.

"Oh, my," I said under my breath.

Arthur dragged two extra chairs into the room, the metal legs screeching across the floor. I nearly covered my ears the sound was so grating. Bill didn't react. Arthur and Mariana kept their places across from Anthony, and Bill and I sat at either end of the table.

"Thank you for coming," Anthony said to us as we sat down.

"Of course, dear," I said, reaching over to squeeze his forearm. "I'm not sure what we can do, though."

"Don't touch him," Arthur barked.

I snapped my arm back and clutched the handle of my purse with both hands.

"No need to be rude, Arthur," I said.

"I haven't slept," he said, as though it excused his behaviour. "If this kid had talked, we could all have slept soundly last night."

"We gave you what you wanted," Mariana said quietly. "Are you ready to talk?"

Anthony nodded.

"Did you complain to Professor Blake that Professor Volk was stealing your research?" Arthur asked, pulling a pack of cigarettes from his pocket.

"I did," Anthony said.

"How did you know he was stealing?" Arthur pulled a single cylinder from the open pack.

I said nothing, but poked Arthur hard with my finger. He looked at me, rolled his eyes and put the cigarette back inside the pack. I didn't like the smell of smoke and Arthur knew it. Beyond that, medical research had demonstrated a causal link between smoking cigarettes and lung cancer.

"It was the end of August, before the term officially began." Anthony looked to me, then to Arthur. "Professor Volk is my supervisor, so I was helping him organize some artifacts in his office. He had gone to the washroom, and I wanted to know what he was working on. Professor Volk was always very secretive about what he was doing until it came time to publish and then he told everyone who would listen. Now I know why. There were some typed pages on his desk and one of them had his name, nobody else's, but the topic of the paper was something I had been working on. He knew that. It was a side project I decided to put some time into back in the spring and Professor Volk had approved. However, by mid-summer he said I should drop it and focus on my thesis.

Then by the end of summer I saw that he was about to submit an article on the exact topic he'd told me to drop. I was livid."

"What happened then?" Arthur asked, scribbling a few shorthand notes onto his pad.

"I didn't want to confront Professor Volk directly," Anthony said, resting his elbows on the table. "So, I went to see Professor Blake. He told me he would speak with Professor Volk about it. Get things sorted, he said. Next thing I knew, Professor Blake was telling me that he spoke to Professor Volk, who denied the whole thing, and that I should keep my mouth shut because nobody would believe me anyway. He didn't use those exact words, but that's pretty much what he meant."

"What did you do?" Mariana asked. "You must have felt angry."

"Of course, I was angry," Anthony sputtered, his forehead wrinkling. "Wouldn't you be? Professor Volk stole my work and there was absolutely nothing I could do about it. If I were Christopher Pearson, it might have been another story, but looking the way I do, who was going to believe the only coloured student in the department?"

"Were you angry enough to kill Volk?" Arthur asked, shifting his gaze from his notepad to Anthony.

"I didn't kill him," Anthony said slowly, enunciating each word carefully. "I was mad, but I wouldn't hurt someone like that. I hoped that one day, in the distant future, I'd have my revenge. I knew now wasn't the time. I wanted to get through the program, graduate without any trouble and move on somewhere else."

"Didn't you ask Professor Volk to demonstrate how to load a musket?" Arthur said.

"I did," Anthony gripped his head in his hands. "Obviously now I wish I hadn't, but don't you think I would have been smarter than to kill him with the exact weapon I asked him to show us how to load?"

"Murderers aren't always smart," Mariana interjected. "And murder is often passionate and opportunistic."

"Didn't you tell us you liked Professor Volk, that he respected students?" Arthur asked.

"That's how I felt about him until I discovered what he was doing," Anthony replied.

"So, you lied to us?" Arthur leaned closer and glared at Anthony.

"I did," Anthony spread his fingers open on the table. "I wanted to tell you everything, but I figured if I told you he was stealing from me, I'd be the prime suspect. I hadn't done anything wrong, but I didn't want to end up exactly where I am now. You can understand that, can't you?"

"Was Evelyn stealing from others, as well?" I asked, not looking at Arthur or Mariana to avoid the sharp glance I knew they were giving me.

Anthony shrugged. "I don't know, Mrs. Forster. It's possible, but nobody said anything to me."

"And your side project was a study of clay pipes from the 19th century?" I continued, still clutching my purse.

"What?" Anthony's eyes grew wide. "No, not at all. I was intrigued by some of the works of Childe, and I was applying a Marxist lens to the interpretation of Fort York. How did the class struggle play out in a highly regimented military context? That's what I was working on that Professor Volk stole."

It was my turn to be surprised. I had assumed the clay pipes article was his original work.

"What is it, Beatrix?" Bill asked.

I saw Arthur open his mouth to protest, but Bill held up his hand. Arthur had always held Bill in high esteem, so he kept silent.

"I don't believe Anthony killed Evelyn," I said simply as all eyes turned in my direction.

Chapter 78

"How do you know that?" Arthur demanded, tapping his pen on his notebook.

"The burned article," I said. "It was about clay pipes, not about class struggle at Fort York."

"So?" Mariana said, pulling her chair closer to the table.

"I suspect," I began, pulling my handbag closer to my bosom, "that this was a crime of passion. The person who killed Evelyn wasn't planning to kill him. When the new issue of Historical Archaeology came out, the student or professor whose original work it was had no idea that Evelyn had stolen his research. It would have been in that moment, when he saw the article, that he understood what had happened and he snapped, grabbing the closest weapon on hand and killing Evelyn. Without thinking much, he ripped the article from the journal in anger and burned it either before or after killing Evelyn. Then he hid the body in the closest accessible place, the cellar in the officers' quarters. I believe that finding out what Evelyn was up to triggered some extraordinary rage in the murderer."

Mariana and Arthur were silent for a moment. Perhaps they thought that Anthony, or Margaret, or Walter were still the best suspects. I, on the other hand, knew that we needed to track down the original author of the clay pipes article.

"Well, I'll be..." Arthur said finally. "You might be on to something, Trixie."

Anthony smiled for the first time since we'd arrived.

"I knew it," he said.

"Knew what?" Mariana asked, looking from Anthony to me and back again.

"That Mrs. Forster would figure it out," he replied. "Everyone knows the Forsters solved the murder at San Miguel. I knew they'd come up with something if I could just get them to hear me out."

I smiled and patted Anthony's hand on the table.

"You're very kind," I said. "But you took a big risk, Anthony. Bill and I didn't really solve the crime at San Miguel. The truth eventually came out with some probing. Please promise me, if there ever is a next time you find yourself a suspect in a police investigation, and I sincerely hope there isn't, you'll ask for a lawyer not a couple of retirees."

Mariana and Arthur stood up from the table, but I wasn't quite finished with Anthony. He might know more than he thought he did.

"One last question for you, Anthony," I said. "Who was researching clay pipes?"

Anthony considered the question for a moment and shook his head.

"I wish I could help you, Mrs. Forster. From what I know, Christopher, if he's doing anything at all, is supposed to be surveying battlefield sites in Ontario. Nadya is researching food pathways at military sites. Brian is looking into historical Indian sites; he wasn't even supposed to be at Fort York, but Professor Volk needed extra hands. And Marco is focused on historical archaeology methodologies. Nobody is studying clay pipes, that I know of."

Chapter 79

On the sidewalk outside the police station, I turned to Bill and looked up at him.

"It feels as if we're so close," I said, sliding the strap of my purse over my shoulder. "Any ideas who might have been working on clay pipes?"

"Unfortunately, not," he said, searching for the car keys in his pocket. "But surely someone knows."

"That could be it, though," I said. "With Anthony, Evelyn didn't steal from his master's research but from a side project that probably few people knew about. Evelyn may have had a dry spell with his own research, but he was an intelligent man. Graduate students present to the department about their chosen area of research. Everyone knows what everyone else is working on. But if you have something on the side, which many do because they want as many publications as possible, you might not discuss the topic with everyone. Evelyn knew that and he exploited it the best he could. It would be more difficult to take advantage of a fellow professor, so I think we must be looking at a student."

Bill and I walked toward the car.

"Now what?" I asked.

"I think you've done most of Arthur's job for him," Bill said. "It won't be that hard for them to extract the information about the clay pipes. They have their ways, and they have the Fort York students now as prime suspects."

I shuddered at the thought of police techniques for extracting confessions. Like Arthur said, not everyone was treated with kid gloves.

"I hate the thought of any of them being guilty," I said, thinking of the students we'd only just barely gotten to know over the past week.

"Except Christopher," Bill replied. "If he were the guilty one, I wouldn't be too upset. It could still be him. We know now to take what he says with a grain of salt."

Chapter 80

With little else to do while we waited for the police to solve the crime, Bill and I picked Muffin up from home and returned to the university. While Bill went back to the lab, I walked Muffin on the campus. If Sidney Smith Hall were anything but aesthetically appealing, there were many other buildings at the University of Toronto that gave English universities a run for their money. A brisk walk, or as briskly as I could, in the crisp air to clear my mind was exactly what I needed. Muffin ran about, looking up at trees for squirrels and letting students pat her head if they approached. Shirley had wondered if we were too old to care for a young dog from what was considered to be an obstinate breed, but we'd heard nothing of it, sticking to the wire fox terriers we'd had for decades.

"But wouldn't a toy poodle be nice?" Shirley asked, showing us pictures as a sort of temptation.

"No," we'd told her firmly. "We are not decrepit yet, and we want a terrier."

I was glad we'd stood our ground. Muffin had been surprisingly easy to train and made for a wonderful companion. While I reminisced on fond memories of Muffin when she was a puppy, I didn't realize I'd made a circle and was heading straight back to Sidney Smith Hall. I whistled for Muffin and turned around, hoping to lengthen my walk, but I bumped straight into Nadya.

"Goodness," I said. "I'm sorry, I didn't see you there. I've been a little preoccupied."

Nadya smiled and said, "I don't blame you. There's lots to think about these days."

There was still an unfortunate yellow bruise around the scab I'd noticed yesterday.

"Aren't you supposed to be at Fort York?" I asked.

"We're getting close to finishing there. With Chris and Anthony absent, I decided to give Brian and Marco the afternoon off so I could do some research. That's ok, isn't it?"

"It's not up to me, Nadya," I said, hoping to reassure her. "I'm sure you can organize your own time."

She lit up suddenly, eyes wide, a toothy grin on her face.

"I found something," she said.

"About Professor Volk's murder?" I asked.

"Oh, no," Nadya stopped smiling. "Not about that. It was about the scalp."

"Ah, yes," I replied, tucking a loose end of scarf back inside my coat when it began flapping in the breeze. "I'd forgotten about that. Let's go find Bill in the lab and you can tell us all about it. Come, Muffin. Let's go."

We began walking toward the building, Muffin keeping a keen eye out for any opportunity of one last escapade before we went inside.

"Nadya," I said, "what can you tell me about clay pipes?"

"Well," Nadya said slowly. "They aren't my area of expertise, but clay pipes are ubiquitous at historical sites throughout North America. They were cheap and broke easily so you find them frequently in areas of refuse. I believe that by the 19th century, the manufacturers, which were mostly in Europe, were putting their name and place of origin on the pipe. Archaeologists often use them for dating at sites. They're very useful."

"That's quite interesting," I said, moving my purse from one shoulder to the other. It tended to feel heavy if I didn't alternate arms from time to time, the leather strap digging into my muscles despite my thick wool coat. "I remember there was one in the tray you showed me that first day at Fort York."

"Yes, we've recovered quite a few at Fort York. The soldiers and officers probably smoked a lot. In times of peace, beyond their drills and duties, there wouldn't have been a lot to entertain them."

"You wouldn't happen to know who is currently studying them?" I asked.

I looked over and Nadya shook her head, strands of her loose hair flying away from her shoulders.

"Afraid not, Mrs. Forster," she said. "I don't know who would be looking into them at the moment. However, if you're interested, there's a reference collection in one of the labs. I'm sure nobody would mind if you took a look."

"I see," I said, feeling disappointed she didn't know more. "Yes, thank you."

We continued on in silence and I wished very much that, as in George Orwell's famous novel, there were surveillance cameras in the lab. Then it would be easy to know exactly who had spent hours on end with the clay pipe reference collection.

Chapter 81

"Look who I ran into, Bill," I said, as Nadya, Muffin, and I entered the lab.

No response.

"Bill," I repeated. "Bill, I'm back."

Bill's head jerked up and away from the bones he was analyzing.

"Beatrix," he said, waving me over. "I've found some more, very interesting, things."

I wondered if he had even noticed Nadya at my side.

"Nadya has, as well," I said, stepping closer to the work tables. "Let's hear what she has to say."

Bill nodded and waited for Nadya to speak. Suddenly shy, she hesitated.

"I... Professor Forster," she began, "the records and books I read to prepare for the excavation did reference a scalp."

"Ooh," Bill intoned.

Encouraged by his interest, Nadya continued: "Apparently, when the Americans captured Fort York, they were so angry about the explosion of the Grand Magazine and the death of General Pike, they were bent on destruction of public property. They ransacked the parliamentary buildings before they burned them. There's a brief mention of two things they took from Parliament. The parliamentary mace and a scalp. The mace was returned to Canada by Roosevelt in the 30s, but nobody knows what happened to the scalp. It was given to Major General Dearborn, or Granny Dearborn, as he was called, but then it seems to have disappeared from the historical record. Some said it wasn't actually a human scalp but rather the speaker's wig."

"Heavens!" I said. "What a story!"

Bill said nothing and we both watched him process the information Nadya had just provided.

"What are you thinking, Bill?" I asked.

"Hmm," he murmured. "Trying to piece things together."

"What were the things you found on the skeletons that you wanted to show us?" I said, trying to bring him out of his stupor.

"Oh, yes," he said. "There are a few things. Have a look at their dentition. Make sure to hold the mandible up to the maxilla for the full impression. Second incisor, canine area."

I did what I was told, Nadya peering over my shoulder. I repeated the same action of holding the jaw together for each individual. All but one had a complete hole or notch worn into their teeth next to their middle incisors. After the third one, I looked at Nadya, and she smiled.

"Clay pipes?" She asked.

Bill nodded and said: "Yes. Three of the four individuals have pipe notches. They clenched the pipe between their teeth so often over the course of their lives that they wore holes and grooves into their dentition, creating the perfect spot for a pipe to rest."

"Oh my," I said. "That's a lot of smoking. I'm glad people don't smoke pipes anymore. Cigarettes are bad enough, but they don't leave holes in people's teeth."

"There's something else," Bill said, resting his hand on one of the tables. "Come have a look at this. I didn't notice it initially because whoever had unpacked this skeleton left it in the newspaper."

Nadya and I stood on the opposite side of the table from Bill.

"Look at the hyoid," he said.

I saw that Nadya had no idea where she was supposed to be looking, so I pointed at the delicate bone of the throat shaped like a horseshoe or, in my personal opinion, an ugly little horned devil holding its fists in the air. The hyoid was the only bone in the human body that did not articulate with any other bones. It sat superior to the thyroid cartilage and was held in place by ligamentous and cartilaginous attachments.

"It's broken," I said, leaning close to the bone to get a better look.

"What does that mean?" Nadya asked.

"Well," Bill began, picking the two pieces up in his hand and holding them out so Nadya could examine them. "If it had been a post-mortem break, it would mean nothing at all. However, the edges of the break appear to be smooth, and they are identical in colour to the rest of the remains. The staining from the soil suggests that the break wasn't as a result of our excavation work, otherwise the area would be white. A fractured hyoid can suggest various things, but I believe in this case it may indicate hanging."

"Oh, dear," I said. "This is the one that was face down?"

Bill nodded.

"Wow, what a way to go," Nadya whispered, brushing some hair out of her face.

Bill replaced the bones on the table, and I wondered what had happened that this man had been hanged at a time when war raged all around. What had he done to be subjected to such a punishment?

Chapter 82

Nadya departed the lab to pick up some things from her office and Bill, Muffin, and I were left alone.

"I asked Nadya about the clay pipes," I said to Bill. "She said she didn't know who might be studying them."

"Of course," Bill sighed. "Nobody knows anything. And the person who killed Evelyn probably knows that the police have some idea about the article and that Evelyn was stealing research. I don't believe anybody will be coming forward to say that they had been one of Evelyn's victims."

"Nadya also told me there's a reference collection of pipes here." I pulled a chair out from the corner of the room and slowly lowered myself into it. My feet were aching, and I was exhausted. "I don't suppose there's a record of who accesses what collection, and when?"

Bill came over and Muffin followed him. She put her front paws on my thigh. I set my purse down on the ground and patted my leg. She sprang up and sat primly on my lap, her toenails ever so slightly digging into my skin through my skirt.

"There is, in theory," Bill said, leaning against the wall. "There's a sign in sheet. However, from what I've been told, the students either don't use it at all, or leave a fake name, something they find funny. I don't think anybody takes it seriously, so I doubt our clay pipe expert did either."

"Something we haven't considered," I began, running my hand over Muffin's back, "is that Evelyn did the research and wrote the article himself. He was generally considered to be an excellent scholar. What happened that he resorted to stealing ideas?"

"I wish I knew," Bill said. "Some people thrive under pressure and others become so terrified of failure that it becomes a self-fulfilling prophecy. It wasn't just pressure to publish that Evelyn faced. He was also living a double life. One does not simply maintain the façade of a happily married man."

"You're right," I agreed. "He must have been struggling, but it's no excuse to victimize others whose voice is silenced by society."

"Absolutely."

When I said those words, I realized just how many people, who went about their daily lives in Toronto, were essentially invisible. Contributing, but overlooked and unappreciated. Unseen until they committed a crime, that is.

"I have an idea," I said. "Stay here with Muffin and I'll be back."

Chapter 83

I went to Donna's office to ask her where the graduate students worked. I'd never had a reason to go there, and the location of the graduate student offices was unfamiliar to me. Donna greeted me politely and asked me if we'd learned anything new.

"Unfortunately, not much," I replied, noticing that the framed picture she'd had on her desk when the police first interviewed her was missing. "Your photograph is gone."

"Oh, yes," she said. "I'm so clumsy I knocked it over and broke the glass. I thought it best to put it somewhere safe. Ever since Professor Volk was killed, I've felt a little jumpy myself, as though the murderer might walk through my door at any second. I'll feel much better when he's caught."

"I think we all will," I commiserated. I could understand why she might be frightened after everything that had happened. Though I hoped she wouldn't have to be fearful much longer. "Do you happen to know which student was researching clay pipes? I have a question I think they might be able to help me with."

Donna thought for a moment. She ran her hand over her smooth grey hair, following it until she reached the knot at the back of her head.

"I'm sorry," she said finally. "It doesn't ring a bell. Is it important?"

"Not particularly," I replied. "I have an idea. Could you tell me where I might find the graduate student offices?"

She began to explain where they were located and then thought better of it. She locked the door to her office behind her and led me through a series of corridors and up a flight of stairs before we arrived at a room with a pale, wood door. She didn't knock. Donna walked in and waved her arm around the room.

"This is it, Mrs. Forster," she said in a low voice. "Most of the grad students have a desk in here. Do you need anything else?"

"That's all, thank you, Donna," I replied, scanning the space.

They weren't really offices at all, but cubicles separated by wood panelling. There were hardly any people in the room, just a few heads here and there hovering over a piece of paper or a book. One student had fallen asleep on his desk. I looked around until I found Nadya. She smiled when she saw me and set aside the book she was reading.

"Hi, Mrs. Forster," she whispered, probably trying not to disturb the other students.

"Hello, Nadya," I said, keeping my voice quiet, as she had done. "I wanted to ask you about the book that talked about the scalp. I'm feeling a bit faint, though, probably all those stairs I had to walk up to get here. Would you mind getting me a glass of water?"

Nadya's expression grew serious, and she stood up immediately. I wasn't really feeling faint, but I needed her to leave her desk for a few minutes.

"Why don't you sit down?" She suggested. "I'll be back in a jiff."

I sat down in the chair she'd just occupied. As soon as she was out of sight I started shuffling through her papers. I felt guilty rifling amongst her things without her permission. All the papers on her desk were notes about food, agriculture, cooking, recipes. It all made perfect sense given the topic of her PhD research. I was starting to wonder if I'd made a mistake. As a woman, I naturally thought she would be one of the people easily overlooked in the department. Her ideas and research passed off as the work of a male colleague or supervisor. Had I been wrong? I didn't have some clever tactic to get her to confess or confirm she was the one we'd been looking for all along, just old-fashioned nosiness. I was about to give up when I noticed a very slim drawer just under the top of the desk. It wasn't locked and I easily pulled it open. There were pens, pencils, paper clips, erasers, pins, and a tube of lipstick. I slid my hand to the back of the drawer, which from my angle in the chair, lay in shadowy darkness. I felt something tucked away out of sight. Wrapping my fingers around it, I slid a small notebook out from the drawer.

"What're you doing?" Nadya snapped, the water in the glass she carried spilling over the side.

She startled me so badly I dropped her notebook on the floor. We both looked down to where it had fallen, and I gasped audibly before she could snatch it up. When I saw the sketches of clay pipes, carefully drawn with detailed markings, I knew I had been right. Evelyn stole the research from Nadya and shamelessly published an article with her work.

"Nadya," I said, standing up.

There were already tears forming in the corners of her eyes. She shakily set the glass on her desk and crumpled to the floor.

"I've made a terrible mess of things," she cried, covering her head with her arms. "I didn't mean to be dishonest, Mrs. Forster, but I was afraid."

"Stand up, dear," I said grasping her arm and helping her get to her feet.

Every one of the students in the office was staring at us, except the sleeping student, who, I guessed, would later be disappointed to have dozed through the most exciting thing to happen in the Department of Anthropology in years.

"Let's go for a walk," I suggested. "Get some air."

Nadya sniffled as the tears streamed down her cheeks. Her face was scrunched up and a deep shade of red.

Once we were alone in the hallway, Nadya collapsed into my arms. I held her tight while she sobbed. Too tall to use my shoulder as support, she hovered above me, shaking unsteadily.

"There, there," I said, patting her lower back. "Let it all out."

Chapter 84

"Hear her out," I said to Arthur, as we sat with Nadya, Bill, and Mariana in the lab.

Nadya had regained her composure and stopped crying, but her eyes were still swollen and the skin on her nose was pink.

"Go ahead," Arthur said, without emotion. "Tell us what happened."

Nadya twirled her long hair around her finger and stared at the ground.

"After Professor Volk demonstrated how to load the musket, he took it back to his office with Donna. I went to work at the test pit, like I said before. The students were scattered a bit all over, but that was normal. They usually use the time Professor Volk takes after the morning lecture to have a coffee, go to the bathroom, make a phone call, or whatever else pops into their mind. I typically work through that time, but while I was digging, I remembered something I needed to ask Professor Volk. I thought it was best to catch him in his office, and I went over to the officers' barracks. When I got there, both Donna and Professor Volk were gone. I assumed he'd gone back to the excavation area. I would have left, but I saw the new issue of Historical Archaeology on his desk and thought I'd have just a quick peek. When I saw the article on the clay pipes, I realized he'd stolen my research. I was furious. How could he do something like that? I thought he liked me and respected me. Apparently, it was all a charade and I'd been a fool. I ripped the article out and without thinking, I burned it in the fireplace. There was little else I could do. I only realized how stupid I'd been when we found out the next day he'd been murdered. I knew immediately if anybody found out about the article, then I'd be the main suspect. It was stupid, but I was terrified of being arrested for his murder and I staged the attack in the blockhouse. I thought if everyone thought I'd been attacked by the murderer that they wouldn't suspect me of the crime. And yet, here I am, talking to the police again, and everyone thinks I killed Professor Volk."

Nadya hung her head limply for a moment. I wasn't sure she would be able to carry on, but then she sat back in her chair.

"What happened after you burned the article?" Arthur asked, propping his elbow on his knee to take notes.

"I went back to the excavation area, assuming he would be there. I knew I'd have to confront him about the article, but it couldn't happen until we were away from the students. It probably wouldn't have mattered. Nobody would believe me over him, but I wanted him to know how angry I was. At the time, I wanted him to suffer. When I got back to where the students were, he wasn't there. That's when I realized something wasn't quite right. The students said they hadn't seen him. I went back to his office just to make sure, but he wasn't there either. After that we all looked for him together and everything else I told you is true. I promise."

Everyone was silent for a few minutes. Muffin came up to us and Bill quickly scooped her up and placed her on his lap. The last thing we needed was a distraction. I didn't know whether to believe Nadya or not. If not she, with an obvious motive to be furious with Evelyn, then who? Was this an elaborate ruse to convince us of her innocence or was she telling the truth? Most everyone had lied to us during the investigation, including Nadya. Did someone else have something to hide?

"Go on," Arthur urged her. He spoke softly as though he, too, felt sorry for her.

"I swear I didn't kill Professor Volk," Nadya mumbled. "I don't know who did, but it wasn't me. I swear. I'm telling the truth this time."

"This is quite the story, Miss Shevchenko," Arthur said. He paused for a moment, then turned to me. "What's your take, Trixie?"

"You want to know my opinion?" I asked, genuinely surprised.

"I do," Arthur said, tucking his notebook into his pocket.

I sat in silence, watching Nadya wipe a tear from her eye. There was something small, some little detail, that was bothering me, but I couldn't quite put a finger on it. I glanced around the room as everyone but Nadya stared at me, waiting for me to speak.

"I'm inclined to believe Nadya," I stated. "Perhaps I'm a naïve old woman, but I think she's telling the truth."

"I agree," Arthur nodded. "Though I have to say smashing your face into a glass cabinet was a pretty dangerous thing to do, young lady."

"I'm sure she doesn't need a lecture, Arthur," I said, looking at the glass cabinets against the far wall in the lab.

I thought about the sound of glass shattering, the sharp tinkling sound it made as the sharp fragments collided with one another. That's when I realized what the small detail that bothered me was. I clasped a hand over my mouth.

"What is it, Trixie?" Arthur demanded.

"I've thought of something," I said. "I think I may need your help this time. An intimidating presence might make this go faster."

Chapter 85

When Arthur and I walked into Donna's office she looked up, startled.

"Detective, Beatrix," she mumbled, "how may I help you?"

"Mrs. Ewen," Arthur said, approaching her desk. "We'd like to see the photograph you had on your desk the day we interviewed you."

"Oh, that old thing?" She asked, waving a hand dismissively. "Why would you want to see that? I told Beatrix already I broke the glass and now I've taken it home. It's less likely to get bumped there than here on my desk."

"That's fine," Arthur said. "We can accompany you to your house."

Donna stood up from her chair. I could see her hands were trembling.

"What's this about?" She asked. "It's just a photograph. Beatrix?"

She looked at me, pleading with her eyes.

"Please cooperate, Donna," I said. "It will be easier for everyone. I didn't notice it at the time, but when we came to your office for Arthur to interview you, you purposely hid the photograph from our view, knocking it over so even if someone went behind your desk, they wouldn't see it. Frankly, that was clever; it seemed accidental at the time. Yet, when you told me you had knocked it over and broken the glass, I realized it fell over in our presence and I never heard glass breaking. I don't believe that photograph is framed with glass, is it?"

Donna's eyes widened and she wrapped her arms around her body for a moment. She said nothing, then pulled open the top drawer of her desk. She produced the framed photograph, kissed it gently and then handed it to me. I wasn't sure what I would find, but I knew there was something in the photograph that Donna didn't want us to see. Something that was important to her. The moment I beheld the people in the photograph, I realized what we'd overlooked all along.

Chapter 86

I held the wooden frame in my hands and stared at an old photograph of a woman and a child in black and white, smiling at the camera. Though much younger, the woman was clearly Donna. The child was the spitting image of Sandra, Evelyn and Margaret Volk's adopted child. The photograph had clearly been taken long before Sandra was born, and I knew immediately I was looking at a childhood photograph of Sandra's biological mother.

"You're Sandra's grandmother," I whispered.

Donna nodded but she stayed quiet.

"What?" Arthur demanded. "But your name doesn't match the birth mother's name. I would have noticed something like that."

Donna looked down at her desk. "When Marjorie, my daughter, got pregnant out of wedlock and she had to go to Bethany House, we gave them a false name, hoping that once the whole ordeal was over, she could start fresh. We didn't have a lot of money, and we knew that having a baby at eighteen would make her life unlivable. Everyone would judge her, and she'd never have a normal life after that. She wanted desperately to keep her daughter, but the unwed mothers' home insisted she give the baby up for adoption. At the time, my husband and I both agreed that it was best. She was so traumatized after the birth, and hopeful that one day her child would find her, that she officially changed her name to the one we'd used at the home for unwed mothers. After Marjorie died in a car accident, I decided I wanted to meet my granddaughter. I used the money we'd saved for the wedding we hoped Marjorie would celebrate one day to bribe a secretary at Bethany House for the name of the adoptive parents. It wasn't difficult; she was eager for something extra on the side."

Donna paused and pulled a handkerchief from her purse. She dabbed at the corners of her eyes.

"I didn't think I had any tears left to cry," she said, staring sadly at the photograph I still held. "It wasn't hard to get a job at the university. The last secretary was retirement age, and I convinced her to put a good word in for me. I wanted to be on friendly terms with the Volks before I told them who I was and what I hoped for. I liked Professor Volk and thought he would be kind and reasonable. I just wanted to see Sandra, meet her, and hoped one day she would know I was her grandmother. I regretted terribly that Marjorie had been coerced into giving her up and that my husband and I had helped make it happen. Life wasn't really fair to Marjorie, and I knew she would have wanted us to try to be a part of her child's life."

"Did Volk know you were Sandra's biological grandmother?" Arthur asked.

Donna shook her head. "When he asked me to bring the journals to Fort York he was in such a good mood, I thought it would be a good time to reveal the truth. He's always been friendly and kind to me. I trusted he would do the right thing by his daughter. As soon as we got to his office, I told him about Marjorie and that I hoped he would consider, with time, letting me be involved in Sandra's life."

"What happened then?" I asked gently.

"He was shocked of course," she replied, "which I expected, but I hoped he would understand my position. Professor Volk told me I was a liar and a trickster, that he would have me fired from my job for dishonesty and that he would never allow me to see Sandra. In fact, he told me he would take me to court if I tried to make contact with her. He walked out of the room, and I saw the musket. It was so stupid, but I thought maybe I could frighten him with it, make him hear me out. I grabbed the gun and followed him into the dining room. When I pointed the musket at him, he just laughed at me and said I would never pull the trigger. He was right, I wouldn't have pulled the trigger. I didn't want to hurt him. I realize now that he was turning away from me, but I was so nervous I thought he was going to try to grab me. I stepped back but I must have squeezed the trigger without meaning to. Then he was dead. I'd never committed a crime in my life and now I was a murderer. It seemed unlikely the police would believe it was an accident, so I hid the body, hoping I'd have time to figure things out. He was heavy, but I managed to drag him over to the cellar and push him down the stairs. I cleaned as quickly as I could with what little was available, wiped the musket of fingerprints, and left. I nearly bumped into Nadya on my way out of the fort, but when I saw her heading toward the gates, I hid in one of the soldiers' barracks until she passed. Fortunately, nobody noticed me leave, so I knew I could say I'd only been with him for five minutes. I'm so terribly sorry for what I did and for lying to everyone. I just didn't want to go to prison, even though I'm aware it's what I deserve."

Donna was right, she did deserve some form of punishment. She'd taken the life of the only father her granddaughter had ever known. Yet, I felt sorry for her and wondered if things would have been different if young, unwed mothers were treated kindly in our society. I hoped the judge would take her unfortunate story into consideration when handing down the sentence.

"One more question," I said, feeling Arthur's disapproving gaze on me. "If you had the photograph on your desk all this time, did nobody ever notice it?"

Donna laughed quietly. "No, Beatrix. Sometimes I thought perhaps that's how Professor Volk would learn who I was. The photograph was always there, in plain sight for anybody to see, but nobody ever asked about it, and the only time anybody came to my side of the desk, they weren't looking at the photograph. I'm sure you know what I mean. I realized eventually that Professor Volk wasn't going to find out by accident, the way I'd hoped, and that I'd have to reveal my identity myself."

Chapter 87

"What are you thinking about?" I asked Bill over dinner that evening.

We sat across from one another, the table filled with dishes of vegetables, meat, potatoes. I'd wanted to get lost in some task or other and cooked enough for a small army.

"The soldiers..." his voice trailed off and he looked up to the ceiling.

I waited a few moments until his eyes met mine. He tapped his knife on the table rhythmically.

"Are you going to share?" I asked, scooting my chair closer to the table. The scraping over the hardwood floors made Muffin pull her ears back.

"Oh, yes. Sorry, Beatrix," Bill said, releasing the knife. "I was just trying to piece together a scenario in my mind. According to the buttons on the uniforms they were wearing, all four men belonged to the American army. So why bury three with dignity and one in a way that clearly showed disrespect?"

The question was rhetorical, so I held my tongue and waited for him to continue.

"Of course, this is pure speculation, and this could never be proved archaeologically. However, my thought is that the three men who died in the explosion were buried in the days after the battle, as was customary and the opportunity presented itself. Only high-ranking officers might be taken back for burial in a military cemetery as they did with Zebulon Pike. They put him in a casket of whiskey to keep him from decomposing, and he was buried in the U.S. A regular soldier would not have received the same treatment. Mostly they were buried where they fell. Those were the original burials in that grave. Then we have the other individual, the prone interment. My best, educated guess would be that the local people of York knew exactly which soldiers burned the parliamentary buildings, government house, other public places, looted and ransacked the town. It was a small community and while the Americans occupied the town the people got to know some of the soldiers. Though most relations were civil between the troops and civilians, the citizens might not have taken kindly to the burning of their town. I think it's entirely possible that during the chaos of preparations for the Americans to leave York, some members of the civilian population or militia, which remained in York on parole, might well have taken one of the men responsible for stealing the mace and scalp and perhaps carried out some form of vengeance. He must have had the scalp returned to him at some point by Granny Dearborn or perhaps he simply took it when nobody was paying attention. The Americans may have believed the missing man deserted the army, which wasn't so unusual when soldiers had had enough of being cannon fodder. The local culprits hanged him in retaliation for the burning of York... perhaps he had been particularly harsh to the people. To hide what they'd done, they buried the victim with previously buried American soldiers knowing that when the British returned, they would focus on reburying their own dead and leave the Americans in their battlefield graves."

"That is quite the conjecture, Bill," I said, cutting a piece of chicken away from the bone.

"That it is," Bill replied, smiling at me. "I'll never be able to publish such a tale, but I like to have things wrapped up in my own mind at least, even if the story might be a bit of an embellishment."

"Do you think it really is a scalp?" I asked. "Or do you think we've all been fooled by the speaker's wig?"

Bill took a bite of potato and chewed slowly.

After a moment he said: "It's possible that the glue and textiles used on the inside of the wig might have decomposed in such as way as to appear leather-like. And of course, any wig powder that might have turned the hair colour white or grey, would be long gone after all this time. We'll have to have some tests done to determine the composition of the material, though I do feel confident the hair is very much human. Time will tell."

I shuddered at the thought of a scalp on display at the parliamentary buildings, and hoped the artifact turned out to be a wig after all. The thought of the Americans' outrage over a wig would have made me chuckle, had it not resulted in such tragic consequences.

Epilogue

The week before Christmas, Bill and I were dozing in our armchairs in front of the television, the CBC background noise for our light slumber before we went to bed. Muffin stood up and circled in my lap, finding a new comfortable position for her own forty winks. I opened my eyes and saw that the Justice Minister, Pierre Elliot Trudeau, was being interviewed about Bill C-150, the omnibus criminal code reform bill. If passed, the bill would decriminalize homosexuality in private and allow women to access abortion, if a committee of doctors felt that the pregnancy endangered the physical or mental wellbeing of the mother. There would even be changes in access to contraception for women.

"Bill, wake up," I shouted, unintentionally raising my voice louder than planned. I leaned over and squeezed his arm.

"What is it?" He asked, sitting straight in his chair.

"It's Trudeau," I said.

"It's bringing the laws of the land up to contemporary society, I think," Trudeau said to a pack of reporters, all shoving microphones as close to his face as possible. He wore a slight smile as though knowing his words would be met with either elation or outrage in homes across the country. "Take this thing on uh, on um, homosexuality. I think the, the view we take here is that there's no place for the state in the bedrooms of the nation..."

"Did you hear that, Bill?" I asked.

"I did," he said, reaching over to take my hand. "It looks like it may be just a matter of time before they pass it into law and things begin to change for a great many people in this country."

"A great many, indeed," I said, thinking of all the people who might have benefited from these laws had they been passed in time.

Acknowledgements

First and foremost, I would like to thank my family: Kevin, my husband, who has been there through both the tears and small triumphs of writing this book; Lois Barlow-Wilson, Malcolm Wilson, Niall Wilson, Ross Barlow, and Gloria Barlow for their unwavering support through thick and thin. In no particular order, I'm grateful for all those who contributed to my archaeological education and training, Dr. Tamara Varney, Dr. Angela Lieverse, Emma Bonthorne, Fran Valle de Tarazaga, and the professors and staff of the Department of Anthropology at the University of Saskatchewan. A special thank you to Dr. Kenneth Brown, Professor Emeritus at the University of Calgary for sparking a lifelong love of the Spanish language and for a superior educational experience; and to two remarkable women who always offer their unconditional support, Rachel Reardigan and Sadaf Farookhi.

DANEE WILSON grew up on the prairies in Regina, Saskatchewan. She completed a BA Hons in Spanish at the University of Calgary before moving to Spain to teach English. Inspired by the unidentified remains entombed in the Valle de Cuelgamuros (previously the Valley of the Fallen) and hoping to work in the recovery and identification of victims of the Spanish Civil War, Danee returned to Canada to study archaeology at the University of Saskatchewan, where she received a BA Hons and an MA. During her studies, she travelled to Spain each summer to volunteer in the search for the victims of Franco's regime. In 2016, Danee began work as Assistant Director of a small archaeology company in the Basque Country, where she spent three field seasons excavating the medieval cemetery at San Miguel de Aralar, and one season excavating the ossuary at Roncesvalles, in Navarre. After more than three years abroad, Danee once again returned to Canada, completing a post-graduate diploma in public relations and communications management from McGill University. She is the author of Murder at San Miguel and Death at Fort York. Danee currently resides in Toronto, Canada, with her husband and toy poodle.

www.ingramcontent.com/pod-product-compliance
Lightning Source LLC
Chambersburg PA
CBHW030600180626
46816CB00005B/1615